SANCTUARY ISLAND

Lily Everett

St. Martin's Paperbacks

This is a work of fiction. All of the characters, organizations, and events portrayed in this novel are either products of the author's imagination or are used fictitiously.

SANCTUARY ISLAND

Copyright © 2013 by Lily Everett.

Excerpt from *Shoreline Drive* copyright © 2013 by Lily Everett.

For information address St. Martin's Press, 175 Fifth Avenue, New York, NY 10010.

ISBN: 978-1-250-01837-3

Printed in the United States of America

St. Martin's Paperbacks edition / August 2013

St. Martin's Paperbacks are published by St. Martin's Press, 175 Fifth Avenue, New York, NY 10010.

10 9 8 7 6 5 4 3 2 1

Bestselling authors agree that *Sanctuary Island* is a breathtaking debut by an incredible new talent!

"*Sanctuary Island* is a novel to curl up with and enjoy by a crackling fire or on a sunny beach. It's a beautifully told story of hope and forgiveness, celebrating the healing power of love. Lily Everett writes with warmth, wisdom and deep insight. The island, with its wild horses and natural beauty, is a place of dreams, and the story will live in your heart long after the book is closed."

—Susan Wiggs, #1 *New York Times* bestselling author
of the Willow Lake series

"I didn't read this book; I inhaled it. *Sanctuary Island* takes the classic elements of romance and women's fiction and weaves them into an incredible story of love, forgiveness, healing, and joy. Lily Everett is a wonderful author and a great storyteller."

—Debbie Macomber, #1 *New York Times* bestselling
author of the Blossom Street series

"I loved it! A rare find."

—Lori Wilde, *New York Times* bestselling author
of *The First Love Cookie Club*

"A heartwarming, emotional, extremely romantic story that I couldn't read fast enough! Enjoy your trip to Sanctuary Island! I can guarantee you won't want to leave."

—Bella Andre, *New York Times* bestselling author
of the Sullivan series

For Ronai.
Thank you for helping me find this book's happy ending.
And, of course, for your son—my own, personal happily
ever after.

Acknowledgments

The Sanctuary Island series wouldn't exist without my editor, Rose Hilliard. From helping me come up with the original idea to pushing me to dig deep in revisions, you inspired, encouraged, and supported me. I can't imagine a better editor.

I'm also blessed to have the amazing, savvy Deidre Knight on my team! D, your faith in my work and your steadfast friendship have meant the world to me. I love you.

I also love my friends and sisters-in-writing, Roxanne St. Claire and Kristen Painter, without whose advice, laughter, sympathy, and butt-kicking, I would be nothing. Thanks, girls! In fact, a big thank you to the entire Blonde Mafia, especially Lara Santiago and Kresley Cole, for always telling it straight and never holding back. You rock!

Another pair of women to whom I owe my sanity are Ana Farrish and Tracie Stewart. My daily writing buddies, you keep me on track, help unstick me, and enable my perfume habit. You're the biggest reason I love our local Austin RWA chapter. Also in the sanity-saving category are the ladies of WriteChat—too many of you to name, but you know who you are! Y'all are the best.

My beta reader, Bria Quinlan, went above and beyond on this book. I feel so lucky to have found you, and that you share your time and experiences with me. My characters wouldn't be who they are without you.

I would be remiss not to personally thank the brilliant bestselling authors Debbie Macomber, Susan Wiggs, Lori Wilde, and Bella Andre for taking the time out of their incredibly busy lives to read this book by an unknown author, and give a quote. I'm honored to have your names on my cover. And a big, special thanks for the ever-gorgeous and witty Sarah MacLean, for all your help!

Last but certainly not least, I must thank my parents for instilling a love of reading and writing in me, and always encouraging me to stretch my imagination and reach for the stars. Thanks to my sister, Baby Horse, and the Jackson Hole Therapeutic Riding Center for helping keep it real.

And of course, my darling husband, Nick. You always tell me the truth, even when you think I'm making a mistake—and then you throw your full support behind me, no matter what. I believe because you believe in me. There is no one on earth I'd rather share my life with. I can't wait to see what happens next!

CHAPTER 1

If one more thing messed with Ella Preston's schedule, she was going to scream.

Tightening her fist around her cell phone—the cell phone which was currently an expensive, high-tech hunk of useless plastic, due to the lack of signal out here in the boonies of southeastern Virginia—Ella put on her best negotiator smile for the white-haired lady behind the counter.

"Exactly *how* late is the Sanctuary Island ferryboat?" Ella asked sweetly.

"Aren't you cute?" the lady said, putting another placid stitch in the square of embroidery she'd spread out over the ticket counter. "Don't worry yourself. The ferry'll get here when it gets here."

That's not an answer. She smiled again and thanked the lady for her help before turning to stare out at the dark green-gray of the water splashing against the concrete pier. If she squinted, she could see a long, narrow smudge against the horizon.

Sanctuary Island.

For the hundredth time since embarking on this trip, Ella wondered who the hell would choose to move to a remote island so tiny it didn't even have a causeway connecting it to the mainland.

The only way on or off Sanctuary Island was by ferry. And when said ferry finally chugged up to the dock at the edge of Winter Harbor, Virginia, more than twenty minutes later than the printed schedule indicated, the sight of its peeling paint and barnacle-covered hull didn't exactly fill Ella with joy.

Neither did the grizzled, salty-looking older gentleman in the shiny bowling shirt with BUDDY stitched across the left breast, who sucked on an unlit pipe as he opened the gate into the ferry's lower level.

Ella gripped the wheel of her rented sedan and inched it over the rusty, pitted ramp leading into the cavelike bowels of the boat, suddenly glad she'd told her sister to get out and walk up the passenger ramp.

She honestly wasn't sure the vehicle ramp could take the combined weight of herself, the beige four-door, and one seriously pregnant Merry Preston.

She followed the pickup truck ahead of her and wedged into the last space on the lower level, right beside the wall. Before she'd even managed to turn the car off, the ferryboat engine came to life with a shuddering roar.

Ella cracked her door, careful not to scratch the rental car's paint on the metal hull of the boat. Sucking in her stomach, she squeezed out of the car just as the ferry lurched into motion. She fought down a swirl of nausea, nerves, and dread by repeating her mantra.

You are in control of your reactions. No one and nothing can hurt you unless you allow it.

The mantra was slightly less reassuring than usual, but then Ella usually took care not to put herself in situations this stressful. She was only here now because of her sister.

This is all for Merry, she reminded herself. Maybe it was the pregnancy, maybe it was the messy end of yet another relationship Ella had warned her from the get-go was doomed to failure, but Merry was determined to visit Sanctuary Island and reconnect with the mother they hadn't seen since their parents' long-overdue divorce fifteen years ago.

Personally, Ella could think of plenty of things she'd rather do than plan a trip to some godforsaken island completely cut off from civilization, to visit a woman who'd cared more about her next drink than fighting to keep custody of her young daughters—but if Merry was going, then so was Ella.

The past was the past, and Ella was completely over it. She'd make sure Merry got over this when it inevitably imploded, too.

Protecting her reckless, impulsive baby sister while Merry barreled forward with one of her harebrained ideas was an ingrained, lifelong habit.

The past was the past—but some things never changed.

Clutching the scarred, pitted wooden railing, Ella climbed the stairs to the upper deck. After the stale, gasoline-drenched air of the parking deck, the first breath of fresh, salt-sparkling ocean breeze buoyed her spirits.

Ella paused at the top of the staircase and inhaled deeply, lifting her face to catch a thin ray of chill spring sunlight.

"Ella! Over here!"

Ella opened her eyes to see her sister waving at her

with both arms, her roundly pregnant bulk propped against the rail on the far side of the boat.

"Hold on," Ella instructed as the ferry jounced over the choppy waters of the Atlantic. "I don't know where the life preservers are if you go pitching over the side."

Merry flapped one dismissive hand, but obediently gripped the railing by her hip. "Pssh. There's no flotation device in the world big enough to fit me these days. Besides, you know you'd jump in after me and tow me to safety."

Ella had to acknowledge that this was probably true, even though she wasn't a strong swimmer. But if Merry went overboard, Ella would, too. That was the way it had always been.

"Let's skip it, huh?" Ella reached her sister and curled an arm around Merry's shoulders, bracing them both. "A near-death-by-drowning incident would really throw off my schedule."

"It's a vacation, Ella." Merry sighed in the long-suffering way she'd perfected as a teenager. "You're not supposed to have a schedule."

"The unscheduled life is not worth living," Ella quipped, but she kind of meant it. In her experience, surprises were vastly overrated. Let other people expect the unexpected—Ella would take boring predictability any day of the week.

They stared out over the water at the strip of tree-lined shore in the distance.

Their mother had moved to Sanctuary Island after her husband walked out and took their daughters with him. Ella and Merry had never seen the island in person, only in the pictures Jo Ellen included in the letters she'd sent them every week since she got out of rehab.

Ella shivered, a chill racing over her skin. *Just the wind,* she told herself, and discreetly spat out one of Merry's loose curls. Ella's hair was pulled back into a sensible knot, which the wind was doing its best to unravel.

Beneath Ella's sheltering arm, Merry felt small, almost fragile. Delicate, in spite of the pumpkin-sized bulge of her belly stretching out her lipstick-red T-shirt.

The need to be strong for her sister stiffened Ella's spine. There, that was much better than contemplating the uncertainty ahead. Whatever happened with Jo Ellen, the number-one priority for this particular plan was that Ella would be there for Merry.

Sweet, sunny, all-too-trusting Merry, who squirmed in a familiar, restless dance, faux-leather leggings squeaking.

"Again?" Ella pitched her voice to be heard over the breeze and the incessant clanking of the engine. "Really?"

"You try standing around with a watermelon constantly pressing down on your bladder, then come talk to me."

"No, thanks." Ella tried, but she couldn't completely erase the fervor from her voice. Not that she never wanted to have kids, but to be in Merry's situation? Low-level job, no savings, abandoned by the baby's father—who'd been as big a loser as Merry had ever dated, so no real loss there.

With an effort, Ella downgraded from a ferocious frown to a subtle tightening of her lips, but when she glanced over at her sister, Ella realized she could've saved herself the trouble.

Plucking absently at the zipper of the jacket that wouldn't quite close over her pregnant belly, Merry had zero attention for anything but the hazy outline of the island town on the horizon.

"I thought it would be warm here," Merry said, a little wistfully, as she wrapped green-glitter-polished fingers around the deck railing and strained up onto her toes to peer over it into the white-foamed water below.

Subtly maneuvering both of them a few cautious inches back from the edge, Ella said, "It's only April—spring is just getting started. According to my research, the weather's supposedly fairly variable until June or so. Some warm days, highs up in the seventies, but lots of storms, too."

Storms like the one that had kept this old bucket of a ferry from running last night, and forced Ella and Merry to spend an unscheduled night at the airport Hilton.

Merry wandered over to the bench seat in the center of the deck and lowered herself down carefully.

The ferry hit a swell that made it pitch alarmingly, and Ella staggered a few steps before managing to grab onto the bench and get herself seated.

Okay, seriously. Is this thing even seaworthy?

She'd been annoyed at the extra expense of the hotel room last night—her nest egg was only going to take them so far, and considering how things were going at work, she might soon need to stretch her savings even further—but now that the single thing between Merry and the frigid water of the Atlantic Ocean was this ancient, rusted-out tin can, Ella was glad whoever ran it had the sense to shut it down in bad weather.

If the ride was this bumpy on a clear morning, she'd hate to see it during a storm.

"It's got to be warmer here than in D.C., at least." Merry sighed, petting unconsciously at her abdomen.

Ella resisted the urge to point out that they'd had record-breaking high temperatures in Washington this winter.

She knew Merry wasn't talking about the temperature.

Putting aside her own misgivings, Ella made her voice as gentle as she could. "I'm sure it will be. And hey, I think I saw a ladies' room sign on the lower deck when we first got on the ferry. Want to go check it out? I'll help you down the stairs."

Merry sat up straight, giving Ella the same bright, plucky grin that had wrapped her around her baby sister's little finger since they were kids.

"No, thanks. I want to stay on the top deck where I can get a good look at the island. I can't believe we're the only ones up here! I guess this must be the off season. I can't wait to see it in a couple of months—I bet it's packed!"

Ella felt as if her body had frozen to the metal bench. "A couple of months?"

Merry's shoulders hunched up slightly and the grin dropped off her face, but Ella couldn't back down.

"Merry. You can't seriously be planning to stay that long."

"Can't we play it by ear?" Merry pleaded. "I mean, she's our mother. And we haven't seen her in fifteen years. You really think two weeks is going to be enough time to get to know each other?"

"I've only got two weeks of vacation," Ella hedged. Two weeks of forced leave thrust on her by her worried, frustrated boss was more like it, but Ella didn't say that. "Come on, we need to stick to the plan."

"Oh, the almighty *plan*. Screw your plan! I'm perfectly happy to throw myself open to destiny and see where it takes me."

Sure, because that always turns out so great for you.

The words stung the tip of Ella's tongue, sharp and bitter, but she swallowed them back.

"Besides, it's not like you're happy at that stupid job, anyway," Merry said, defiance trembling through her low voice.

The unconscious echo of the speech Ella's boss gave her only days ago jolted Ella like a slap to the face. Merry couldn't know what Paul Bishop had said that afternoon when he'd called her into his elegant, wood-paneled office and closed the door. When he'd shaken her carefully constructed world down to its foundations.

Ella gave her sister the same reply she'd given Bishop. "I'm good at what I do. Yes, commercial real estate is slumping, but it's a cyclical business. I'll be back on top before you know it."

Underneath the firm answer, though, Ella was aware of the same puzzling sense she'd had in the meeting with Bishop—the sense that there was something she wasn't understanding, some concept just outside her grasp.

Because all she could honestly think was, *What the hell does my happiness have to do with anything?*

Her job at Bishop Properties paid well, offered benefits, and until recently, had provided the kind of security Ella had been looking for her whole life.

Silence was a weird thing, Ella reflected as the next couple of minutes brought nothing but the rush of the wind and the low thrum of the engine vibrating through the deck.

She knew Merry better than anyone in the world. They had the same blue eyes, the same slight dimple in their chins, the same brown hair—although Merry had dyed hers a deep, purplish magenta this week, and next week it could easily be platinum blond—but that's where the similarities ended.

Still, at only three years apart, they were closer than any sisters Ella knew. As close as twins, with their own shorthand language, mannerisms, and expressions, and the ability to communicate volumes with just the quirk of a brow. They could talk for hours or sit in a completely companionable quiet together, and just be.

But even as close as they were, Ella couldn't bring herself to admit exactly how near she was to freaking out about seeing Jo Ellen Hollister again.

Merry squirmed in her seat, mouth turned down in an unhappy curve, and Ella blew out a breath. "Just hold on, sweetie. If you don't want to use the bathroom on the ferry, that's okay. I think we're almost there, and the ferry bathroom is probably a health inspector's nightmare, anyway."

"No, that's not what . . . Look. Ella. I know I'm kind of a mess, but you're not the only sister who gets to worry. For the last year or so, I've wanted to say something about that job. When you told me you were taking a vacation, I was so relieved, because you were, like, *this close* to burning out. All you do is work. You don't go out, you don't have friends, you don't date." Real concern laced Merry's husky voice, and one of her slim hands fluttered almost unconsciously to rest on the hard roundness of her stomach.

"Hey! I have friends," Ella protested, ignoring the comment about her dating life. Who had time to date? She couldn't imagine devoting precious hours to the awkward, messy, pointless process of dating. Someday, maybe, but now? When the job she'd fought and studied and lived for was in jeopardy, and her baby sister was about to have a baby of her own?

No. Ella had more important things to worry about than dating.

Merry gave her the patented Little Sister Eye-roll of Doom. "Please. We live together. I know everyone you know. Your best friend is your therapist. And when you're not at work, you're at the apartment on your laptop, researching properties."

"Adrienne hasn't been my therapist for years and you know it, so it's completely fine that we meet up for lunch every now and then as friends. As for the rest of it, you've got enough hobbies for both of us," Ella said fondly. "Maybe I'm a workaholic. But I'm trying to do better! An island vacation ought to get me off the hook for a year, at least."

She was trying to make a joke out of it, mostly to avoid having Merry press any harder on the reasons behind Ella's abrupt willingness to use vacation days to visit the mother she'd long ago written off, but Merry didn't smile.

Ducking her head, Merry said, "I know this isn't exactly the vacation of your dreams—I know you're only here because of me, and I want you to know I appreciate it. I can't imagine going through this alone."

Ella swallowed around the lump thickening her throat and leaned in for a hug. "Don't worry about me—I graduated from therapy, remember? I worked through all my issues about this. And sure, maybe for me that means being fine with the status quo of turning down all of Jo's attempts at reconciliation. But I understand why you don't feel the same way. And, sweetie, you'll never have to be alone," she said into the soft hair at her sister's temple. "Not as long as you have me."

The ferry blared its low, bleating horn. Merry pulled back, her eyes filled with excitement and nerves.

Craning her neck, Ella saw that they were pulling up to a wide wooden dock that ended in a gravel parking lot. A small, whitewashed building squatted at the top of the gravel hill stretching a barrier arm across the narrow road that led to the interior of the island. The words "Summer Harbor" were painted across the side of the building in flowy script, the letters scoured to a faded blue by the salty breeze.

The dock had been built up from the beach where a tumble of large, red-brown rocks formed a sloping wall between the flat circle of gravel and the surprisingly long stretch of untouched sand. Squinting, Ella made out a rickety set of steps connecting the two.

After the incessant ebb and flow of the crowds thronging the streets of Washington, it was almost surreal to stare down at what seemed like miles of pristine beach, empty of everything except a couple of sandpipers hopping comically through the foam of receding waves.

The wind was so briny Ella could taste it on the tip of her tongue. Gulls swooped and shrieked, their white wings glowing in the morning light, and Ella stood up to latch on to the railing.

Even though her feet were firmly planted on the rumbling deck, she somehow felt pitched forward, poised on the brink of something she couldn't name.

Ella didn't believe in fate or destiny. She didn't believe in much of anything beyond the need to work for independence, the security of having a good plan, and the unbreakable bonds of loyalty and love that tied her to Merry. Believing in things was more in Merry's line.

But as a shiver of surprising anticipation traced down Ella's spine, she couldn't escape the feeling that Sanctuary Island was exactly where she was supposed to be.

CHAPTER 2

Ella carefully navigated their car's slow, painstaking way down the corroded ramp, very aware of the precious cargo of Merry and her unborn baby strapped into the passenger seat.

She drove across the parking area to the little white shack and paused in front of the red-striped automatic arm. Rolling her window down to try and get a better look through the uncovered window cut into the side of the building, Ella wondered if she was supposed to honk to get someone's attention.

A large, hulking figure with a strangely shaped head stirred in the shadows of the gatehouse. The figure moved with an odd, shambling gait, and when a meaty fist slid back the glass window in the side of the booth, Ella jumped.

An older man beamed out at them, sunlight sparking red and gold off the points of the scratched, dented metal crown cocked at a rakish angle over his left eyebrow.

"Good day! I'm King of the Gateway to Sanctuary. How can I help you ladies?"

He spoke in a rich, plummy, obviously fake British accent, his underlying Southern diphthongs twanging through the words.

Ella opened her mouth, then closed it again. The self-proclaimed royal leaned a companionable elbow, regally clad in a red-and-black checked flannel, on the windowsill and regarded the two women with considerable interest.

"We . . . would like permission to enter the island," Ella said, flicking a glance at the rearview mirror where the few other cars that had come over on the ferry were forming a line behind them.

The king turned on the high beams, smiling widely enough to reveal crooked, tobacco-stained teeth and a disarming pair of dimples. "Well, of course! That's what everyone wants. But we can't just let any old so-and-so in, now can we? So. Who are you?"

Rattled, Ella reached for her purse and dug through it for her driver's license. What was this, Communist Russia? Was she going to have to produce her papers next? But when she held out the license, the king merely gave her a pitying look and made no move to examine it.

"No, no, no. I don't need to know your outsider name—I need to know your insider name. Who you are. Deep inside."

Beside her, Merry stifled a giggle, then winced uncomfortably as she pressed a hand to her lower stomach.

Please don't have an accident in this car, Ella thought frantically. *I need the deposit back!*

Turning back to the gatekeeper, Ella put on her best calm, authoritative smile—the smile she used to convince real estate developers to sign on the dotted line. She sized up the King of the Gateway the same way she'd size up anyone she faced across the negotiating table.

First, establish a rapport.

"What's your name, sir?"

"King Sanderson," he replied, puffing out his chest.

Of course it was. "Well, your highness, it's been a very long drive, and my sister is in dire need of a ladies' room. If you could tell us what we need to do . . ."

"I see," he said, stroking his nonexistent beard meditatively. "Travelers from afar . . ."

"Is there a fee of some kind?" Ella swallowed, mentally tallying up the price of the rental car plus the ferry, the unexpected hotel, now this. "I've got cash. I think. Somewhere—Merry, can you grab my purse?"

"Sisters," the king mused. "A pair of sisters . . . hmmm . . ."

He banged his hand suddenly against the wall of the booth, startling the wallet right out of Ella's hand.

"By Jove, I've got it!" The man pointed one fleshy finger at them triumphantly, crowing, "I knew I'd get it! You've come a long way, through wind and rain, to see someone special—the woman who gave you life—for the first time in years."

Ella stared, an echo of that odd, fated feeling reverberating through her chest. "How did you know that?"

He slapped the outer wall of the booth again, apparently tickled. "Shoot! Because your mama told me, that's why! You're Jo Ellen Hollister's girls, I should have known from the get-go—you've got the look of the Hollister women about you. Come on in! We've been expecting y'all."

"Thanks," Ella said with some relief. She eased her

foot off the brake, but his royal highness wasn't quite finished yet.

"I hope you girls are ready for this." He shook his grizzled head slowly, like a sleepy lion.

Stomach tightening into a knot, Ella wanted to ignore him—but, of course, Merry had to lean across her and ask, "Ready for what?"

His eyes took on a sharpness that somehow made him seem more there, all of a sudden.

"This island . . . it's good for what ails you. It'll change your life, if you let it, but like any great healing—it comes at a price."

Ella felt the hairs along her arms lift and prickle. Plastering on a determined smile, she said, "Okay, thank you for the warning. Bye now!"

"Well, that was weird," Merry said after Ella rolled her window up. "I wonder what he meant."

"He meant," Ella said firmly, "that he's an elderly gentleman who probably ought to be in an assisted living home somewhere, instead of manning that gatehouse all by himself. I wouldn't worry about anything he said."

"I guess it's good, though, right?" Merry licked her lips nervously as the wooden arm of the guard booth slowly lifted and the king waved them through with a benevolent smile. "That she talked about our visit?"

"Sure, otherwise we'd be stuck baring our souls to his highness back there," Ella said, summoning up a smile to soothe her sister's palpable anxiety.

The narrow paved road took them straight through the heart of downtown Sanctuary—which they knew because there was a banner splayed over the road that said THE HEART OF DOWNTOWN SANCTUARY in faded red lettering.

Ella kept her breathing steady and even. So what if every heartbeat brought them closer to the moment when she'd look her mother in the eye for the first time since she was thirteen years old? She'd worked hard to move past the lingering issues of her childhood, and she'd succeeded. In the grand scheme of her life, Jo Ellen Hollister was completely unimportant.

Ignoring the wave of nerves that implied otherwise, Ella studied the quaint clapboard buildings that lined the street.

From what she could see, this place had a ton of untapped potential. Ella couldn't help wondering how different the town might look if the island's founders had seen fit to build a causeway. Without that link to the mainland, Sanctuary Island was a butterfly trapped in the sticky amber glow of times gone by.

They drove slowly past a grass-covered square in the center of town. A white gazebo perched in the middle. People went about their lives, strolling the paths of the square and the wide sidewalks lining the streets, chatting in pairs or singly holding shopping bags. A lanky young man on a bicycle pedaled past Merry's window with a cheerful grin and a wave.

In fact, everyone they passed smiled and waved, as if Ella and Merry were long-lost friends returning home. Ella wanted to find it creepy, but she couldn't. It was nice. Friendly. Welcoming.

And the work-obsessed corner of her brain lit up with possibilities. A good developer could do a lot with raw material like Sanctuary Island.

"I don't know what I was expecting," Merry said as they circled the town square, complete with pavilion and bandstand. "Maybe I thought it would look like Virginia

Beach or something, kind of cutesy fakey touristy? But this place feels . . . real."

Ella knew what she meant. Part of her wanted to stop the car and get out, explore the town and all it had to offer. But instead she said, "Do you still need me to find a gas station or a rest stop?"

"I'm okay." As if to prove the words a lie, Merry's fingers clutched at the map in her hands, crinkling the paper. Giving Ella a rueful smile, she smoothed out the page and said, "I kind of just want to get there, you know?"

Trying to resign herself to the fact that she wasn't going to be able to put it off much longer, Ella made the turn off Main Street as Merry directed her, driving deeper into the island.

The car emerged from a section of road shaded by tall pines, and the sudden brightness blinded Ella. She slowed the car, shading her eyes against the glittery splendor of the marsh laid out before them. Raindrops sparkled on the tall grass waving in the breeze. Everything had been washed clean by the recent storm, even the air.

"So pretty," Merry said, delighted. "In the city, rain just means cabs splashing you with dirty water every time they hit a deep puddle."

"Yeah, but even our old neighborhood didn't have potholes like this," Ella said, clutching the steering wheel tightly as they followed the winding road deeper into the trees. "Is your seat belt still on?"

"You are such a worrier. I'm perfectly fine!"

"Your navigation skills might be less than fine." Ella made a grab for the map in her sister's hand, but Merry held it teasingly out of reach. "Are you sure we're going the right way? This looks like the middle of nowhere."

"Of course I'm sure! At least, I think this is the right

way. We might have made an extra turn somewhere, but Ella, come on, look where we are! Who cares if we're lost? We should be soaking it all in, and . . . oh my God, pull over, pull over!"

"What?" Ella cried, slamming on the brakes. Her arms reflexively spun the wheel to get the car onto the side of the road while Merry scrabbled at the buckle of her seat belt and pushed open the passenger side door.

Merry's boots were squelching in mud before Ella had even thrown the car into park, and by the time she managed to wrestle her way free of her own seat belt, all she could think was that her sister had gone into premature labor or something.

But no. Standing a few feet away from the car, Merry stared out over the marsh with her hands clasped rapturously under her chin. Her eyes were shiny, with joy or tears, Ella couldn't quite tell, but she definitely didn't appear to be in any pain.

"What on earth are you doing?" All of Ella's fear and worry exploded out of her in a burst of exasperation.

"They're just so beautiful," Merry whispered, staring off into the distance. "I had to get a closer look."

Trying to get her heart to settle back into her rib cage where it belonged, Ella wrapped her arms around herself for warmth and stood next to her sister. Merry pointed, and that's when Ella caught her first glimpse.

A band of half a dozen wild horses foraged through the scrub grass on the other side of the marsh. Still shaggy with their winter coats, the horses ranged from darkest black to white spotted with big brown splotches.

"I was afraid we wouldn't get to see them," Merry whispered.

"The entire island is a nature preserve for the wild

horses that live here," Ella said, quoting the sparse ency-
clopedia entry she'd memorized when that first letter
from Jo arrived. "We were bound to see horses at some
point."

And personally, this was about as close as Ella wanted
to get to them.

Looping one arm through the crook of Ella's elbow,
Merry leaned her head on Ella's shoulder and sighed.
"Oh, Princess Buzzkill. Can't you just enjoy the moment?"

Ella pressed her lips together and went back to watching the horses pick their way through the grass. It wasn't
as if she was completely unaffected by the sight—there
was something tantalizing and exhilarating about the animals. They'd look amazing on the cover of a brochure.

But it was breezy out here, Merry didn't have her jacket
on, and Ella couldn't shake the knowledge that their
mother was waiting for them.

However, Merry was determined to immerse herself in
the moment, so Ella decided to give her a few minutes to
get it out of her system.

While they watched, the largest of the horses raised its
head and perked its ears. Wind caught and tangled in its
flowing black mane as the horse scented the air for a long,
breathless moment before taking off at a loping canter,
tail streaming behind like a pennant.

The other horses, cued by their leader's sudden flight,
raced to catch up, and even from a hundred yards away,
Ella felt the drumbeat of their hooves reverberate through
the earth and up into her chest.

Her breath caught as the horses galloped free and un-
fettered across the freshwater marsh. They crested a hill,
and the big, black horse paused for a moment while the
rest of the herd streamed past and out of view.

Ella stared, transfixed, as the black horse turned and disappeared over the swell of the hill. Beside her, Merry hummed appreciatively, then did a little shimmy with her hips.

"You know what? Since we're stopped anyway, I'm going to sneak behind a bush and pee."

"What? You can't do that! Merry!"

Ella made a grab for her sister, who danced out of reach. She was surprisingly light on her feet for an about-to-pop pregnant chick.

"Back in a sec," Merry called out. "Keep watch for me!"

Closing her eyes, Ella turned her back and scanned the stretch of empty road. The echo of the horses' hooves still pounded through her chest, setting a rhythm for her heartbeat.

Whirling back to face the marsh, Ella nearly stumbled against her car as a rangy, reddish-brown horse paced along the edge of the meadow and up to the side of the road.

This wasn't part of the band of wild horses, though—this one had a rider.

A very tall, very broad, very male rider.

And he was heading straight for her.

CHAPTER 3

Ella backed against her car door as the horse paced closer. She willed her gaze not to dart around searching for Merry—no need to draw attention to her sister, who might or might not be baring her behind to the breeze at this very moment.

The man made a soft clucking noise in the back of his throat, and the horse stopped walking.

"Are you lost?"

The man's voice was as rough as his stubbled cheeks, low and deep in a way that reached into Ella's chest and messed with her breathing.

He was big. Broad through the chest and shoulders, with powerful thighs that gripped his mount's flanks, effortlessly controlling the huge, snorting animal he rode. Most of his face was shadowed by the brim of a battered white baseball cap, the fringe of hair spiking out from under it dark gold, like antique coins.

Ella flinched when the horse stomped one massive hoof and blew out a loud breath. Large animals made her nervous. Heck, big men who appeared out of nowhere, in the middle of nowhere, made her nervous.

Falling back on her tried-and-true method of dealing with nerves, Ella swept the man with a swift, assessing gaze, sizing him up in a single glance.

She couldn't get much of a read on his expression under the cap, but his honeyed Southern drawl had sounded . . . carefully neutral. Not particularly friendly, but not threatening, either. His body language was noticeably loose and relaxed, especially considering he was sitting on top of two thousand pounds of rawboned muscle.

So he was comfortable in his skin, comfortable in the outdoors—but even as she thought that, she noticed the way his leather-glove-clad hands were clenched tightly around the horse's reins.

Interesting. Maybe he wasn't as comfortable as he seemed. But that was a mystery she didn't have time to solve.

Shooting for a sunny smile, Ella found it best to appeal to the manners hopefully ingrained in this Virginia gentleman since he was a much littler boy.

"As a matter of fact, I'm a bit turned around. If you could point me in the right direction, I'd be so grateful. And then you can get back to your ride."

He crossed his arms casually and leaned forward over the horse's heaving neck. The morning light caught a gleam in his shadowed gaze that sent a shiver of awareness down Ella's spine.

"Well, ma'am, I surely do appreciate you giving me permission to keep riding on this land, but I'm not the one who needs it."

Ella blinked at the edge in his tone. Wow, it had been a

while since she misread someone so completely. "Needs what?"

"Permission. Fact of the matter is, you're trespassing."

The rustling sound from the bushes behind her had Ella stiffening. Willing Merry to have the sense not to come charging into this tense little standoff, Ella said, "I'm just passing through."

A slight sneer twisted his mouth, drawing Ella's attention to the sensual, masculine curve of his lips. "Is that right?"

He sat up tall in the saddle once more, his gaze moving to something over Ella's shoulder as he went on, voice bland as butter. "That's not what I heard. Jo Ellen said you and your sister were coming to stay a while. Get to know the island. And her."

This man knew their mother. The knowledge struck Ella like a blow to the head.

As if he could read the complex stab of emotion under Ella's ribs, he shrugged and sat back in the saddle. "Then again, maybe I heard wrong. And maybe that's a good thing. God knows, Jo doesn't need any more trouble than she's already got."

He was sending out waves of disapproval strong enough to nearly knock Ella off her feet. "Who the hell do you think you are?"

"Just a friend of your mother's. And I have to tell you, darlin' . . ." One leather-gloved finger tipped up the brim of his ball cap, and for the first time, Ella got a glimpse of his handsome, hard-jawed face and burning green eyes.

Those eyes skewered her, pinning her in place as he told her, "You look like big trouble to me."

"Well, hello, gorgeous!" Merry's delighted voice shattered the tense, shocked silence as she sidled up next to Ella, her lips parted in a happy grin.

The man's dark gold brows winged up, a maddening smirk twisting his lips. Ella clenched her fingers against the itch to slap that mocking half smile off his face.

"She's talking to your horse," Ella said in the most withering tone she could muster.

"I am," Merry agreed, with stars in her eyes, all her attention zoomed in on the big, dark reddish-brown horse. "What a beauty. Not that you aren't nice-looking, too, mister."

"Hey, don't do me any favors," he said, clearly amused.

Merry had worked her magic once again. Since they were kids, people had been drawn to Merry's bubbly personality, the vivid, reckless sense of fun and life that beamed out of her bright blue eyes. Within moments of meeting most people, Merry had them eating out of her hand.

A thin sliver of something oddly like jealousy pierced Ella's belly. Reminding herself she didn't give two shakes if this unfriendly stranger fell all over himself for Merry, Ella turned determinedly away from him.

"We need to get going," Ella told her sister. "Apparently, we're trespassing on this man's property."

"I never said it was my property."

"Then what, exactly, is your problem?" Ella couldn't help the sharpness of her voice, even when it made the horse eye her nervously and prance in place.

"Shhh," Merry cooed, before the man could respond. She held out one calm hand, green-tipped fingers curled under to let the horse bump its nose against her knuckles.

Ella fought the urge to snatch her sister's hand away

from the horse's whuffling nostrils and big teeth. Merry had always loved animals. The horses on the island were a huge part of the draw for Merry in coming here, Ella knew. This was part of the plan—the sooner Merry got her fill of the horses, the sooner they could go back to D.C.

"You must be Merry. You're good with him," the man observed.

"Is he a gelding?" Merry was all eagerness, the unguarded innocence of her voice at odds with the sullen darkness of the makeup ringing her eyes, the streaks of punk-rock red highlighting her brown hair. "What's his name?"

"Yep, he's a gelding. I call him Voyager. Do you ride?"

Merry shook her head, hand still outstretched and that enchanted look turning her pixieish face soft and dreamy. "Never had the chance to learn."

Ella squeezed an arm around her sister's shoulders, a pang hitting her heart.

"It's not too late," the man observed, watching them. "I'm sure your mom would love to teach you. Or I could."

Time to take control of this encounter. Sending the rider a frosty smile, Ella said, "Oh, I think we've taken up enough of your no doubt valuable time. Just tell me how to get to Jo's house, and we'll be out of your hair."

With a reluctant sigh, Merry gave the horse's nose one last stroke and said, "Guess I'll start the ten-minute process of squishing this blimp of a body back into the car. Nice to meet you and Voyager."

Ella waited until Merry was in the car before whirling to face the unnamed stranger who felt he had the right to meddle in their relationship with their mother.

"Look. I understand you're a friend of Jo Ellen's," Ella

said, striving to keep her voice even. "But that doesn't give you the right to pass judgment on me or to put ideas in Merry's head about what this visit is going to be like. You don't know us. You don't know our family history, and frankly, it's none of your business, anyway. So tell me how to get out of here, and hopefully that will be the last we'll see of each other."

He studied her for an endless moment, the heat in his green eyes taking away the chill of the storm-washed morning air. There was something new on his face, an expression she couldn't read, as he stared down at her.

A pulse of feminine awareness pulled at Ella's consciousness, but she didn't allow herself to break eye contact.

"You're right," he finally said, his drawl slow and rough as honey over gravel. "I don't know you, but I do know your mother. And if you're here to break her heart, then the only directions I'm going to give you are for how to get back to the mainland."

Fire kindled in her blue eyes—that same clear blue she shared with her mother and sister. Grady Wilkes stood his ground in the face of Ella's shocked anger, but it wasn't the easiest thing he'd ever done.

After five years on Sanctuary Island, surrounded by friends and family, he was a little out of practice when it came to dealing with strangers.

And despite how much Ella and Merry looked like their mother—from their wavy dark hair right down to the fact that their mouths were made for smiling—and despite the fact that he'd never seen Jo Ellen happier than the day she found out her daughters were finally accepting her standing invitation to visit, Grady was worried about his friend.

Jo wanted so badly for this to work out, and he understood better than anyone that guilt and regret could make a person do crazy things. It was a tough situation, because Jo definitely had plenty to feel guilty about, and Grady realized her daughters had every right to hold a grudge.

But he didn't want to see Jo get hurt.

Blood ties don't make a family. Family are the people who are there for you when you need them most.

Even though she'd turned down every one of his uncle's marriage proposals, Jo Ellen Hollister was the closest thing to a mother that Grady had left. And he'd do whatever it took to protect the vulnerable heart she tried so hard to hide. Getting taken in by a pair of opportunistic scam artists who hadn't shown any interest in her until she inherited Windy Corner and the valuable land it sat on—that would kill Jo Ellen.

"Sorry to disappoint you," Ella tossed out, crossing her arms over her chest in a way that had his eyes skimming over her curves without any help from his brain. "But we're not leaving. Not until Merry has the chance to work through her obsession with getting to know Jo Ellen."

Grady frowned. "So it's all about Merry. Right."

As if she hadn't picked up on the sarcasm dripping off his words, Ella shrugged. "Hey, believe me, I tried to talk her out of this trip. But Merry is a force of nature when she has her heart set on something."

Grady couldn't fight the tug of curiosity. It was his besetting sin. "What about you? What's your heart set on?"

He didn't know what answer he thought he'd get—if she were really a gold digger intent on hooking her claws into her mother's recent inheritance, she'd hardly be likely to admit it straight-out.

Ella stared up at him, an unreadable expression on her

pretty face. "All I want is to get Merry through the next few days and be there for her when she realizes the fantasy of a mother that she's dreamed up in her head is nothing close to the reality. And then I want to get us both back to D.C."

That, at least, sounded like the truth.

An unwelcome spark of respect kindled in Grady's chest. He knew all about protective urges and how deep they ran, and he couldn't fault Ella for wanting to take care of her very pregnant younger sister.

In return for her honesty, and in recognition of the fact that he clearly wasn't going to have much luck running them off before they ever got to Jo's, he pointed at the road where her car was pulled over.

"You missed the turnoff for Jo's place about a mile back," he said, instinctively rebalancing his weight as Voyager danced under him. "Her land is the last acreage inhabited by humans on the east side of the island. Once you get out this far, it's all dedicated as a nature preserve and wild horse sanctuary. We try to keep nonislanders—and their cars—out of here, to ensure the safety of the horses and their habitat."

She arched a brow. "You sound like a public service announcement. Do you get paid to patrol the marsh for trespassers? Are you authorized to shoot on sight?"

"Obviously not, since you're still here."

"Right," Ella said. "I never did catch your name, Mr. . . ."

She trailed off expectantly, those blue eyes wide and intent on his face. Grady had the unfamiliar urge to mess with her—he'd been known around the task force for being a prankster, but he'd always kept his sense of humor to the guys, or his cousins. People he knew well, who knew how to take a joke.

Not prickly, put-together women he'd known for all of thirty seconds.

Shaking it off like a dog emerging from a lake, he offered her his gloved hand and said, "Wilkes. Grady Wilkes."

She hesitated before stepping closer, and he wondered if she was nervous about the horse or about taking his hand. Whatever it was, it didn't stop her from reaching out.

"Ella Preston," she said, and the moment their fingers touched, Grady had to clamp down on a shudder of sensation.

Even through the thin, supple leather of the work gloves covering his scarred hands, Grady felt electricity arc between them in a flash of heat and awareness. Her eyes widened with it, and she stumbled back a pace.

Sudden panic had him curling his stiff fingers into as tight a fist as he could manage, keeping his leather glove from peeling away from his hand with her jerky movement.

Ella blinked at him, the moment spinning out between them as fine as spider silk strung between two pine trees as Grady's heart banged against his rib cage.

"Ella! Are you coming? We need to go, because I didn't. Go, I mean. And it's starting to get dire up here."

Without another word to Grady, Ella whirled and hustled around her car, calling out, "I'm coming, and I've got directions."

Grady watched her walk away, unwillingly fascinated by the sleek, sexy movement of her rear end in those conservative khaki pants.

There was a time, he remembered, when even this

loose fist would've been more movement than his hands could deal with. When he'd thought he'd never get any range of motion back, or be able to use his hands as more refined instruments than paddles.

The memory had him gripping the reins more tightly than he needed to as he wheeled Voyager around and pointed him in the direction the car had disappeared in.

Nothing about this situation was as cut-and-dried as he'd thought when he fielded that happily tearful phone call from Jo telling him her daughters were finally coming to visit.

If Grady was going to figure out where to go from here, he needed to see how Merry and Ella reacted to Jo, and to the big, rambling, falling-down plantation house she'd inherited. And he needed to be there for Jo if it all went to hell.

It had nothing to do with wanting to see more of gorgeous, strong-willed, overprotective Ella Preston before she hightailed it off the island back to the city where she belonged.

Nothing at all.

CHAPTER 4

Jo Ellen Hollister stared across the gleaming expanse of the polished mahogany desk and fought the feeling of relief washing over her. She wasn't here to lay her troubles at this man's feet.

She'd given up the right to expect his help.

"I know I said we needed to take a break, but . . ." Paper crinkled in her grasp, and she had to force herself to unclench her fingers, to smooth out the wrinkles in the letter from the county.

Harrison McNamara shifted his tall body, making the tufted leather of his chair creak. "Stop that. I hope you know you can always come to me. No matter what."

Jo closed her eyes briefly, then forced herself to meet his gaze. "Thank you."

He leaned forward, his dark eyes full of the intent focus and attention that never failed to send Jo's pulse into overdrive. Her heart kicked against her rib cage with bruising force, but this time she was pretty sure it had nothing to do with Harrison's deep-set brown eyes.

"Honestly, I can't believe you're only coming to me with this now," he said. "I know we haven't exactly been on the best of terms these last few months, but if you needed money to get the stables up and running . . ."

"She didn't tell me." Ridiculous. It was intolerable that out of the whole mess, this single fact could make Jo's throat squeeze tighter than a fist. "I found out when I got this letter."

The words came out whispery and cracked. Jo cleared her throat forcefully and sat up in her chair. "When Aunt Dottie gave me the money—I should've questioned it, but she told me a bond had matured, and I just . . . took it. I wanted my stables so badly."

Those dark eyes of Harrison's softened at the corners. "You wanted to make her proud of you, to show her you were independent."

"And instead, I made her think she had no other option than to go to the meanest, nastiest old man on Sanctuary for a loan."

Harrison smoothed his close-cropped salt-and-pepper beard with a jerky, agitated hand. "I don't understand why she didn't come to the bank."

Jo sat back, her shoulders bending down under the weight of new knowledge. "There's no way she could have gotten a bank loan without you knowing about it. Maybe she thought you'd tell me, and then I'd stop her from putting up the house as collateral. Which I would have. Or maybe she thought she could talk old man Leeds into better terms—she knew him her whole life, ever since they were kids. Who can say?"

They certainly couldn't ask Dottie now.

Grief reached up and slapped Jo in the face, sharp and shocking. Grief faded, everyone said. Time healed all wounds. But Jo had mostly found that as her sadness faded from a constant pain to a dull ache, it had become an even more painful surprise when it flared back up.

"I'll look into the lien for you," Harrison said, reaching across the desk for the letter.

Jo surrendered it reluctantly. With everything else she had going on, there was no way she'd have time to do as full and thorough an investigation into this situation as Harrison would do. Without even breaking a sweat, because the man was a genius with finance.

"I appreciate it. You can keep that letter—it's a copy. I have the original at home in a safe place."

Expectant silence stretched between them for a long, agonizing minute before Harrison's mouth went flat and hard. Keeping his eyes on his own hands shuffling papers around on his desk, he said, "All right, then. I'll let you know what I find out."

Jo ached at the distance between them. "Harrison, this means a lot to me. You mean a lot to me."

He snorted out an unflattering breath. "Sure. Not enough to marry me, but enough to come running when you need something."

Jo stiffened, but before she could snap out the retort burning her tongue, Harrison held up a big, blunt-fingered hand.

"Forget I said that." His voice was gruff and tired, burrowing tendrils of guilt into Jo's heart. "I'm glad you came. I'll be even gladder if it turns out I can do something to help. And I'm not doing it for thanks, or to guilt you into changing your mind about us. But I suppose I'm enough of an optimist to hope this situation might show you there are some benefits to going through life as a couple, to having someone to rely on."

It pissed her off that she couldn't hold his gaze. "I used to believe that."

"Not all men are as easily scared off as your ex-husband—"

She stood up, unwilling to listen to the rest of that thought. "It has nothing to do with Neil Preston. This is all me. I'm just not at a place in my life right now where I can commit to anything other than getting my girls back."

He spread his arms wide, exasperated. "How would being with me keep you from reconnecting with your daughters?"

"When my mother died, my father remarried so fast, it made my head spin. I was so young, already dealing with the loss of my mother, and then to have a brand-new person thrown into the mix . . . it was more than I could manage. It broke us. Things were never the same between Dad and me. I know this isn't the same situation, but it's going to be tough enough to overcome years apart without adding any more layers of complication. I can't risk it. I won't. And besides . . ."

You're a distraction I can't afford.

She stared into his eyes for a beat. "You know what? We've been through all of this before. You know exactly how long I've wanted this, and how hard it was to respect their wishes and leave my girls be when all I wanted was to camp out in front of their apartment building and hope for a glimpse of them. But every time I asked if I could come—for Ella's college graduation, for Merry's birthday, for dinner, for anything, they asked me not to. They weren't ready, and I hated it, but I understood. I had to wait for them to come to me." Moving briskly for the door, Jo kept her voice as light and steady as possible. "And now

they are. Ella and Merry are arriving on the evening
ferry. They'll be here for a couple of weeks at least, and
it's the culmination of more than ten years of prayers and
wishes. Let me have this time with them. And when they
leave, we'll talk. I promise."

"What if I find out something about the lien? Should I
sit on it until your daughters leave? I mean, God forbid
that in all this reconnecting and forging of new relationships, they should find out that you had a whole life—a
damn good life, Jo—after your husband took them and
left. You weren't alone. You had Taylor, and you had me."

She flinched, hand on the cold cut crystal of the door-
knob. His barb hit its target in her chest, certainly—but it
was the weary pain and frustration in his voice that hurt.
Worst of all, though, was the use of the past tense.

You had Taylor, and you had me.

Swallowing down the litany of apologies that nearly
choked her, Jo managed to keep her tone admirably
steady. Addressing the glossy wood of the office door, she
said, "If you find out anything about the lien, give me a
call. Otherwise . . . it's only a few weeks, Harrison."

"It's more than that, and you know it. But I can wait.
God knows, I'm used to it."

His low tone vibrated through her. Jo dropped her
forehead to rest for an instant against the door panel.
"Thank you."

Without pausing to hear his reply, she pushed open the
door and escaped before he could make it any clearer that
his legendary patience was strained to the breaking point.

She just had to get through the next month without
Dabney Leeds taking her to court over Aunt Dottie's debt.
Or anyone finding out how far the renovation and opening

of Windy Corner Stables had depleted her savings. Or
Harrison finally getting fed up and washing his hands
of her.

Most of all, she needed to make sure none of those
problems surfaced to scuttle Ella and Merry's visit.

Jo Ellen Hollister had waited fifteen years for the
chance to get to know her own daughters and to try and
make up for the sins of her past. Now that they were finally ready to see her, she couldn't let anything stand in
the way of this chance.

She might not get another opportunity to say what had
to be said.

CHAPTER 5

"I am in agony," Merry moaned as soon as Ella got back to the car. "Screw the suspension or the shocks or whatever—just get us to a bathroom!"

"Why didn't you go in the bushes?" Ella demanded as she buckled in, silently impressed with how steady her voice was. Considering how fast her heart was thumping in her chest, it was an accomplishment.

"I got all the way over there and wrestled my leggings down before I remembered the TP problem."

"What—"

"Toilet paper," Merry clarified. "As in, I didn't have any. And I know hikers and whatever use leaves, but I don't exactly have a degree in horticulture. It'd be just my luck to wipe my hoo-hah with poison ivy. So rev it up, Dale Earnhardt Jr.! Before my bladder splatters the inside of this ugly rental car."

"Yikes." Ella checked the rearview mirror, but they'd already turned off the main road. There was nothing behind them but sassafras trees, loblolly pines, and a muddy dirt track.

That's definitely not a pang of disappointment, she told herself. *The less you see of Grady Wilkes while you're here, the better.*

"I'm not sorry we stopped, though," Merry gushed. "If we hadn't stopped, we would've missed meeting Voyager!"

She went on to describe the horse they had both just seen in loving detail, reliving the moment when he'd nosed over her hand looking for a lump of sugar or a stray thumb to chomp on, and Ella didn't feel more than a passing tickle of guilt at tuning the recitation out.

Her mind was too full of Voyager's rider to do much more than add the occasional "Hmmm" to the monologue.

Grady Wilkes, the watchdog at her mother's gate.

Why now? Why him?

Because of course, of freaking course, this was the way it went. It had been months since she could think about anything other than her dwindling portfolio of clients and inability to land a deal, mere days since her boss booted her out of the office to get her head on straight . . . and here she was trundling down this pitted mud trap of a road toward a reunion with the mother who'd abandoned her family in every way that mattered.

So of course, now was when Ella was suddenly walloped in the head with an attraction she couldn't deny.

The fact that the man in question was a friend of her mother's, and had already decided that Ella was out to hurt her somehow? That was the cherry on the crap sundae of Ella's life.

Seriously, Fate. If you exist, I hope you know you're a stone-cold witch.

As she wheeled the car carefully down the nearly hidden side road Grady Wilkes had mentioned, it occurred to her that maybe she was fixating on that weird, surprising spark she'd felt with Grady in order to avoid thinking about the fact that she was moments away from seeing Jo Ellen Hollister.

Merry's voice trailed off uncertainly in the middle of a sentence about the way she could tell from Voyager's teeth that he was at least six years old, and Ella thought maybe her sister was doing the exact same thing—fixating on something, anything, to avoid hyperventilating and passing out from stress and nerves.

The car bounced over a deep rut and Merry put one hand on the dashboard to brace herself as she peered through the windshield. Ella pressed her lips together and tightened her grip around the steering wheel, easing her foot off the gas and letting the car roll to a stop.

A canopy of budding branches stretched overhead, turning the thin spring sunlight into dapples of green dancing across the hood of the car. It was quiet, almost eerily so, with none of the ambient street and car noises Ella had grown so used to in the city. The silence was broken only by the low hum of the rental car's idling engine and the too fast, almost panicky breathing coming from the passenger seat.

"It's okay," Ella said, giving Merry a reassuring smile. "Everything's going to be fine." Except she wasn't at all sure it would be.

"I just . . . I was only eight when Dad took us away. I barely remember her." Merry's voice, usually so vibrant and full of life, was a fraying thread. "What if she thinks I'm a giant slut for getting knocked up and then dumped?"

"She won't." And if she did, Ella vowed, she'd make sure Jo Ellen kept her mouth shut about it.

Merry hesitated. Then, in a small voice, she asked, "What if she doesn't like me?"

It's not too late to back out of this, Ella yearned to say. *We could leave right now, make a seven-point turn on this ridiculous, narrow path that passes for a driveway, and head straight back to civilization.*

But that wasn't what Merry needed right now. "I don't think that's going to be a problem. You have everyone you meet eating out of your hand within minutes! And anyway, you know how much Jo Ellen wants to see us."

Merry nodded slowly, her breathing beginning to even out. "All those letters asking to be allowed to visit." Ducking her head so that her purple hair swung forward and obscured her face, she asked, "Do you think Dad's going to be mad that we're here? I know he was glad when we asked her to stay away."

Ella swallowed, emotion burning behind her eyes. "Oh, kiddo. Dad loves you no matter what, you know that. He just doesn't want you to get hurt."

That wasn't strictly true. Not the part about Dad loving them, but the implication that he wouldn't be angry when he found out about this impromptu visit . . . and Neil Preston knew how to hold a grudge.

Not that he wasn't justified when it came to his ex-wife, Ella thought.

"Every time she floated the idea of coming to visit, I wanted to say yes," Merry confessed. She gave Ella a side-long glance. "I know you didn't."

Ella struggled with how to respond. She didn't want to make Merry feel bad or wrong about trying for a relationship with Jo. It was natural, especially now that Merry was having a baby of her own, to wonder what it would be like to have the support and comfort that supposedly came from the mother/daughter bond.

But unlike Merry, Ella had been old enough to be very aware of what was happening during those final tempestuous years of their parents' marriage. The drinking, arguing, drinking, crying, and more drinking.

She remembered Jo Ellen Hollister, and no matter how penitent the woman seemed in her letters, no matter how many times she'd begged for the chance to make it up to them, Ella wasn't interested in adding that much chaos and unpredictability to her nicely ordered life.

Now, if only this trip could help Merry finally move on and put a stop to all the *what if*s . . .

"It's okay that we have different needs," Ella said gently, determined to be supportive. "Are you ready?"

Merry pulled in a deep breath and let it out slowly, tapping the fingers of one hand against the swell of her belly. "Yes."

"There's my girl." Ella mustered up every ounce of approval she could find as she put the car in gear and started inching forward once more.

In the privacy of her own brain, all she could think was, *Let's get this over with.*

But as they rounded a bend in the road and came to a break in the tree line, the view that rose in front of the car took Ella's breath away.

Gravel covered the last five hundred yards of the driveway as it wound away from the trees and up a slight, grassy hill to the house . . . although "house" hardly seemed like the right word.

"It's a mansion," Ella realized, staring stupidly.

A huge, tumbledown red-brick mansion with a front

veranda and white columns reaching for the third-floor balcony, paint peeling sadly from railings and shutters hanging askew at the dark, curtainless windows.

"Wow. This is where she lives?" Merry said, awe creeping into her tone.

"It's a gorgeous place. Good bones, lots of old-fashioned Southern charm." Ella stared up through the windshield at the dilapidated building, her brain automatically cataloguing the salable features.

"Stop."

Torn from her mental calculations of what it might cost to rehab a house like this, Ella blinked. "What?"

"You've got that look," Merry accused. "That how-can-I-turn-a-profit look. This isn't one of your clients' properties."

"I know that."

Merry huffed and crossed her arms over her chest. Ella pressed her lips together, sorry she'd snapped. Gentling her voice, she said, "Sorry. It's habit."

It was more than habit, according to Ella's ex-therapist, Dr. Adrienne Voss. Adrienne had built her career working with adult children of alcoholics, and she'd explained that her patients often became overachievers in an attempt to create security outside of the home.

Ella didn't know how much she bought into the theory. All she knew for sure was that she didn't love the idea of so much of her personality having been formed by her mother's alcoholism.

Pulling around the circular drive, Ella threw the car into park and hopped out to help Merry extricate herself from the low-slung seat. When she squeezed her baby sister's cold hands, Ella felt the flutter of Merry's pulse jackrabbiting away.

She didn't have time to do more than haul Merry to her feet with a grunt—*wow, is the girl carrying triplets?*—before a screen door banged open behind them.

Bracing herself and putting a sheltering arm around Merry's stiff back, Ella turned them both to stare up at the woman standing on the sagging porch steps.

Ella blinked.

It wasn't Jo Ellen Hollister.

This was a girl, just a kid, really, and she was completely unfamiliar. Sunny blond hair, rosy fair skin, coltishly skinny arms and legs, startling eyes the color of warm brandy.

Although there wasn't a lot of warmth to those eyes, Ella noticed as the unknown girl crossed her arms over her chest.

"Welcome to Sanctuary. How was your trip?"

The words were polite, even friendly, but somehow, they conveyed the exact opposite of a welcome. Ella felt as if the girl had thrown up her hands to keep them at arm's length.

"Great," Merry exclaimed, enthusiasm cranking her vivaciousness up to about a thousand. "It's so insanely beautiful here, I can't stand it."

Whoever she was, the blonde reacted to Merry the way everyone did. The thaw was perceptible in her voice as she confirmed, "I'm Taylor McNamara." She paused for an odd, expectant moment, then finished with a sullen, "I work at the Windy Corner Stables."

Now that they were closer, Ella thought the girl couldn't be more than sixteen years old. "That must be a nice summer job," she said politely. "I'm Ella Preston, and this is my sister, Merry. We're here to see Jo Ellen Hollister."

Those golden-brown eyes cut to Ella, wariness cooling Taylor's voice. "I know who you are. And Jo's not here. We expected you on the evening ferry, and she had an appointment this morning, but she should be back any minute."

This was so awkward. In all her worrying about how emotionally draining and upsetting this trip would be, why had Ella never considered the awkwardness factor?

"Okay, thanks." Ella straightened her shoulders, determined not to show how uncertain she was. They were expected; they'd been invited. There was no reason to feel so unwelcome, just because this teenager hadn't even asked them up onto the porch with her, much less inside.

Merry did an uncomfortable little shimmy, reminding Ella that they were in danger of an accident if they didn't find a bathroom soon. Plus, how long had it been since Merry ate anything?

"Come on, kiddo," she said, grasping her sister's elbow to steady her for the climb up the sagging porch steps.

"No," the young woman said sharply, and Ella looked up to see that she had literally stuck a hand out, as if warding them off. "Don't come up here . . ."

Dropping Merry's arm, Ella planted her hands on her hips to keep them from curling into fists. None of this ridiculous situation was Taylor's fault, but Ella'd had about enough.

Reaching for the porch railing, Ella put her foot on the first step. "Look, my sister and I have been traveling for what feels like a week. We're tired, we're hungry, and Merry needs to find a bathroom. All we want is to wait inside until Jo Ellen gets back. She knows we're coming; she wants us here. I can't imagine she'd object."

A strange expression, a blend of hurt and resentment, twisted Taylor's pretty face for a split second before she said sweetly, "Suit yourself."

"Thank you." Ella started marching up the stairs. "Merry? Come on."

But as Ella reached the top of the steps, there was a loud crack of breaking wood. The world lurched sickeningly and dropped Ella with a scraping thud, her right leg buried up to mid-thigh in a hole in the porch floorboards.

Before Ella could even catch the breath that had been knocked out of her, Taylor strolled over to stare down at her with folded arms.

"And that would be why I told you not to come up here. The stairs have rotted through in the center."

"Why did you let me?" Ella gritted out, pain streaking up her calf and throbbing through her left leg where it was doubled under her, bearing most of her weight.

"You were so determined." Taylor gave a little shrug of her slim shoulders. "And who am I to stop Jo's daughters from doing whatever they want? Nobody."

Ella shook her spinning head, unable to even begin to untangle all that. "Ever think about getting this porch repaired?"

"It's on the list, believe me."

"Are you okay?" Merry cried.

"I'm fine. Stay down there," Ella warned her sister. "I'll be out of here in a jiffy."

Except . . . she wasn't.

Even when Taylor leaned down to give her a hand, Ella couldn't budge more than a few inches before the rotten, splintered wood gouged at her skin.

"It's no good." Taylor straightened with a guilty

grimace, wiping her hands on her denim-clad thighs. "Let me run inside and call our handyman. I'm sure he'll be able to get you out of there in no time."

"Umm, I hate to be a focus-puller," Merry began, a hint of tension tightening her voice, and Ella pushed down the pain in her leg to concentrate on her sister.

"Right. Taylor, would you mind taking Merry in with you? She needs a bathroom, and she should probably sit down and put her feet up with a glass of water. And maybe a sandwich. If it's not too much trouble." Ella injected a good amount of *it better not be too much trouble* into her serious glare. Taylor had the good grace to squirm a little before nodding.

"I don't want to leave you all alone out here," Merry protested, but Ella could hear the relief in her tone.

"I'll be fine," Ella said soothingly, keeping any hint of pain out of her voice. "The sooner you go in and call the handyman, the sooner I'll be out of here. Go on. You need to stay hydrated, and I know you're hungry. Don't make me worry about you."

Taylor led Merry around to the side of the porch where there was a hole in the railing, and helped her take the giant step up onto what was evidently a more solid portion of flooring.

The screen door banged shut behind them, leaving Ella to contemplate exactly how uncomfortable and embarrassed she was. Thank goodness she'd worn pants to protect against the spring chill—she could only imagine how scraped up and raw her trapped calf would be if she'd been wearing a skirt.

Not to mention that she'd be a lot closer to flashing the whole world right about now.

This couldn't be further from the way she'd imagined meeting her mother for the first time as an adult.

Ella had visualized herself as strong, independent, completely in control. Instead, here she was, stuck half in and half out of a hole in the woman's front porch like Winnie-the-Pooh after too much honey.

After the longest fifteen minutes of her life, a heavy tread crunched on the gravel behind her. Ella couldn't force her head to turn far enough to see who was there. Was it *her*?

Ella stiffened all over, every muscle clenching in anticipation of hearing the voice she'd never quite forgotten, the voice that visited her dreams—sometimes to scold, sometimes to weep, but sometimes to croon sweet lullabies that left Ella awake in the dark, memories shuddering through her in painful waves.

But instead of her mother's low, husky drawl, the voice that spoke sent a shudder of a different kind down Ella's curved spine.

"Somebody call for a handyman?"

Ella closed her eyes and counted to ten, but she knew it wouldn't make any difference.

As her friend Adrienne liked to say, the truth was the truth, no matter how inconvenient or painful . . . and the truth was that the handyman who'd been called to help her was none other than Grady Wilkes.

CHAPTER 6

Grady saw Ella Preston with her leg stuck between two broken floorboards, and instinct surged up, flooding his bloodstream with adrenaline.

His spine straightened as if a giant hand had slapped him on the back, his movements sure and purposeful as he reined Voyager to walk in a circle so Grady could assess the situation from multiple angles.

It had been a while, but his keep-the-victim-calm voice came out of him without any effort at all. "Are you injured? Are you in pain?"

Not that Ella seemed to need calming. From what he could see of her face, she appeared pale, but composed. Although at the sound of his voice, some tension flowed out of her shoulders. Interesting.

Tossing her dark brown hair back, she watched him come closer out of the corner of her eye. "Grady Wilkes. When you said you were a friend of my mother's, you neglected to mention that you were actually her employee."

Studying her, Grady saw the rise of hot red in her cheeks, the tightness of her lips. She was embarrassed to be caught in this pickle, which he could understand. What he didn't understand was his own gut reaction to witnessing her discomfort.

Grady didn't like it. Not one bit. "Pretty feisty for a lady jammed halfway into a front porch," he said as he threw his leg over Voyager's back and slid to the ground. He looped the reins over the horse's head and tied the trailing ends in a slipknot around a sturdy portion of the porch railing.

"Are you here to gloat? If I'd taken your warning and headed back to the ferry, this wouldn't have happened." Her voice was stifled, as if she were fighting down panic.

So much for teasing.

Pitching his voice to soothe, Grady crouched down to investigate what he could see of the situation under the porch, peering through the rickety wooden lattice fronting the deck. "I'm just here to help, ma'am. We'll have you out of there in a jiff. I know it's hard, but keep calm and breathe deep for me."

She'd gone straight through, all right. Squinting into the dusty blackness of the area under the house, Grady could see that her right leg was dangling, toes barely brushing the dirt foundation. Which meant all her weight was on her other leg, bent and folded under her, and supported by her hands pressed against the splintering floorboards.

Ella sucked in an audible breath, making Grady's gaze swivel to her pink cheeks and downcast eyes.

He'd knelt beside her without thinking about anything more than getting the lay of the land, but the position had him snugged up next to her so tight that when she took another deep inhale, the expansion of her rib cage brushed her shoulder against his hip.

"You're right," she said, still sounding a little choked. "I'm sorry, and thank you for coming so quickly. I do appreciate it. This is just . . . not how I thought today would go."

That makes two of us, sweetheart.

Clearing his throat, Grady did his level best to ignore the spine-tingling awareness of her slim body, so close at hand that his fingers buzzed with the need to reach out and shape her curves from hip to waist to breast.

He also had to ignore the fact that, very shortly, he would be putting his hands on her, to pull her out of the porch. And when that happened, he'd have to dig deep for every ounce of focus his training had ever imparted to keep from getting distracted by the softness of her smooth, pearly skin.

Grady shook his head to dislodge the searingly persistent images. "How did this even happen? Taylor was pretty vague on the phone."

"Right, of course you know Taylor. This is one of those Mayberry-type places where everyone knows everyone else, isn't it?"

She was starting to steady herself, Grady noted, her deep breathing doing its job of distracting her from the fact that she was trapped. To keep it going while he figured the best way out of this fix, Grady absently started up a light, distracting patter. "Well, yeah. But in this case, we happen to be cousins. I've known Taylor since she was born, and your mom has known her almost as long. She's . . . a close friend of the family, almost like a mother to Tay, since my aunt died when Taylor was five."

It occurred to him even as the words flew out of his

mouth that maybe talking up Ella's estranged mother's close maternalesque relationship with another girl might qualify as sticking his foot in it.

So he was watching closely enough to catch the quick shiver of a flinch in Ella's frame, even though she rolled her shoulders and got rid of it almost immediately. And her voice was soft and mostly neutral when she replied, "I see. That explains . . . a lot."

Narrowing his eyes, Grady stood and propped his hands on his hips. "Wait. Exactly how did you manage to fall through this porch?"

Ella tilted her head back, soft waves of dark hair cascading over the shoulders of her bright green sweater. She looked him straight in the eye and said, "It was an accident. Can you get me out, please?"

There was more to this story, he knew it, but he was distracted from ferreting out the whole truth by the white-knuckled tension of her fingers pressed against the floorboards. He frowned. That could be from the awkwardness of this whole conversation . . . or it could be an indicator of pain. "You really didn't answer me before, when I asked if you were okay."

"Aside from being stuck in a porch, I'm fine," she said, firm and no-nonsense. "But I'd like to get out of here, preferably before anyone else sees me like this."

She was lying. Grady knew the look of pain—intimately—and the fine lines bracketing her mouth, the stiff way she held herself, told him there was more going on than she was saying.

Her leg was hurting her, he'd be willing to bet on it, but she didn't want to admit it.

Slapping his hands on his thighs, Grady stood and

swung off the porch. She didn't have to tell the truth about what was going on with her leg—either way, he'd be careful not to cause her any more pain.

And once she was safely unporched, he'd deal with whatever injuries she might have incurred.

Grady was trained to be rational and mission forward, but it had been five years since he'd been face-to-face with an injured rescue. And the last time he'd had to rescue someone who was more than a stranger . . . he shuddered, the kick of memory making him fumble with the buckles strapping his tool kit to the pack across the back of Voyager's saddle.

You've done rescues like this a million times, he reminded himself, flexing his stiff fingers against the compression of his leather gloves.

But when he glanced back at Ella, with her flushed face and glittering blue eyes, her tight shoulders and the determined tilt of her little chin, he knew this wasn't like any rescue he'd ever done.

Grady's instincts for danger had been honed over many years in some of the toughest, most devastated areas of the nation, from the treacherous rubble of collapsed buildings to the sodden chaos of flood plains.

The sharp, devastating slap of desire he felt when he looked at Ella Preston was by far the most dangerous thing he'd faced in a long time.

Ella had no idea what Grady Wilkes was doing— something that involved a scary-looking handsaw and a lot of cursing.

At the moment, it was taking all her concentration not to notice the heat radiating off his big, broad-shouldered body. Her skin was so sensitized by the electricity in the air between them, if he even brushed her shoulder, she jumped.

This is ridiculous, she thought despairingly. *Why is this happening now, of all times?*

But the fact that this surge of attraction was super inconvenient didn't change how much she wanted to lean into the solid strength of him and hide her stupid blush against his neck.

Searching for a way to distract herself, she said, "You should post a sign, at least until you get this porch fixed. It's common sense. This porch is a liability."

He grunted irritably, still working away. "Nobody on Sanctuary is going to sue Jo Ellen Hollister." The handsaw froze for a moment as his gaze shot to hers. "Unless you're planning to."

"Of course not." Ella looked away from that too-penetrating stare. "I don't want anything from her."

She lifted her gaze to the peeling paint of the porch ceiling and held her breath, which had the added benefit of silencing her startled whimper when he bumped a little too close to her and jarred her leg against the jagged edge of a broken board.

Not a sound passed her lips, but he shot her another sharp look anyway, almost as if he knew she was hiding exactly how much pain she was in.

Uncomfortable, she splayed out her hands against the floorboards to keep from doing something crazy like reaching out to touch him. "Has Jo always lived in this house?"

That got her a sharp glance. "Yeah. She took care of her aunt here after she had her stroke. And then Miz Dottie left the place to Jo in her will."

Annoyed by the way he was studying her—what, did he think she was after her mother's inheritance?—Ella did a quick centering breath exercise. "Well, it's a lovely house, underneath the disrepair."

He relaxed enough to smile. "Hey, you'd be in some disrepair, too, if you were as old as this pretty lady. The house dates from 1899."

"Historical building, structurally sound—mostly." Ella craned her neck to peer down the wraparound porch to the wings stretching out to the sides of the main building. "Unspoiled natural setting, zero competition. And those wild horse herds, people love stuff like that. You know, this place would make a great bed-and-breakfast."

Beside her, Grady went completely quiet. Something about his stillness made Ella shiver, like the calm before a storm rolled in off the bay.

"The last thing Sanctuary Island needs is a bed-and-breakfast bringing in tourists to trample all over the wildlife and wreck the peace." His voice was low and devastating, almost a snarl.

Ella blinked, taken completely off guard by the rush of heat down her spine. She'd never been attracted to big, hot-tempered, aggressive guys in the past, but there was something about the passion in Grady's voice and the intensity in his green eyes that got her blood pumping.

Flustered, embarrassed, and more than a little annoyed at both herself and Grady, Ella sputtered, "Look, Mr. Protector of the Island, I'm just making idle conversation here. I certainly don't have any designs on the house or the land, so feel free to stop acting like I'm here to ruin your life, or Jo's, or anybody else's."

Still scowling, Grady loomed closer until their lips

were a breath apart and Ella was sure he could hear the thunder of her heartbeat. "Then why are you here?"

The reminder of what was at stake was like a glass of cold water dumped over her head. Drawing in a shaky breath that smelled like sun-warmed skin and saddle leather, Ella said, "I'm here for Merry. She wants a relationship with Jo Ellen, and I'm here for moral support. Nothing else."

And I can't let you distract me . . . no matter how good you smell.

The scowl faded from Grady's face, but the focused power of his gaze never lessened, even when he cocked his head at an angle to study her. One corner of his mouth curled up, making Ella's stare drop down to trace the sensual shape of his lips. She wondered how he would taste.

"I like the way you talk about your sister. She's lucky to have you."

Ella made her living off her ability to read people, to size them up and figure out the tactics that would work best to get what she wanted in any negotiation. But she couldn't seem to get a handle on Grady Wilkes.

Rattled, she ignored the warm, speculative gleam in his eyes. "Are you almost done?"

"What? Oh. Should be. C'mon, give me your hands."

He stood and she slid her hands against the worn, butter-soft leather of his gloves, suppressing a shiver at the way his eyes darkened as his fingers closed around hers.

"Here we go," he said, lifting.

This time, Ella couldn't bite back a thin cry as the move wrenched her ankle, sending a sickening jolt of pain up her leg.

She was still gasping when sudden, intense heat surrounded her. Grady dropped to his knees and scooted close enough to snake one long arm into the widened hole he'd made around her leg.

"I think my foot is caught on something," she managed, her head still swimming from the pain.

His only answer was to tilt his chin down in concentration. Ella stared at Grady's face bent so close, the solid bulk of his muscular body held still, his power leashed and tamed as his fingers groped her foot and ankle.

"Wait," she cried, suddenly afraid. "I don't think you should be touching that . . ."

"It's okay," he told her. "I'm trained for this."

"You have training in getting women out of porches?" Ella wanted to laugh, but she was afraid to give in to the hysteria bubbling up in her throat.

"Sort of." He paused for a long moment before reluctantly continuing. "Back before I moved here from Dallas, I was part of Texas Task Force One, an urban search-and-rescue team."

Another puzzle piece slotted into place, and it calmed Ella's nerves like nothing else could have. "So . . . I guess this isn't even close to the craziest rescue you've ever attempted."

A half smile tugged at his mouth, but didn't reach his green eyes. "This ain't exactly my first rodeo, no."

Ella took a deep breath, bracing herself. "Okay. Go ahead."

The fingers were back, but before she even had time to tense up, he said, "Got it."

She felt a grating pressure against the bones at the top of her foot and controlled her instinctive wince, but there was no sharp pain, only a swift relief as she realized she could wiggle her foot from side to side.

"Let's try this again," he said.

Grady hooked his hands under her arms in a tantalizing imitation of an embrace that had Ella's heart hammering. At the brush of his cheek against hers, the rough scratch of his golden-brown stubble, Ella had to bite back another sound—but this time it was a moan of need.

Feeling half crazy and dizzy with the onslaught of too many conflicting feelings, Ella let her hands steal up to clutch at his flannel-covered shoulders.

"Do it," she said, bracing herself for another jab from a broken board, but between one heartbeat and the next, Grady hauled her up and out of the hole . . . and straight into his arms.

CHAPTER 7

Okay, Ella, you can do this. Stand on your own two feet.

But the instant she gathered the fraying threads of her self-control and pulled away from Grady's steadying arms, her ankle protested with a ferocious twinge that sent her wobbling.

She nearly fell over before Grady caught her with his large hands wrapped around her upper arms.

Closing her eyes in an embarrassed wince, Ella said, "Thank you. I seem to have twisted my ankle a little. I'm sure it'll be all right in a second."

"Or it could be broken," he pointed out, staring down her body as if he could perform an X-ray with his naked eyes. "What's with the stoic act, anyway? It's okay to admit you might be hurt, you know."

No it's not.

Swallowing back the gut reaction, Ella called up a smile. "Of course. I just don't see what good it does for me to whine about it."

His gaze snapped to hers as if she'd said something

bizarre. Mouth twisting into something closer to a grimace than a smile, he said, "I get that."

Ella stared at him, every inch of her aware of the taut, sculpted muscle beneath his bulky plaid shirt. And all Ella could do was wonder what he'd been through in his life to put that look on his face.

Probably, it wasn't exactly what she'd been through. Chances were slim that he'd spent his childhood with a mother sliding into raging alcoholism and a father who detached himself from his family to save his own sanity. Grady had probably never felt like he had to be grown-up by the age of seven, because he had a little sister who didn't understand what was going on, but still knew something was very wrong at home. He'd probably never dreaded the possibility of teachers or guidance counselors finding out about it, never pushed himself so hard to appear normal, without really knowing what normal even felt like.

But all the same, as she stood there in the circle of his arms and stared up into his eyes, she felt a connection unfurling between them like the tender green vines creeping up the side of the house. A perfect empathy unlike anything she'd ever experienced in years of talking candidly to professional therapists, even Adrienne.

Without warning, something inside her opened up, a tightly closed bud stretching toward the first sunlight of spring.

His gaze dropped to her lips, and Ella's heartbeat quickened. The moment went taut, suspended and fragile between them, as if they were holding something delicate and infinitely breakable in the cradle of their bodies. Slowly, almost in a daze, Ella tilted her head back. Just a little.

Just enough.

As if aware that a sudden movement would shatter the moment, Grady dipped his head to take what she was offering.

His lips moved over hers softly, a questing touch that barely grazed her mouth, but somehow sent shivers of sensation cascading down her spine. Ella's lungs ached and burned until she remembered to breathe, sighing against his lips, and the kiss changed.

Grady's careful grip tightened, pulling her closer, so close she was all but burrowing into the solid warmth of his chest. He made a hungry noise that reverberated through her chest, and when she gasped, he stroked his tongue along the sensitive flesh of her bottom lip.

His eyes darkened, and Ella realized this was the first time she'd ever kissed anyone with her eyes open. It was odd, almost too intimate, and some part of her cowered away from the frightening vulnerability of letting him see what he was doing to her.

But she couldn't bring herself to close her eyes. She couldn't look away from him and what he was telling her without words. Whatever Grady was saying, it was in a language Ella didn't know yet—but with every beat of his heart against hers, she felt herself groping toward understanding.

A truck engine rattled and coughed, heavy wheels churning up the gravel of the driveway.

Ella snapped back into reality with an unpleasant sensation of whiplash. Jerking her head back, she blinked into Grady's intense stare. Her lips were still buzzing and tingling from his kiss. Every part of her body that had been touching his now felt cold and bereft.

Oh dear Lord. What am I doing?

A hot flush crawled up her neck, and she squeezed her eyes shut and pulled out of his arms, desperate to escape the unbearable strangeness of this whole episode.

What had she been thinking? Dreaming up some mystical, spiritual connection with a man she'd known for all of fifteen minutes, letting him save her and then swooning into his arms like some pathetic, helpless damsel offering herself up for a kiss?

It's this island, Ella thought hysterically as she put some much needed distance between herself and Grady. *Sanctuary Island is doing something to me. It's turning me into an insane person.*

The loud, dark blue pickup truck rumbled to a stop in front of the house, and the driver's side door opened. Ella barely had time to smooth a trembling hand over her hair and make sure her shirt was still neatly tucked in before a tall, spare woman stepped down from the truck's cab.

The woman shaded her eyes with one hand as she stared up at the porch, and when she smiled, Ella wished she were still standing close enough to Grady for his strong arms to steady her. That smile made the entire world tilt like the D.C. metro train taking a sharp curve.

That smile. Bright, open, infectious, inviting whoever saw it to share the joke. Ella had seen that smile a thousand times, growing up. But never before on her mother's face.

That was Merry's smile.

"Well, now." The woman's throaty voice, laced with a combination of nerves and amusement, sent a shock of recognition all the way to Ella's bones. "Looks like Grady is making you feel right at home."

Ella gathered the tattered shreds of her dignity around her and drew herself up as straight as she could manage without flinching at the low throb of pain in her stupid ankle. "Yes, he's been very helpful."

And to think, Ella had been sure that when she saw her mother in the flesh for the first time in fifteen years, she'd feel nothing.

The seething well of messy emotions bubbling in her chest was certainly not nothing. Shocked at herself and taken completely off guard, Ella struggled to find some sort of equilibrium.

Eyes sharp on Ella's face, Jo Ellen appeared to be gauging every word carefully. "Ella. It's been . . . you look good. Wonderful, really. How are you doing?"

The stilted question flayed along Ella's raw nerves like a razor blade. It seemed as if Jo were asking for a lot more than an update on Ella's health and well-being.

"I'm fine," she said, schooling her voice and her expression to show nothing. She didn't want to give this woman anything, and wow, did she ever need a minute to catch her balance. "You should go inside. Merry is looking forward to seeing you."

Next to her, Grady lifted a hand to her shoulder, and the warm, heavy weight of it was an anchor in a stormy sea. Ella straightened her spine and lifted her chin, pathetically grateful for the surprising show of support.

"And you weren't," Jo clarified, her voice quiet but unsurprised. "Well. That's certainly . . . understandable. Thank you for coming anyway—it means a lot to me to have you here."

"Look. I don't mean to be harsh," Ella found herself saying, even though she did mean to. Didn't she? "But I don't think there's any point in beginning this visit under false pretenses."

"So tell me, what you do want from this visit?" Jo Ellen said.

"I'm not here to act out some movie-of-the-week tear-jerker." Ella's voice had gone raspy, the words ripping from her throat like bolts shot from an arrow. "I'm not going to fall into your arms and call you mom. I'm not here for you at all. I'm here for Merry. That's it."

She saw—actually saw—every one of those words strike home. That smile Jo Ellen had stolen from her youngest daughter melted away, leaving Jo looking up at the porch with an expression Ella couldn't decipher.

"I see." Jo stood tall, solid, completely unlike Ella's memories of broken-down desperation. "In the interest of clarity, let me tell you what I'm expecting from this visit."

Ella braced herself, ready to fend off her mother's emotional demands for a renewed relationship, her desire to reconnect, to rehash the past, to apologize—Ella didn't want to hear any of it.

Apparently, that wasn't what Jo had in mind.

"I want you to get to know the island," Jo said. "This place is part of your family history, and you deserve the chance to discover where you come from."

It took Ella a long moment to switch gears. "Um, sure. It seems like a nice place."

"It is," Grady said. His deep, certain answer was aimed at Ella, but when she glanced at him, he was watching Jo. The two of them seemed to be having a silent conversation using only their eyes.

His hand still gripped her shoulder, and Ella fought a moment of vertigo. Was it weird to feel so much more of a connection to this man she'd just met than she did to her own mother? "And it's small, too, which is nice. I can't imagine it will take me long to see all the sights."

"Oh, I don't know about that. I bet it would take a month, at least, to really plumb the depths of what Sanctuary has to offer," Jo said lightly.

"One week," Ella countered, her inner negotiator zooming to the fore.

"Three weeks," Jo returned, with a hopeful smile.

"Two. And that's my final offer—that's all the vacation time I've got."

Technically true, although this wasn't exactly a vacation. Paul Bishop had told her he didn't want to see her back in the office until she'd put on five pounds and lost the bags under her eyes. But there was no way she was admitting that to Jo Ellen.

"Okeydoke." Jo's smile widened into a grin, and there it was again, that so familiar, much-loved smile looking completely out of place . . . and yet, right at home on Jo's angular face. "I can work with two weeks."

Somehow, Ella realized, she'd gotten the short end of this deal.

"I know you don't want to hear this," Jo said, staring up at Ella. "And I know you won't believe me right now, because I destroyed any trust you ever had in me a long time ago. But I'm going to make sure you don't regret coming to Sanctuary Island. That's a promise."

Ella felt herself seize up with tension, as if someone had strung a wire through her shoulder blades and pulled it taut. Grady, who obviously noticed, stepped up to stand beside her. His voice was a deep rumble in her ear. "And when Hollister women make a promise, they never break their word."

Something like pain and regret shadowed Jo's blue eyes. "I didn't always live up to the Hollister name. But these days, I do my damnedest."

Despite herself, Ella felt a twinge of curiosity. She knew almost nothing about her family on Jo's side. It might not be a horrible chore to find out more.

"For now," Jo said, reaching into the cab of her truck and hauling out a couple of plastic bags, "let's go inside. I'm dying to see your sister."

Grady walked over to the side of the porch as Jo came around, stretching an arm to help her up. Instead of taking his hand, however, Jo passed him the pair of shopping bags and vaulted lightly up onto the porch under her own power.

When Jo saw the gaping hole in her porch floorboards, she froze so suddenly that the shopping bags Grady had been handing back to her slipped through her fingers.

"What happened?" Her concerned gaze shot to Ella, raking her from head to toe as she took a step forward. "Are you all right?"

Ella retreated a step before she could force herself to hold her ground, her injured ankle wobbling and slicing lines of pain up her calf.

When Ella sucked in a short breath, Jo froze in place, dismay carving lines into her face.

"It's nothing." Ella drew on her reserves and carefully controlled the image she presented. Self-sufficient, dismissive, poised. "Twisted my ankle a little. Go ahead and find Merry, she's waiting for you. I'll follow you in a minute."

Ella forced herself to straighten out her ankle and plant her foot firmly on the floor.

Don't fuss, she mentally warned Jo. *I don't need your sympathy or your concern.*

After a long moment, Jo reluctantly looked away. She turned her gaze on Grady, who nodded once, silently.

Which was apparently the reassurance Jo needed. The screen door banged behind Jo as she slipped past them, and Grady turned back to Ella with a wry twist to his mouth.

"Let me walk you in. No sense hurting yourself worse just to prove a point," he drawled as he held out his arm.

Heat scorched her cheeks and neck. Even Ella wasn't sure if it was anger at his insistence on misunderstanding her or the thrill she got every time they touched.

"I'm not proving any point," she declared, defiantly taking his arm. "I didn't want to get Taylor in trouble for not warning me about the porch."

Grady's tawny eyebrows shot up in surprise. "Why not? The brat deserves it."

"Maybe." Ella shrugged, hyperaware of the hardness of his bicep under his soft flannel shirt. "But she's just a kid, and if she and Jo are as close as you say, then it can't be easy for her to suddenly come face-to-face with Jo's biological daughters."

"That's . . . incredibly perceptive and sensitive of you." Grady moved toward the door, keeping pace with her slower steps.

Ella laughed, her throat raw and tight. "Don't sound so shocked. I'm not the villain here, Grady."

He stopped short, pulling her off balance so that she leaned more of her weight on his shoulder than she'd intended.

"I know that." Grady's arm was like solid steel beneath her fingers. "For what it's worth, I'm sorry about earlier. I shouldn't have tried to run you off."

The lump in Ella's throat was hard to swallow around.

"Jo is important to you. To a lot of people on Sanctuary Island, apparently. Including Taylor."

"That doesn't give us the right to attack you. And you should know, this isn't Jo's fault. I mean, it's not like she's been bad-mouthing you and Merry all over town or anything."

"Don't." Ella winced at the sharpness of her own voice. "Look, I don't want to ruin this nice moment we've got going on, but I can't listen to you sing Jo's praises or make excuses or apologies for her."

A muscle ticked in his rigid jaw, but he met her gaze squarely. "Fair enough."

"And thanks," she said, as they restarted their painfully slow progress across the porch.

"For what?"

"For getting me out of the porch." Ella paused, then gritted her teeth and finished. "And for not making a big deal about . . . before."

He stilled under her touch for the briefest of moments before circling a steadying arm around her shoulders. Despite how close he stood, Ella felt his withdrawal before he even spoke.

"You mean the kiss."

The kiss was a mistake, a blip in the smooth, predictable course of Ella's organized, sensible life. She wasn't here on Sanctuary Island to make friends. Or to make out with handymen.

No matter how handsome that handyman might be. Handsome, intriguingly complicated, fiercely loyal . . .

"I was taken off guard," Ella explained quickly, keeping her eyes trained forward on the front door. "This whole trip has turned out to be a lot more . . . emotional than I was expecting. But it won't happen again."

She sneaked a peek at his face out of the corner of her eye and saw the way his jaw clenched. Catching her looking, Grady smoothed his face into an impenetrable friendly politeness. "Sure. With the whole rescuing-the-damsel thing, we got caught up in the moment. It didn't mean anything."

Ella swallowed, the ache in her throat making it tough to form words. "Good. We agree."

Thick, leaden silence dropped over them like a blackout curtain. Ella hobbled on, every fiber of her being tuned in to the rangy, rough-hewn man beside her. It took almost as much effort to hide her wince every time her bad foot landed on the boards as it did to hop laboriously forward, inch by inch.

After the fourth or fifth step-hop-ow, Grady made an aggravated noise. "This is stupid."

He turned to her, and before Ella knew what was happening, he'd swept her into his arms like a bride, kicked open the screen door, and carried her over the threshold.

CHAPTER 8

This. This was what she'd been missing.

Jo buried her nose in her younger daughter's hair and breathed in, the combined scents of sea salt and whatever chemicals Merry had used to dye her hair magenta coating Jo's brain in the kind of euphoria she hadn't experienced since her last shot of bourbon, fourteen years ago.

The reminder of her past, the things she'd done and choices she'd made that had resulted in having to go more than a decade without putting her arms around this amazing young woman had Jo tightening those arms until Merry squeaked.

"Sorry, sugar." She never wanted to let go, but she had an insatiable need to stare into Merry's beautiful face. One glance had been enough to sear the image onto Jo's brain forever.

During those long years of missing her girls and feeling their absence like an aching hole in her own heart, Jo had prayed for the chance to catch just a glimpse of them. Even from afar, to see how they were with her own eyes—she'd sworn before God that if she could have that, she'd never want for anything more.

And now, here she was with one baby girl in her arms, the other close by, and Jo knew she'd been wrong.

Sorry, God. I lied. One glimpse is not enough. Because I'm weak and greedy, and now that I have them here, on my island, I want more.

Thankfully, Jo was pretty sure God hadn't been fooled. He knew what she needed better than she knew herself—as proof, the fact that Ella and Merry were here on Sanctuary.

But for how long?

Already dreading the moment when Merry would be out of her reach, Jo let herself have one last squeeze before easing back and staring down into her daughter's wide blue eyes.

I have them for at least two weeks, she reminded herself. *Ella agreed to it.*

And there was nothing in that agreement that said Jo couldn't do her darnedest to make them both want to stay longer.

"Um, hi," Merry said, tucking a strand of reddish-purple hair behind her ear. "It's good to . . . meet you? Although I guess we've already met. Wow, could I have come up with a dumber thing to say? Sorry."

Ignoring the tightening of her throat, Jo smiled. "Let's say we're happy to see each other and leave it at that."

Merry ducked her head, a grin tugging at one corner of her mouth. "I guess you saw Ella outside. Was she out of the porch yet? Is she okay?"

"She looked fine to me." Other than the hurt ankle, Ella looked wonderful—every inch a grown woman, sure of herself and ready to fight to protect her sister.

It warmed Jo's heart to know that her daughters had such a close bond, and that Ella's instincts were so caring and strong. It said a lot about her as a person, Jo thought.

"Was Mr. Tall, Blond, and Helpful with her?" Merry popped a dimple in one cheek as she cast a sly look at Jo, who had to laugh.

"Grady? He sure was."

"Good." Merry nodded decisively. "Once Taylor told me who your handyman was that she was calling, I decided to stay in here and let them have a few minutes together."

"That's funny, I had the same thought!" Remembering the way Grady had stepped up and stood with Ella made Jo smile. She left Merry perched on the ancient chintz sofa and walked across the front parlor to peek out the window. She couldn't get a good angle to see what was going on out there, but Ella and Grady certainly did seem to be moving mighty slowly.

As Merry explained how they'd met up with Grady on their way here from town, the sound of her bright, vivacious chatter filled the musty old house with light.

"And when I saw them together," Merry concluded, "I knew. There's something there."

Before Jo could do more than clasp her hands in sheer delight, the front door swung open and the man in question stepped into the foyer.

With his arms full of Ella.

Jo shot a quick look over to Merry, who raised both brows and made a see-what-I-mean kind of face.

Giddy at the feeling of sharing something with her younger daughter, even a potentially silly and baseless hope about what might be going on here, Jo beamed at Grady.

Who barely noticed, what with having to contend with Ella's squirming and loud demands that he put her down this instant.

Grady had that expression on his face, though. Jo had seen that expression countless times after he finally picked himself up and got determined to do his physical therapy and help himself heal. She knew exactly what it meant.

Grady Wilkes was all in.

Hmm. This has possibilities.

"Hush up and hold on. I'm putting you down on the sofa," he said firmly. "Where you can't do any more damage to yourself. God Almighty, woman, who taught you to be so stubborn?"

"Are you all right?" Merry's voice was sharp with concern.

"I'm perfectly fine," Ella said, just as Grady muttered, "Right ankle. Probably a mild sprain."

It took everything Jo had not to fuss over Ella, make her sit down and check her out from head to toe and possibly bundle her onto the ferry for a trip to the emergency clinic over on the mainland. But the "back off" vibes emanating from Ella were clear as day, and Jo had made a private vow that since her daughters were being generous enough to give her this chance, she would not screw it up by presuming too much or pushing too hard.

But it wasn't easy. She'd forgotten what it was like to have this big, consuming love pulling her in more than one direction at a time. For so long now, she'd poured all of those instincts into Harrison's trouble magnet of a teenage daughter.

Where is Taylor, anyway?

As Grady leaned over to settle Ella on the couch be-side her sister, the pocket door to the hallway slid open to reveal Taylor balancing a tray with a pitcher and a bunch of glasses filled with ice.

"There you are," Jo said, relieved. Here, at least, was someone she knew inside and out—someone whose life she hadn't in any way screwed up. Someone who might actually count on the plus side in the balance sheet of Jo's past. "I was worried—did you see that big hole in the front porch that Ella fell into?"

"Uh, yeah, I saw it. Hey, anyone want some iced tea?" Taylor said, and something about the hesitation in her voice made Jo give her a sharper look. Hovering awk-wardly in the doorway, Taylor appeared to take in the scene at a glance.

"Thanks, honey, you didn't have to do that," Jo said, walking over to sling her arm around Taylor's shoulders. "So you already met both my girls?"

The thrill of saying that out loud—"my girls"—was almost enough to distract Jo from how Taylor's neck was strung wire-taut with tension.

"We met." Ella huffed out a relieved breath as she sank into the couch cushions. "Taylor was the one who called Grady when I had my dumb porch incident."

Beside her, Taylor swallowed audibly, and Jo frowned. She had the feeling she was missing something.

"You know what?" Taylor shrugged Jo's arm off with a quick smile that didn't reach her eyes. "I'm going to take off. Y'all have a lot to catch up on, and you don't need me for . . . well, for anything, I guess."

She shoved the tray at Jo, who grabbed it just as the pitcher wobbled. With visions of iced-tea stains splotching

Aunt Dottie's gazillion-year-old hooked rug, Jo spent precious moments getting the tray under control, and missed Taylor's swift exit from the room.

"It was nice to meet you," Merry called after her, and Jo set the tray down on a white-doilied side table before her shaking hands could rattle the ice in the glasses.

Talk about being pulled in too many directions.

Here were her biological daughters, in the same room with her for the first time in years. She'd imagined herself happily busy laying the groundwork for rebuilding her relationships with Ella and Merry.

Instead, she was messing up one of the few relationships in her life that she'd ever been proud of.

Sending Grady an agonized glance, Jo hoped he read her mind as effectively as he usually did.

He gave her a slight nod and went after his cousin . . . but not without a swift look back at Ella, who was struggling to sit up straight on the edge of the overstuffed sofa cushion. Ella's cheeks went pink—the same pink that tinged the tips of Grady's ears as he ducked out of the room—and Jo felt that tingle of potential intensify into the beginning of a plan as she turned back to her daughters.

In recovery, Jo had to take the tools she was handed and use them to the best of her ability. She'd learned not to let anything get in the way of doing the work and achieving her goals.

Merry wanted to be here, Jo knew that much from the precious letters they'd exchanged. But Ella was a tougher nut to crack. Jo had been counting on the magic of Sanctuary to make her eldest daughter's visit a success.

But maybe Jo could find a way to help the old island magic along . . .

* * *

"Hold up, Tay."

Grady caught his cousin's arm as she veered away from the hole in the porch and headed for the relative safety of the gap in the railing.

She whirled to face him, red flags of emotion flying high on her pale cheekbones. "I need to get out of here."

"What the hell is your problem? Ella just covered for you in there, in case you didn't notice."

"No one asked her to. And I don't have a problem," she ground out through a clenched jaw. "God. Excuse me if I'm not in the mood to sit around the parlor drinking iced tea."

Grady grabbed onto his patience with both hands. "Jo's worried about you . . ."

Taylor made a miserable, sarcastic sound. "Please. Jo doesn't have time to spare worrying about me. Not now that she has her real daughters back."

"Taylor Elizabeth McNamara," he chided gently. "You know Jo loves you more than life. But Ella and Merry only just arrived, and she wants to get them settled in."

"Right. So she can convince them to stick around even longer." Taylor's fingers were white-knuckled where she clutched the railing to swing herself down to the ground. "Well, thanks but no thanks. She'll have a better chance of getting what she wants if I'm not around, anyway."

Grady started to protest—knew Jo would want him to stop Taylor from leaving like this—but at the same time, he didn't think Taylor was completely wrong. In this kind of mood, his young cousin had once stolen a vacationer's sailboat, beached it on the sandbar south of the island, and managed to set it on fire.

Of course, she'd had an accomplice, and all of that was a couple of years in the past, but still. Taylor could wear herself out trying to convince the good people of Sanctuary that she'd grown up, matured, and mellowed since the bad old days when she and Caleb Rigby used to terrorize the town with graffiti sprees and other hijinks . . . but Grady had known his baby cousin her whole life.

And as far as Grady could tell, people didn't change. Not all the way down to the bone. Which meant that Taylor, right this minute, was an oil slick just waiting for some damn fool to drop a lit match.

"Okay," he said, using the calm, soothing tone he usually reserved for the wild horses. "Should I tell Jo you'll see her at the barn tomorrow, as usual?"

Taylor's shoulders slumped in defeat, but defiance sparked in her voice as she muttered, "She's not going to want me around once Ella tells her I was the one who got her hurt."

Grady scowled. "Yeah, about that. What the hell were you thinking? What if it had been Merry—a pregnant lady could be really badly hurt by a fall like that."

"I didn't know the whole floor would bust open," Taylor cried. "And I wouldn't have let Merry come up there. Anyway, I tried to tell Ella not to."

Grady arched a brow. "Right. But you didn't try all that hard, did you?"

"I wanted . . . I don't even know what I wanted." Taylor's pretty face was set in lines of misery. "I was so mad. I forgot how that felt, the way I used to feel like my head would explode sometimes, and before I even know it, I'm doing something bad."

There was pure dread in her tone, a fear and self-loathing that struck a chord deep in Grady's gut. He knew that feeling. Curling a protective arm around Taylor's slumping shoulders, he walked her over to her car, a much loved little two-door hatchback she kept running by tinkering with it every chance she got.

"You're not bad," Grady told her. "But you can be thoughtless, and a little too quick to believe the worst in people. And I say that as someone who's realizing he might be that way, too—so we both need to do better. Okay?"

She paused for a moment before lowering herself into the driver's seat. "I'll try. But it's not going to be easy, with Merry and Ella around. Merry seems okay, maybe, but I don't care if Ella didn't snitch, she still has a stick up her ass."

Instantly and without warning, a vision of Ella's behind rose up in Grady's mind's eye, round and pert, filling out her sensible khaki pants to perfection. Realizing a long moment had passed and Taylor was still looking at him expectantly, Grady cleared his throat. "Right. I'll watch out for her ass. I mean, I'll keep an eye on things here, take care of Jo."

Taylor made a face like a filly sticking her nose in a clump of ticklish clover. "Gross, you perv. Now I'm really leaving. But I guess I can show up for my shift at the barn tomorrow."

After Taylor drove off, Grady stood in the middle of the driveway for several long heartbeats and thought about the promise he'd asked of her.

It was good advice, to think before acting and not to leap to conclusions about people. He'd met Ella with a heart full of preconceived notions, and she'd turned out to be nothing like he'd expected. He owed her another chance.

As he remembered the shock and wonder of that scorching-hot kiss, he decided he owed it to both of them.

Because maybe it hadn't meant anything to Ella Preston, but it had been a long time since Grady had felt anything like that.

And he wasn't giving up on it without a fight.

CHAPTER 9

"I think you'll be comfortable in here," Jo said, so brightly that Ella could clearly hear the nerves in the older woman's voice.

Ella, who'd limped after Jo down a hallway to a door at the rear of the house, bit her lip as the door swung open to reveal a light, airy bedroom with an old-fashioned four-poster bed pushed awkwardly against the far wall.

"Oh, it's . . . lovely," she said, fumbling it in her momentary confusion over the odd placement of the furniture, the solid mahogany dressers and intricately carved nightstands shoved aside to leave an empty, gaping space in the middle of the room.

"Sorry," Jo apologized, bustling into the room to strip the bed with quick, efficient motions.

"This is your room," Ella realized, dread settling over her like a fog. She glanced around at the scuffed hardwood floors, the bare walls—and found confirmation in one of the framed photographs sitting on the antique dresser.

Picking up the one that had caught her eye, Ella stared down at . . . herself. And Merry, in one of those shots Merry loved to take, grinning wildly at the camera held at arm's length. Merry's hair had blue streaks in the picture, which was how Ella placed it.

"My graduation?" she asked faintly.

"Merry sent it to me. I hope you don't mind."

Jo's anxious voice scraped across the raw places in Ella's spirit. She did mind, but what could she say? "No, of course not."

"I love that one." Jo left the sheets in a pile on the bed and came over to stand at Ella's shoulder. "Merry has a gift for capturing a moment."

The graduation candid was the only shot with Ella, but there were a couple more of Merry—one on the back of a motorcycle, prepregnancy, the other one in what Ella referred to as one of Merry's arty moments. It was black-and-white, a little fuzzy around the edges, but the picture of herself reflected in a music-store window caught the essential wistfulness underlying Merry's playful, buoyant exterior.

"She's very talented," Ella agreed, carefully setting the frame down. "Not that she agrees. She hates every picture she takes; I'm kind of amazed she let you have these."

"It took some begging, but I was motivated."

Ella could feel Jo's searching gaze like a touch to the side of her face. Heart pounding, she pretended a fascination with the other photos on the dresser. There was one of the blond teenager from earlier, Taylor, astride a massive black horse and leaning over the animal's neck as it jumped a fallen log. And the last one was of an elderly woman in a floral-patterned housedress, her white hair impeccably set in curls and a shrewd intelligence shining from her sharp blue eyes.

Touching the glass over the old lady's weathered cheek, Ella was surprised to feel the lump rise in her throat. "Is that . . . ?"

"Aunt Dottie. Your great-aunt, Dorothea Selden Hollister. The room is still set up for her hospital bed—that's why all the furniture is like this. I haven't had a chance to move everything back. She needed around-the-clock care, at the end. I know this house is a wreck, but it's all I have left of her."

Grief throbbed through Jo's low voice, making Ella shift her weight uncomfortably.

She'd thought it was awkward entering her estranged mother's front parlor in the arms of the man she'd bickered with, leaned on, and soul-kissed half an hour after meeting him. But no, this was ten times worse.

Not only did Ella feel a pang of loss for a woman she never had the chance to know, but she almost wanted to reach out and comfort Jo Ellen, who had known and loved and cared for her aunt in her final days.

Suddenly antsy, as if her skin were a badly tailored suit that pinched and pulled, Ella jerked away from the bureau. "I can't put you out of your own bedroom. Really, I don't feel comfortable . . ."

Jo snagged her wrist before she could get more than a few steps toward the door. "No, it's fine! The guest rooms are all upstairs, and with that ankle, you really shouldn't . . . please. Let me do this for you. I want to."

Ella could clearly discern the naked desperation in Jo's voice, and the soft, weak part of her responded to it, wanting to hug and make nice and smooth over this difficult moment.

But that was a crutch, she reminded herself. Years of therapy had taught her to deal honestly with the situation rather than doing whatever it took to cover up the truth. Facing Jo Ellen squarely, Ella forced herself not to duck the real issue.

"I don't want you to think that my taking this room— even for one night—means that I want anything else from you. Or that I'm going to give you anything in return."

Jo took a deep breath. There was pain in her eyes, but she didn't let it crush her, and she didn't use it to manipulate the situation. Ella met her gaze with the first inkling of respect nudging at the back of her mind.

"I understand. And believe it or not, I appreciate your frankness. This is a nearly impossible situation, made worse by the fact that I know . . . God, do I know, that I brought it on myself. I'm not asking for your sympathy, and I'm willing to work for your trust. But I wouldn't be able to live with myself if I didn't match your frankness with a little of my own."

She inhaled again, and panic flared behind Ella's breastbone. "Do we really have to talk about this? Surely we've said everything that needs to be said."

"Almost." Jo lifted her chin in an achingly familiar gesture. "I understand you don't want anything from me, and I respect your feelings. But you deserve to hear this, at least. I'm sorry. I apologize for . . . too many things to name, but most of all for not being the mother I should have been. For not being the mother you and Merry deserved. I regret it from the bottom of my heart, and I completely acknowledge your right to whatever anger you still feel toward me."

Jo made it through the whole speech without a break in her voice, but her eyes were wide and shiny with tears she was too stubborn to let fall.

Drawing in a shuddering breath, Ella hammered all her years of therapy into a plate of armor over her heart. "I'm not angry with you," she finally said. "Anger is unproductive and pointless, and implies an unresolved issue. My issues with you have been resolved. Thank you for the apology, but it's unnecessary. I'm fine."

The light in Jo's eyes dimmed, but she nodded without arguing. "Good, then. We've both said what we needed to say. Let me just get a set of fresh sheets for the bed, and I'll leave you alone. I know you must be tired."

Abruptly aware of exactly how exhausted she was, Ella gave up the fight over which room she should take and nodded. If Jo wanted to displace herself, she wouldn't argue.

But as her mother slipped out of the bedroom, Ella's restless eyes landed on the photo of herself and Merry, in pride of place in the center of the dresser. And she couldn't help the ache that opened up in her chest.

Ella woke to the buttery, tantalizing scent of fresh-baked biscuits and a painful crick in her neck from the flat pillow on her great-aunt's antique four-poster bed. If she'd known last night about Jo's neck-torturing pillow, she might've protested her room assignment more vigorously. Yow.

Gently flexing her ankle, Ella waited for the twinge, but it didn't come. Ha! She'd been right that her so-called sprained ankle was only twisted. She'd be fine, as always.

Ella wished she could throw a bathrobe on over her pajamas and head to the kitchen in search of biscuits . . . but one glance at herself in the bathroom mirror while she brushed her teeth had her rethinking that scenario.

It was a fantasy, she acknowledged with a sigh, wincing at the screech of water through the old pipes when she turned on the shower.

She'd never be able to face whatever fresh hell today might bring in a tank top and flannel pants covered in cartoon frogs.

Half an hour later, Ella was freshly scrubbed and ready to face the day. She made the bed, meticulously tucking in the quilt at the corner of the mattress and smoothing down the sheets.

There. Now you couldn't tell Ella had ever been there. She wished she could strip the bed again and launder everything, but she didn't know where the washer and dryer were, and she didn't want to go poking around the house.

Tidying her things off the nightstand and back into her suitcase, Ella managed to knock her sleep mask to the floor. Bending down to retrieve it, she bumped the wobbly, three-legged antique that served as a bedside table.

She reached out to steady the thing, and the single slim drawer in the center popped open.

Now what?

Ella certainly didn't intend to look inside. It was a complete invasion of privacy and nothing she saw in that room—nothing she learned on this entire trip—was any of her business.

Since she had no intention of building a relationship with her mother, she had no reason to care about what was happening in Jo's life.

Except . . . when she went to close the drawer, she couldn't help noticing that it held a very official-looking letter. A letter that was dated only a few days previous. Words like "lien" and "debt" jumped out at her as if they'd been bolded.

"Delinquent payment." "Court."

Ella closed the drawer with a snap and hurried out of the room, determined not to care, not to even think about that stupid letter.

This house . . . it's all I have left of her.

Distracted by memories of last night's talk with Jo and trying to deal with the fact that her stomach appeared to have tied itself into a knot, Ella got lost twice on her way to the small, white-tiled kitchen at the back of the house.

She braced herself to see Jo, and did her level best to wipe the new knowledge she'd just gained off her face. Breathing out a slow, steadying sigh, Ella opened the door.

But no amount of breathing could have prepared her for the way everything inside her jumped at the sight of Grady Wilkes standing over the old white porcelain stove.

Ella stopped stock-still in the doorway and sent up a fervent prayer of thanksgiving that she hadn't stumbled in here, braless and hair all sticking up on one side of her head.

"Good morning," he said, without looking up from whatever he was doing with the stove. "I hope you like red-eye gravy."

Ella's usual breakfast consisted of a buttered cinnamon raisin bagel from the coffee cart on the corner, so she didn't consider herself a connoisseur of breakfast foods. And she certainly wasn't a cook—the apartment she rented in Alexandria boasted a kitchen approximately the size of the claw-footed enamel bathtub she'd just showered in.

Red-eye gravy didn't sound particularly appetizing. Still, she had manners.

"What are you doing here?" Ella demanded.

Okay, so maybe this one time, manners could take a backseat to finding out why Grady Wilkes was in her mother's kitchen at eight o'clock on a Tuesday morning.

"Fixing breakfast." His response was short and clipped, as if he weren't any happier to be here than she was to see him. "Do you want some or not?"

Ella's stomach answered for her with a long, embarrassingly audible gurgle. A smirk tugged at the corner of Grady's mouth.

Lifting her chin, Ella sank down on one of the ladder-backed wooden chairs and folded her hands on the scarred pine tabletop with as much dignity as she could muster.

"Breakfast would be delightful. Thank you."

Two chipped platters in the center of the table were mounded with enough food to feed a family of ten. Flaky, golden biscuits steamed gently on one, while the other was piled with thick slices of dark red meat—maybe ham?

Ella swallowed as her mouth started to water. "Shouldn't we wait for everyone else?"

"They're not here."

She blinked, her interlocked fingers tightening until the tips went numb. "What?"

Grady turned away from the stove and faced the table, leaning one hip on the counter. Tall and rawboned, his dark blond hair shaggy and his jaw rough with stubble, he should've looked silly with blue-and-white striped oven mitts covering his hands.

But instead, he looked completely at home, in his element, and it didn't matter that he was holding a cast-iron skillet and a long-handled wooden spoon instead of a handsaw and a crowbar. He leaned across the table to ladle a thin, darkly fragrant liquid over the waiting ham and said, "Your mom and sister. They were up early—I guess they wanted to catch the sunrise over the eastern marsh."

Something inside her shriveled at being left behind, but Ella firmed her jaw and nodded. This was what they were here for, and she'd been very clear and forthright with Jo the night before. If anything, she should be pleased Jo was respecting her wishes and wasn't pushing her. "Good. That sounds nice."

Grady gave her a look from under his lowered brows, a lock of hair falling over his forehead and making him seem younger, somehow. "The island is better than nice. And dawn breaking over the water . . . it's a sight that can change your life."

"Maybe you can show it to me sometime." She grabbed a biscuit off the top of the pile and set it on her plate before she realized how unintentionally flirty that sounded.

She sneaked a sidelong glance at Grady, pulling off his oven mitts and tossing them to the counter, to see if he'd noticed. The slight red flush at the tips of his ears said he probably had.

Ella blinked. Underneath the mitts, Grady was still wearing those leather gloves.

He pulled out the chair next to hers and reached for the platter of breakfast meat. "I'd be happy to, if you're here long enough. There's a lot to see on Sanctuary Island."

"Like the wild horses." Ella couldn't remember her dreams from the night before, but she had a shivery awareness of the sense of freedom and majesty she'd felt, watching that band of horses sweep across the field. "Where did they come from, anyway? I couldn't find anything about their origin online. Is there a mystery to it?"

"Not a mystery, exactly." Grady piled so much ham onto his biscuit, it was going to take two hands to get it to his mouth. "But there are a few different theories. No one knows the truth, for sure."

"That would drive me nuts," Ella said, laughing. "Don't you want to know?"

"I know everything I need to about the horses. The rest, I take on faith."

There it was again, something uncurling in her chest and turning toward Grady like a flower seeking sunshine. "What's your favorite theory about the horses?"

A half smile quirked up the corner of Grady's mouth, and the look he slanted her way made blood throb heavily in her veins. "Some people say the horses are descended from livestock the British colonists hid on the island to avoid paying taxes to the crown; some say the first horses on Sanctuary belonged to the Harringtons of New York, who owned the whole island back in the thirties and used it as a summer home."

Ella propped her elbow on the table and leaned in, fascinated by the rich warmth of Grady's voice as he spun his tale.

"But what I believe," he continued, "is that the horses were here first, before the colonists, before the millionaires. The Spanish explorers brought horses to North America in the fifteenth century, sailing them across uncharted seas to the eastern shores of a newly discovered land. The voyage was dangerous, and many a crew came to grief on the rocky shoals off the coast of Virginia . . . including a Spanish galleon with a herd of Arabians in the hold. When that galleon foundered and sank, those horses, bred for toughness, elegance, and survival in the harshest conditions on earth, refused to go down with the ship.

They swam and swam until they found land . . . a small, uninhabited island that the horses made their own. Now, hundreds of years later, they've adapted to the island's conditions and learned to flourish here."

"I love that story," Ella told him, dazzled. She could almost see the terrified horses kicking out into the storm-tossed waves, pushing through exhaustion to reach the beach.

"That's why I spend so much time looking out for the wild horses and their habitat." Ella tried not to melt at the way Grady's jaw went hard with determination. "Sanctuary is their home, just as much as it is ours."

A pang shot through her. This wasn't her home, and she didn't know why it hurt a little to be reminded of that. "Thank you for cooking," she said, trying to drag the conversation back up to the surface.

Ella wasn't great at accepting help, but she was trying to do better. "I'm not an invalid, though—my ankle must have only been twisted, like I said, because it's fine today. So if Jo asked you over here to babysit me, you don't need to feel obligated."

Grady paused in the act of building the perfect ham biscuit. "You're not an obligation. I'm here because I want to be."

CHAPTER 10

Ella had been joking, or trying to, but the way Grady said that, so seriously and with his eyes intent on her face, sent a shiver of awareness skating over her skin.

She could actually feel herself getting pink in the cheeks, so she dipped her head and got busy with her own breakfast. "Okay. Well, thank you, anyway. This is really . . ." She paused to take a big bite, and had to close her eyes as the rich taste of smoky ham and intense salt exploded across her tongue. "Oh. Wow."

She tried not to be warmed by the glint of approval in his smile, but it was hopeless.

"Real country ham, fried up nice and crisp," Grady said, tearing into his breakfast while Ella did the same. "Then you take the hot drippings, add some strong black coffee, and boil it down until it's the saltiest, most perfect flavor on the planet. Soak it up with good buttermilk biscuits, and you've got yourself a slice of heaven, right there."

She popped the last bite in her mouth and contemplated

copying Grady as he reached for a second biscuit with a brown-leather-gloved hand.

Without meaning to, she tracked his movements while her mind clicked through the possibilities, the reasons a man like Grady might have to keep his hands covered at all times. He was pretty covered up, in general, she noted. Her eyes skimmed the broad shoulders under layers of cotton undershirt and unbuttoned flannel shirt. The soft, forest-green-sleeves were buttoned tightly at his wrists, leaving not even an inch of bare skin to peep out between the edge of his gloves and the shirt cuff.

"Noticed the gloves, huh?" His mouth twisted in a crooked smile, as if her answer didn't matter much, but Ella had the sense that if she said the wrong thing, he'd be out of his chair, maybe even out of the house, in the blink of an eye.

Even though she was embarrassed to be caught staring, Ella knew the worst possible reaction she could give him would be to make a big deal out of what was so clearly a hot-button issue for him.

So she shrugged as casually as she could manage, and reached for another biscuit. "They're nice. I like the stitching. Pass the red-eye gravy, please."

She deliberately didn't look at him, concentrating most of her attention on getting her ham biscuit together. But she could feel the moment the tension left his big frame, like air escaping from a tire.

Ella ate her biscuit and tried to think of something to say that wasn't "So what are you hiding under those gloves?"

But maybe Grady could feel the question hanging in the air over their heads the same way she did, because after a minute or so of silent eating, he abruptly started talking.

"I received an injury a few years back. For a while, I had to wear gloves for protection, and I got used to it."

Ella wondered if the injury happened during his time with Texas Task Force One. Peeking up at him, she tried to gauge whether sympathy would be welcome.

"So . . . your injury is all healed up now? Good as new?"

A muscle ticked in his jaw. "Not exactly. But as close as it's going to get."

There was definitely something he wasn't saying, but Ella didn't get a chance to dig deeper because he sat back in his chair with a determined glint in his straightforward green gaze.

"Actually, I'm as healed as I am because of your mom. I owe her a lot."

This time, Ella was the one stiffening up. "Oh?"

"Your mom, and Sanctuary Island. When I first moved here, right after I got out of the hospital, I was kind of a mess." He lifted one shoulder in a dismissive jerk. "I mean, I had it better than . . . a lot of folks. At least I'm still alive and walking around, right? It was stupid to be so screwed up about it. But I was a mess, all the same."

"It's not stupid," Ella felt compelled to say. She couldn't dial back the fierceness in her voice, so she settled for keeping it short. "Whatever happened to you, however you got hurt . . . Trauma is never stupid. Don't play the game of comparing who had it worse and how much suffering earns you the right to be upset. No one wins."

"You sound like a shrink."

Ella lifted her chin. She hadn't missed the way his open expression shut down. "That's probably because I've been in and out of therapy since I was about fifteen."

Staring into his wide eyes, Ella could see the moment

he realized why she'd needed therapy. But if he wanted more details, he was out of luck. She'd stripped herself bare enough already—sitting in her mother's kitchen comparing painful histories, Ella felt like a single exposed nerve.

"Anyway," he went on, as if realizing that the topic of Ella's therapy had been closed. "I think you're right. I got there eventually on my own, with some help from Jo."

"Got where?"

He shrugged, making a face like he was trying to do a complicated math problem in his head. "I guess . . . it is what it is, you feel how you feel, and you can't control it. All you can really control is what you do about it—that's what the island taught me."

"It sounds like Jo was here for you at a time when you really needed someone," Ella said, with some difficulty. "And I'm glad, honestly. But you have to understand—she was never there for me. For us."

"But she wanted to be," Grady protested, resting his elbows on the table and leaning in as if warming to his subject.

"But she *wasn't*." Ella flinched a little at the sharpness of her own retort, but she wouldn't take it back. Trying to moderate her tone, she said, "Look. I know you're trying to help. But I can't . . ."

He shook his head, looking pissed at himself. "No, I'm sorry. I didn't mean to go there. What's between you and Jo is your business. I'm not here to meddle in that."

It took a few tries to swallow down the lump in her throat, and even Ella wasn't sure if it was tears or relief.

Ever since they arrived on the island, she'd felt like all the stress fractures in her psyche were showing up. And Grady Wilkes seemed to have an uncanny ability to strike at them. "Then why are you here? Do you cook breakfast for my mother every morning?"

"No. And I should tell you, I can't take credit for these biscuits. Jo made them before she left."

"They're pretty good," Ella had to admit. Light, fluffy layers of buttery perfection, with the slightest hint of buttermilk tang inside to contrast with the salty richness of the golden toasty outside.

"Pretty good? Your mama makes the best biscuits on Sanctuary."

"All right!" Ella had to laugh at Grady's fervent declaration, grateful for the sudden lightening of tension in the air. "They're amazing. She'd make a bundle serving these for breakfast at a B and B."

Grady's jaw went granite hard, and Ella threw up her hands.

Pushing back from the table and carrying her empty plate to the sink, she couldn't help saying, "What on earth is your problem? This is Jo's house, not yours."

It was Ella's great-aunt Dottie's house. It had been in her family for generations.

The memory of that letter from the county floated in front of her eyes as she ran the faucet to wash the crumbs off her plate.

"My problem," Grady growled, "is that you keep bringing up this damn B and B idea, and eventually Jo might decide it's a good way to keep you and your sister on the island, helping her out with it."

Ella froze. She hadn't considered how Merry might react if she knew Jo was in trouble.

But Grady wasn't done. "Your mother would die if she actually had to spend all her time cooped up in this house playing hostess to a bunch of vacationing mainlanders, no matter how much money she might make. What is it with you and money, anyway?"

The scorn in his tone raised the small hairs at the back of Ella's neck, and she whirled to face him.

"First off, I don't have a thing about money." She hated the way that sounded, as if she were shallow and mercenary, or judgmental of people who didn't wear the right clothing brands or something. That wasn't it at all. "But I don't think it's somehow wrong to expect stability and security in return for hard work. What have you got against the hospitality industry, anyway?"

Shaking his head, Grady stretched his long, denim-clad legs out under the table and regarded her contemplatively. "Hospitality isn't an industry. Around here, it's a way of life . . . a dying one, maybe. But it's how we still look at the world, down in backwater places and small towns like Sanctuary. And the last thing hospitality ought to be about is making money."

"I still don't get why it's such a big deal to you," Ella protested. "Surely the island attracts plenty of tourists. You said yourself, your family used to come for the summers!"

He tipped his head back and blew a sigh up at the ceiling. "It's hard to explain in words." Tilting his chin in her direction, he smiled. "But I could show you."

Ella narrowed her eyes. "I was kidding before, but maybe I was right—you are here to babysit me. Did my mother put you up to this?"

She expected him to hedge, but instead he said, "I've ridden over every inch of this island, and I love it. So, yes, your mom asked me to play tour guide because she wants you to get to know Sanctuary. And she's smart enough to accept that you're not ready to see it with her."

Deep down, Ella wasn't at all sure touring the island with Grady instead would pose less of a hazard to her heart, but she had made that promise to learn about her family's legacy on the island.

And unlike some people, Ella took her promises seriously. Plus, this would give her time to figure out what to do about the letter.

Not that she owed Jo anything, but now that she'd spent time here, she found she hated the idea of the house leaving the family. After years of convincing herself she didn't need anything from her absent mother, the magnetic pull she felt toward her family history surprised her. This house was a part of it, and so was Sanctuary.

"Fine," she decided. "Show me what's so special about this island of yours."

Surprise and delight fired Grady's gaze with a brilliant light, and as the smile stretched across his face and crinkled at the corners of his eyes, Ella couldn't help thinking that no matter how picturesque Sanctuary might be, it would be hard to find a more appealing view than the one right here in her mother's kitchen.

CHAPTER 11

Jo fiddled with the truck's climate controls, trying to find the perfect temperature to stop Merry's teeth from chattering.

Early April mornings were still pretty nippy, but she'd made sure they were both bundled up before they drove away from the house in the gray predawn light.

Forty-five minutes and one spectacularly pink and orange sunrise later, there was still enough of a chill on the air to have Jo and Merry shivering.

"That was awesome." Merry sighed. She didn't seem to notice or mind the cold, in spite of the fact that her lips were tinged a worrying blue. "Do we have to go back to the house yet?"

"We probably should. Don't you need to eat?" Jo didn't want to cut this outing short, but she wanted her baby girl warm and comfortable more than she wanted to drag out the sweetness of this moment.

Besides, she told herself, *I'll have at least two more*

weeks of sweet moments with my Merry, and the hope of more with Ella, eventually.

Be grateful for what you have, she reminded herself, *even if it's not everything you want, as fast as you want it. There was a time when you thought neither girl would ever let you back into her life, and now here they are.*

"I had three biscuits before we left," Merry pointed out. "I mean, Baby and I will be hungry again before too much longer—I swear, it's like I swallowed a tapeworm—but we're good for now."

Jo wasn't going to argue too hard. "Well, what were you hoping to do instead?"

Merry's shy smile cracked Jo's heart in at least three places. "Last night at dinner, you said something about stables?"

"You want to see my barn? That's pretty convenient, since it's just behind Aunt Dottie's house."

Merry blinked. "Really? I didn't realize it was so close."

"It's screened pretty well by a stand of red cedar trees."

"I love how green it is here. The whole island feels so alive."

Jo shifted into drive, hiding a wince at the grinding of gears. "The old gray mare, she ain't what she used to be," she said with a rueful smile.

Merry shrugged. "Hey, at least you own your own car. And house. And business. I think that's cool." Her hand drifted up to rest against the roundness of her tummy. "I haven't got much of anything except Baby, here."

Fighting the urge to ask about the baby's father, Jo gripped the wheel until she lost circulation in her fingers. "When I first came to Sanctuary, I was like you—I had nothing. Not even my babies, because when your father left, I wasn't fit to be near you, and I knew it. I gave up my rights . . . and then you were gone. And I was all alone, until your great-aunt Dottie took me in."

"You miss her a lot." Merry's voice was muffled and a little choked. Jo took a chance and reached out a tentative hand to her younger daughter, who grabbed it and held on with a strength that surprised Jo.

"I do miss her. She was an incredible lady, although she hated that term." Jo managed a damp laugh. "Aunt Dottie always referred to herself as 'an old broad,' and she was proud of it."

Merry's dimples popped out. "She sounds like someone I would've liked."

"She was. Dottie would have loved you; I'll always regret the fact that my mistakes deprived her, and you and Ella, of the chance to know each other."

"Mom," Merry choked out, and Jo felt a sob rise up in her throat.

"It's been so many years since I heard that word from one of my girls." The shock and joy of it stole her breath—but it wasn't surprising that it had come from Merry.

Almost too open and trusting—and oh, how Jo shuddered to imagine the target that innocence painted on Merry's back. Jo felt Merry's yearning for closeness as if it were the mirror of her own emotions.

"Well, you are my mom," Merry said, almost defiantly, as if she expected Jo to snatch back the right to that relationship.

"Call me whatever you're comfortable with," Jo hurried to say. "Personally, I love 'mom.'"

Merry's shy smile made Jo want to laugh and cry and jump up and down, but all she could do was lace her fingers tightly with her younger daughter's, and hold on.

"Tell me more about Aunt Dottie," Merry said, tilting her head back against the passenger seat's headrest.

Jo cleared her aching throat. "There have been Hollister women on Sanctuary since the town was first built up, after the Great Depression. Dottie's mother, Eleanor, is who Ella is named after."

"I always thought she was named after you! Jo Ellen."

Shaking her head, Jo smiled a little. "Nope, she's named after your great-grandmother, Eleanor Hollister. Who was quite the broad, herself—she ran a boarding-house in town, and she never married because, back then, marrying meant giving up her independence. Which is something a Hollister woman would never do."

Jo laughed, but Merry was noticeably quiet beside her.

"I'm not very good at being independent," Merry confessed. "Every time I try, I screw up my life in the worst possible way. Sometimes I feel like a lost cause."

"Sweetheart." Jo's heart burned against her ribs. "There's no such thing as a lost cause. Sanctuary Island and your great-aunt taught me that. And believe me, if I could build a life to be proud of out of the wreckage of my weakness and fears and terrible mistakes, so can you."

Merry's smile was hesitant, but it lit up her eyes. "Thanks, Mom."

Jo debated with herself for all of ten seconds before the offer came tumbling out. "You can stay here as long as you need to. I want you to know, you're always welcome here. You and Ella both. This island has always been good to the Hollister women."

Merry ducked her head, a swath of wavy magenta hair swinging forward to hide her expression. "I . . . thanks. That means a lot to me." Her voice grew fierce, and Jo caught a glimpse of the spunky girl who matched the rock-and-roll edge of the clothes she tended to wear. "But I want you to know, that's not why I came here. I'm not looking for a handout."

"I never thought you were. But it would mean a lot to me to be able to help you, any way I can. I've got quite a few years to make up for. You don't have to decide right this minute, but think about it."

"I will," Merry promised, as the truck turned onto the back road that circled up to the barn, and Jo caught sight of the cars parked out front.

Uh-oh.

One of the cars was a regular fixture out at Windy Corner Stables. The dented green covered-bed truck with the salt-corroded wheel wells and the shiny, brand-new trailer hitched to the back belonged to the island's resident large-animal vet and farrier, Ben Fairfax. He came out about once a week to see who'd thrown a shoe, who needed shots, and so on.

But the other car . . . that was a surprise, and Jo felt her heart kick at her ribs like a startled mule.

She pulled up beside the white SUV and squinted at the dark, smoked windows. There was movement inside, and Jo closed her eyes, wondering if this was the moment when her worlds collided.

Then, like an answer to a prayer, Ben stuck his dark, curly head out the barn's double doors. Hopping down from the truck cab, she flagged him down with a perky wave.

"Benji! How's my favorite vet today?"

His scowl made Jo grin. "Terrible. I'm taking White Lightning back with me. I need a closer look at that cut on her forelock, but stitches are going to be the only way to get it to close right. And don't call me Benji."

Jo's smile faded. Stitches. Damn it. That would mean antibiotic ointment, special leg wraps—more stuff she couldn't really afford.

None of which was Ben's fault, so she rallied. "No worries. But before you go, let me introduce you to my daughter Merry."

Dr. Ben Fairfax had a reputation for being gruff and difficult with anyone who wasn't one of the animals in his care, but he was still a good Southern boy. With those long, lanky legs of his, he easily beat Jo to the passenger side of the truck so he could open Merry's door for her.

Jo glanced over at Harrison's SUV, trying to keep his doors locked and closed with the power of her brain.

When she looked back, she had to blink twice to make sure the look on Ben's face wasn't an illusion.

Terse, taciturn, perpetually cranky Ben Fairfax was staring at Merry as if he'd never seen anything so amazing in his life.

Well, goodness. These girls of mine sure are heartbreakers.

Ben's gray eyes were wide and shocked as he held out a hand to help her down from the tall truck cab. "Here, let me just . . ."

Merry took his hand as she levered herself out of the seat, but the moment she was on the ground, she jerked away as if she'd grabbed onto a live wire, her eyes wide and startled.

Ben's face closed down at once, resuming its normal stern lines. He stomped off without another word, heading back to the barn. Merry watched him go, and Jo noticed her baby girl's cheeks were flushed a bright, pretty pink.

Jo didn't have time to do more than note this very interesting development before the sound of a car door opening had her moving to intercept Harrison before he could climb out of his SUV.

"Ben, can I ask for a quick favor?" she called, moving swiftly to herd a visibly reluctant Merry in the direction of the barn's entrance. "Merry's interested in seeing the horses, could you give her the short version of the tour? I'll be along in a second, honey, I just need to speak with this gentleman about some business matters—it won't take but a minute."

Jo hoped.

Ben threw her a glance that was part fury and part gratitude, and part something indecipherable. But all he said was, "You owe me. Big-time. Come on . . . Mary, was it? Let me guess, an angel came to you in a vision and nine months later . . ."

"Not the saintly kind of Mary. Merry, as in short for Meredith." Merry's hands went protectively to her baby bump, but her voice was full of brittle humor. "And trust me, there's nothing holy about my ex. Unless you count his god-like sense of self-importance. Which reminds me, hey, if you're too busy to give me a tour, feel free to go about your business with the horses. I can take care of myself just fine."

Jo blinked. That was the most she'd ever heard Merry say about her baby's father.

"I guess it won't be the worst chore in the world. You seem marginally less objectionable than most people."

"Wow. Put away the charm, Mr. Suave, I'm getting all faint and swoony."

"Hey, that was my highest compliment. People suck, which is why my patients are animals, and I'm amazing at treating them. Come to think of it, you should be swooning. Only don't, because then I'd have to catch you and maybe mess up my hands—and these are the hands of a certified genius."

Merry narrowed her eyes. "How about your face. What happens if someone messes that up?"

Ben's jaw ticked once before he let out a short, sharp bark of a laugh. Merry had managed to surprise him. "Come on, I'll introduce you to White Lightning, so long as you promise to be sweet to her. She could use a little extra TLC today."

Even the knowledge that Harrison was getting out of his SUV behind her, his solid, looming presence like a second sun at her back, couldn't get Jo to tear her eyes off the interaction in front of her.

"I'll be sweet to White Lightning," Merry said, color high and eyes bright. "But I make no promises when it comes to arrogant, jerkface veterinarians."

She marched up the hill toward the barn, with her head up and her hair whipping in the breeze like a flag. Ben's gaze followed her for a long moment before he turned to Jo and said, "Damn you to hell, Jo Ellen Hollister."

He looked as if someone had set him on fire, his face a mask of agonized disbelief. It was only in this moment of seeing him so alive and electrified that Jo realized she'd known this young man for years, and had never seen any emotion in his expression beyond sardonic humor, boredom, or disgust when talking to another person.

When he talked to his furry, four-legged patients . . . well, that was something else entirely. The gentleness she knew Ben had buried deep inside was what made Jo say, "You're welcome."

With an incoherent snarl, Ben stormed after Merry. Mind whirling, Jo felt an almost irresistible compulsion to follow them and watch them strike more sparks off each other. But Harrison cleared his throat meaningfully, and Jo turned to face him instead.

Her heart sank. He didn't have his casual-conversation face on. No, this one was more like the we-need-to-talk face.

Harrison raised a brow. "That one of your girls?"

A pang of guilt splintered through Jo's rib cage. "Merry. My younger daughter."

There was a look in his eyes that Jo could barely stand to read, and not for the first time, she wished this man knew just a little bit less about the sins of her past and her hopes for the future.

"Pretty girl," he said, his gaze never leaving Jo's. "When's she due?"

"About six weeks, she tells me."

"Think she'll still be here then?"

If Jo's fervent prayers were answered, Merry and Ella would both still be on Sanctuary when Baby showed up. And since Jo believed wholeheartedly in the power of positive affirmations, she smiled and tossed her long ponytail over her shoulder. "Yes. That's not the plan, as of now, but plans change."

"They sure do," he agreed, tone drier than the sawdust blanketing the barn floor, and Jo grimaced.

She'd kind of stepped in that one.

There was a moment of heavy silence before Harrison took pity on her. "I spoke with Dabney Leeds's representative, a lawyer over in Winter Harbor."

Jo's mouth went dry. "And?"

The sympathy in Harrison's deep-set eyes tipped her off before he spoke. "Given that you didn't know about the debt until after Miz Dottie passed, I talked them into giving you a monthlong grace period. But if you can't come up with the full amount to cover the debt within thirty days, the house will belong to Mr. Leeds."

The blow made Jo want to stagger, her knees weak with horror. "I can't be the Hollister who loses Windy Corner. What about the stables?" She was grasping at straws and she knew it.

"They haven't turned a profit."

"Not yet, but by the end of the year . . ."

"You don't have until the end of the year." Harrison crossed his arms over his chest, his brawny biceps straining at the material of his gray suit coat. He'd loosened the knot of his striped tie on the drive out from town, and Jo's gaze caught on the triangle of sunbaked skin exposed by the open top button of his crisp white shirt. "But I may have a solution."

A ray of hope broke through the nausea and panic swirling through Jo's brain. "What? I'll do anything, whatever it takes to save Windy Corner."

The corner of his lip quirked up sardonically, as if he knew already that she was going to regret saying that.

His steady gaze had Jo's heart rate picking up. "Then marry me."

There went her knees again. "What?"

He took a step forward, close enough to enfold one of her limp, bloodless hands in his big, warm clasp. "Be my wife, and all of this goes away. I'll pay off the lien, we'll save Windy Corner, and everything else will work itself out."

Jo's mind went blank, as if every thought and emotion had been washed away by a torrential flood of disbelief. This couldn't be happening. The answer to her money problems couldn't be so simple . . . so impossible.

She stared down at their joined hands, his long, deft, dear fingers as familiar to her as her own, and she knew exactly what she had to say.

CHAPTER 12

"I may not have the best sense of direction," Ella said, curling nervous fingers around the roll bar stretched under the canvas roof of Grady's green Jeep, "but I'm pretty sure the town of Sanctuary is back the other way."

"We're not going into town."

The Jeep bounced and shuddered over the rough, backcountry road, but Grady made no concessions to the terrain. Pedal to the metal and barely slowing down for curves, the line of his body was entirely relaxed and confident. He could've been kicked back in his recliner in front of his flatscreen.

Her gaze dropped to the loose grip of his gloved hand around the gearshift. She was supposed to be looking at the island, the beautiful scenery flashing past the car in a blur, but all she could see was Grady.

Needing to distract herself from errant thoughts about what it would feel like to be touched by a man wearing leather gloves, she said, "This is not the plan. You're supposed to be showing me around the island. Surely any good tour starts in the 'Heart of Sanctuary.' "

He smiled a little at her air quotes. "I hate plans. And trust me. The town square is not the heart of Sanctuary Island."

The Jeep churned its way up a sandy hill and shuddered to a stop at the top. Ella had to blink furiously to clear her vision of the dazzle of sunlight on water as the never-ending vastness of the ocean stretched beneath them.

A snowy white egret lifted its beak from the shallow tidal pool at the bottom of the hill and stared up at the Jeep. As if finding them boring, it went back to grooming its feathers. Ella's breath went ragged, her ribs squeezing hard around the beauty of the wide, open meadow, the tall grass waving down the shore to meet the lapping of the waves.

"This, on the other hand." Grady's voice was quiet, almost reverent. "This is where I feel the heartbeat of the island."

The look on his face was one she'd seen before, she realized with a shiver.

He looked like someone who'd just made a break-through in therapy—emotional and almost overwhelmed, but somehow at peace.

Ella had seen that expression in the mirror, once or twice, after a particularly difficult session—one of the few times she'd managed to push herself to open up and be really honest about how she felt.

Amazing that for Grady, all it took was a glimpse of this serene, breeze-ruffled meadow.

Shaking himself free of his reverie, Grady smiled over at her, the wide, carefree grin of a little kid. "Want to get a closer look?"

Ella regretted her choice of shoes almost immediately. Her brown ankle boots were eminently sensible in the city, low-heeled and comfortable for walking, but they were no match for the soft, sucking ground or the razor sharpness of the salt-marsh cordgrass.

She picked her way after him, reluctant to say anything to break the spell of contentment this place had woven around Grady. He moved through the thigh-high grass as if following some path only he could see. Every few steps, he'd glance over his shoulder to check on her progress, and if she fell too far behind, he'd grin and wait for her to catch up.

To her surprise, Ella couldn't help grinning back at him even as sweat began to prickle at her hairline and dampen the spot at the base of her spine. Sure, her tender ankle gave her a twinge or two, and she was pretty sure this field was crawling with ticks, but there was also something indefinably exhilarating about being out here.

In the middle of nature—practically covered in it, in fact, she mused as she swatted at a mosquito—bushwhacking through soggy patches and heading steadily for the coastline.

"I don't know why I'm having such a hard time keeping up," Ella panted apologetically, scurrying the last few steps to where Grady stood watching her patiently. "It's not the ankle, I swear. And I walk everywhere in the city. I don't even own a car!"

He shrugged easily. "City walking is different. But don't worry your head, pretty city mouse." Grady's mouth kicked up in a teasing smile. "We're not in a hurry to catch a train or something. We've got all the time in the world."

She blinked. "I guess you're right."

"Been a while since you took some time off, I bet."

She was watching where she put her feet, hoping to avoid another patch of sticky mud. The fact that she was also avoiding Grady's too perceptive gaze was just a bonus.

"I'm not big on downtime." She smiled, trying to keep it breezy and light. "I like to work."

"What is it you do, exactly?"

Ella cast him a searching glance, but he seemed sincerely interested. Most men who asked that question, on a first date or at a bar, tended to glaze over the minute she started answering.

Keeping tabs on his reaction from the corner of her eye, Ella said, "I'm in commercial real estate development, hotels and office buildings, mostly. Lots of wheeling and dealing, contract negotiations, scouting potential properties . . ."

Nothing about that description conveyed the excitement of pitting herself against other developers or talking indecisive buyers into signing on the dotted line. It also, she admitted to herself, didn't describe quite how exhausting the whole process could be, how easy it was to get lost in the minutiae of contract details. How easy it was to start making mistakes.

"So, basically, your life is a giant, never-ending game of Monopoly."

That surprised a laugh out of her. "More or less."

Of course, one bad roll of the dice hadn't landed her on Free Parking—it had gotten her banished to this tiny island.

There was a pause where Grady paced her, slowing his loose, long-limbed stride to match her more cautious steps. The line of his body along her side radiated warmth more intensely than the morning sun reflecting off the water.

For the last few years, Ella had brought in more business than anyone else in her firm. That wasn't an accident. She knew an opening when she saw it, and she never hesitated to press an advantage.

Out here in the sunlight, with Grady in an open, sharing mood, was her best chance at getting more information about Jo's financial situation.

"Actually," she began, deliberately casual. "I know how you feel about the whole idea of a bed-and-breakfast bringing tourism to this island, but I have to tell you—in my professional opinion, Jo is sitting on a potential gold mine."

He stiffened, his movements losing that easy, loping grace and going jerky. "Leave it alone," he growled.

The intensity in his tone brought Ella's head up to study his face. But his expression had closed down, the ease of the morning shuttered away as he gazed off into the distance. He looked like a stranger all of a sudden, hard-faced and wary.

Ella was surprised to find herself wanting to tailor her questions to draw him back out into the sun—even if that wasn't really necessary for her goal of getting information.

"It could be a wonderful thing for the island," she said, as if she hadn't noticed his shutdown. "But even more than that, it could be great for Jo Ellen."

She watched him closely as he stomped along at her side, but he didn't appear to be moved. "Jo will be fine. We take care of our own here on Sanctuary."

His words had a conviction that told Ella she'd butted up against one of his unshakable beliefs. Every person in a negotiation had at least one or two ideas that they couldn't be talked out of—beliefs so strong that they were considered capital *T* Truth.

It was pointless to continue a line of discussion that would entail contradicting one of those Truths. Ella veered around it.

"Must be nice to live in a community like that. Especially if something unexpected happens—when something unexpected happens, I should say." She forced a laugh. "Goodness knows, into each life a little surprise catastrophe must fall, right?"

He rolled his shoulders as if trying to warm up to lift something heavy and unwieldy. "I told you already that your mom helped me a lot, when I first moved here after the accident."

The accident. His injuries were the result of some sort of accident.

Ella's brain greedily snatched at the crumb of information, adding it to her hoard of facts about Grady Wilkes.

"But it wasn't just Jo," he went on, his jaw like iron. "It was the whole island, the horses, the peace. How much it felt like nothing could touch me here, like the outside world stopped mattering and I could finally stop running. All the things that a B and B, or anything that brings tourists to the island, would ruin."

"I understand all that, but what if Jo truly needed the money?"

He gave her a look that bordered on pity. "Not everyone cares about money as much as you do."

The slap of shame rocked her back on her heels, the sensation of being seen through, and found lacking, almost enough to distract her from the fact that she'd achieved her goal.

Grady didn't know about Jo's money troubles.

The success of her plan wasn't enough to dull Ella's urgent, immediate, foolish need to slap Grady back with one of her own personal Truths.

Raising her chin, Ella gathered the scraps of her dignity like spare change dropped on the street. "You're probably right. But then, not everyone has been working since they were sixteen to help support their family because their divorced single dad couldn't make enough to cover rent and food at the same time. And trust me, when you get home from double-bagging groceries and stocking shelves only to dig into a mountain of homework so you can get a desperately needed scholarship, well. It gives you a strong appreciation for what money can do."

He stilled, the hard planes of his angular face softening ever so slightly. "Ella . . ."

"Save it," she told him, picking her way through the marsh and leaving him behind, along with every drop of joy she'd taken in the beauty of the day. "I don't need your pity."

"Will you take my apology?"

She didn't stop moving. If she stopped walking, she'd have to face him, and somehow she wasn't quite ready for that. "Only one way to find out."

"Ella. I'm sorry. I hate when people make assumptions about me—I shouldn't have done it to you. Not today, and not when we met." The quiet sincerity in his simple words melted the angry lump in her throat.

The problem was that without anger as a shield, Ella was all too aware of just how much this whole conversation meant to her. She cared way too much about what Grady thought of her. She needed to get control of this spiraling need, this awful vulnerability.

She slowed enough to allow him to catch up with her. "Apology accepted. If you tell me what assumptions people tend to make about you."

The least he could do was put them back on some sort of even footing, she reasoned. Except when she glanced over her shoulder, ready to make a mood-lightening joke about how he was the one falling behind now, Grady wasn't even looking at her.

He stared out over the field toward the water, every muscle in his lean, rangy body tensed. His brows drew together, a troubled frown tugging at his mouth, but instead of baring his soul and his vulnerabilities, he bolted past her.

He took off for the beach at a dead run, his long legs eating up the distance as Ella's heart jumped into her throat.

Shading her eyes, she watched him cut a path through the grass and emerge onto the strip of sandy beach about fifty feet in front of her.

Ella squinted. There was something happening down there, the tall grass waving jerkily. Did he need help?

She pushed herself into motion and took off after him, moving as quickly as she could with her heart pounding out a sharp, staccato rhythm.

For such a peaceful, sleepy little island, Sanctuary was turning out to be a thrill a minute.

Gritty pebbled sand ground into the knees of Grady's jeans as he dropped down beside the heaving mare.

She snorted nervously, rolling her eyes to track his approach. Her dappled gray flanks were flecked with foam, the distended mound of her belly straining with contractions.

"What's wrong with it?" Ella gasped from behind him.

He spared her a quick glance as she hit the grass line and froze as if one step onto the beach would trap her in sucking quicksand.

Ella's face was pale with worry, and maybe a little fear. He hadn't missed the way she kept her distance from Voyager when Merry introduced herself. Ella was afraid of horses.

Well, she was going to have to get over it in a hurry. "She's in labor. The wild mares come down to the beach to foal."

"So this is normal." Relief throbbed through Ella's voice. "Surely she knows what she's doing, right? Instinct takes over?"

"Normally, yeah." Grady passed his hands over the horse's sweaty side, feeling the heat rising from the dark patches of hair even through the thin leather of his gloves. "But I think something's wrong here. Her hind muscles are all relaxed, as they should be, but that means things should be moving really fast by this point, and nothing much seems to be happening. I can see a hoof, but it's not . . ."

He ducked down to check the progress of the foal's emergence from the birth canal and swore under his breath.

One hoof instead of two. Not good.

Ella swayed and her skin went from parchment-white to faintly green. That was enough to convince Grady not to give her a play-by-play of what was happening at his end of the struggling mare.

Adrenaline poured into Grady's system, speeding his heartbeat and narrowing his focus. "I left my cell phone in the Jeep. Do you have yours with you?"

When she nodded, he recited a number and asked her to call it. "We need help. Tell the guy who answers to get down to the west end of the cove, south side of the watering hole, as fast as he can."

Ella pulled herself together pretty well, Grady noted with approval. Her fingers only trembled a little as she obeyed his instructions to the letter.

But at the end of her conversation with Ben, she nodded at something he said and held the slim black phone out to Grady.

"He says he's on his way, but he needs to know what's happening. He might have to talk you through assisting the mare."

Her eyes were as big as dinner plates. Grady could relate—he wasn't exactly qualified for this, and the idea of screwing it up and letting anything happen to this mare or her foal sent chilly fingers of anxiety skittering down his back.

Snagging the phone from Ella's hand, Grady barked, "Ben, come on. I know I'm kind of the boy who cried wolf here, but this time it's serious."

"I believe you." Ben was doing that soothing thing with his voice, where he got extra super calm to combat the drama and chaos around him. Even recognizing the tactic for what it was, Grady felt his shoulders loosening.

"But it's going to take me a while to get out there; I'm up at Windy Corner now, so at least half an hour. I need you to be my eyes. What do you see?"

Having a clear mission settled Grady's nerves more than anything else could have. Using brief, terse sentences, he described the width of dilation he was seeing, and the worrying appearance of just one of the foal's little hooves. He'd been around enough equine births to know that wasn't optimal.

Ben's sigh confirmed it. "Yeah, sounds like the foal is going to need to be turned in the birth canal. Can you tell how long the mare has been in labor?"

"She's pretty sweaty and exhausted. Barely twitched when I touched her."

Which was another hint that something was wrong, because as much as Grady loved the wild horses of Sanctuary, as much as he'd appointed himself their protector, he kept his distance. The horses weren't tame pets— they were truly wild animals, unused to human contact. This was the closest he'd ever been to any of them.

"Once the foal first appears, the rest of the birth should only take about half an hour. Sounds like she's been working a lot longer than that, which isn't good—if she gets too tired . . . Listen, here's what I'm going to need you to do."

Ben got brisk and businesslike, going through the list of things that had to happen immediately, if not sooner, and Grady snapped to attention. It was exactly like gearing up for a rescue. He memorized every last instruction, visualizing the actions that would be required and not allowing himself to dwell on the possible negative outcomes.

Ben paused, then said, "Grady. We need to keep things as clean and sanitary as possible. You're going to have to take off the gloves. Maybe your overshirt, too, or at least roll up the sleeves to above the elbow. Can you do that?"

Darkness encroached on his vision, tunneling the world down to the glaring bright spot of the task ahead.

He'd be exposed. All those scars, the living memory of pain and terror, and Ella would see it all, and she'd get that look, that pitying horror-struck look . . .

"Grady!"

He blinked at the bark of his best friend's voice in his ear, and swallowed down the nightmare. The mare moved under his hands, straining hopelessly against a contraction, and Grady reached for the inner core of peace he'd found with the horses before.

It didn't matter what Ella saw or how she looked at him after. He'd do it, because he had no choice. He couldn't let this mare suffer, or take the chance that the foal might suffocate before it ever had a chance to breathe the clear island air.

His voice was a painful rasp in his throat, but he forced the words out. "Get here, Ben. I'll do my best, but—"

"I'm on my way. You'll be fine," Ben promised, then hung up.

Grady stared at the silent phone in his hand for a long moment, wishing he could hate Ben for making promises there was no way he could be sure would come true. But since Ben was one of the few friends Grady had managed to make after his accident, he knew he'd end up letting it go.

Ella took a tentative step closer to the mare. "How can I help?"

Light pushed back some of the darkness dragging at Grady's heart and mind. Even though Ella was scared, here she was, her chin tilted up and a determined glint in her blue eyes.

"The foal is twisted in the birth canal—the mare's not going to be able to push him out on her own." Tamping down the fear of failure, Grady kept his voice firm and matter-of-fact. "I'm going to have to physically locate the foal's other leg and pull him into position. Hopefully she'll be able to take it from there."

He could see the gulp of her swallowing down her nerves even from across the expanse of the mare's rounded belly. "That sounds . . . messy."

Grady had to grin. "Don't worry, city mouse, any mess will be getting all over me, not you. But I'm going to need you to hold her head, keep her quiet and still while I work. If she decides to freak out and stand up while I've got my arm inside her up to the elbow, we could both be in trouble."

"Wow. Better you than me." She wrinkled her nose, pulling a grossed-out face, but Grady caught the hint of a smile curling her mouth. Warmth washed through him at the realization that she was doing her best to break the tension.

"Just don't faint," he told her.

Ella waved an airy hand and folded down to kneel beside the mare's head. "No worries. I've never fainted in my life."

Grady sincerely hoped this wasn't an instance of there being a first time for everything.

Especially since she'd be confronted with worse things than the miracle of life in a second, here.

Any minute now, Grady was going to have to quit stalling, strip off his gloves, roll up his sleeves, and expose his scars to the open air and the sight of another human being for the first time in five years.

The mare groaned, a drawn-out, exhausted expulsion of air that shoved Grady into action.

He couldn't think about it. He couldn't watch for Ella's reaction when she saw the ruin of his hands and arms. He just had to rip off his protective coverings, like tearing off a bandage, and keep moving.

Holding his breath, Grady ground down on his back teeth and took off his gloves.

CHAPTER 13

Thin and white, raised in some places, puckered in others, the scars patchworking the skin of Grady's large, square hands stole Ella's breath and every scrap of her attention.

And he didn't stop with the gloves. Moving stiffly, almost mechanically, he unbuttoned the cuffs of the green flannel shirt and shrugged it off his shoulders.

Ella's gaze traced the marks of his injury up his strong wrists and over the tensed, corded muscles of his forearms. The scars stopped below his right elbow, but on the left side, they kept going, a vicious, slashing pattern of violence that disappeared under the short sleeve of his cotton undershirt.

"I know they're ugly, but if you're going to pass out, try not to fall on the mare."

Her eyes snapped to his. The hard-jawed face was shadowed with a wariness that hurt Ella's heart. Grady appeared braced for some theatrical fit of horror.

And she did feel horrified, but not because the scars

were so ugly. They weren't pretty . . . but what caught at
her chest and stole her breath was the amount of pain they
represented. Imagining what he must have suffered to
cause scars like that tightened a vise around her chest.

She wanted to deny it, tell him the scars weren't ugly,
but she knew he wouldn't believe her. Just by looking at
him, she could tell he was poised on the verge of a total
shutdown.

Her reaction to these scars meant something to him.
And even if it was only that he'd clearly been hiding them
for a long time, Ella still felt the full weight of responsibility bearing down on her next words.

The last thing Grady Wilkes wanted was her pity.

Lifting her chin, she leveled him with a stern look. "I
already told you, I don't faint. Now come on, focus. This
horse needs our help. What can I do?"

The lines at the corners of his eyes smoothed out. In
fact, Ella saw a lessening of tension in his entire face,
down his neck and into the line of his shoulders, making
him suddenly look both younger and more vulnerable
than she'd ever seen him.

Grady blew out a breath, stirring the burnished gold
lock of hair that fell boyishly over his forehead. "Okay,
you kneel down and hold her head. Keep her from moving around too much."

Trying not to think about what was going to happen, or
how close she now was to the mare's large teeth, Ella
dropped to her knees and placed tentative hands on the
horse's sweat-flecked hide.

"You can do this," she muttered, half to Grady and
half to herself. When he nodded once and pressed his lips
together firmly, Ella braced herself for something dis-
gusting.

Grady crouched behind the mare, muttered something under his breath that sounded like "in and up"—*oh no*—and before Ella could do more than curl her hands loosely around the horse's head to stop her thrashing, Grady had one arm inside the mare up to the wrist.

After a tense thirty seconds that felt more like an hour—and Ella could only imagine how the poor horse felt—he gasped and twisted his torso, exerting steady pressure as he pulled backward away from the animal in time with her contraction.

The mare's nostrils flared, her large head heavy and warm in Ella's lap. Ella found herself stroking the velvety soft nose and humming nonsense words as Grady sat heavily on the sand and propped both arms on his raised knees.

With a quick glance at Ella, he grabbed his flannel shirt from the ground and used it to wipe at his right arm. "I found the other leg and got the foal repositioned. I think she's going to be okay now."

Peering down the length of the horse's shivering body, Ella couldn't really see anything. Which, actually, was fine with her.

She didn't need to see what was happening to know that nature had taken over, and things were moving quickly.

"We need to stick close and monitor her," Grady said, his low, wrecked voice causing a strange clenching tightness in Ella's body.

"She's tired," he went on, "so I might have to help pull the foal out. But you could probably let go of her, if you want."

Ella's sore ankle was throbbing a bit, folded under her. There was sand in her shoes and a line of sweat trickling down her back that she desperately wanted to itch away.

"I'm okay, actually."

Grady nodded, looking a little surprised, but he couldn't have been as shocked as Ella, because it was actually true.

She wasn't ready to give up her spot holding the horse's head. Every shudder, every heartbeat, every contraction that racked the mare's body reverberated through Ella. And every time she bent over the mare's neck to murmur into the long, sensitive ears, and the horse calmed, Ella felt a wash of something like awe melting her minor aches and expanding her heart until it felt like it would burst through the cage of her ribs.

The next half hour was one of the most intense of Ella's life. After letting the mare rest for a few minutes, Grady gently wrapped his flannel shirt around the foal's exposed hooves and tugged to help the mare deliver the head and shoulders.

The shoulders were the worst part, and when it was over, all three of them needed another rest.

Grady threw himself down beside the mare, stretching his back in a big arch like a jungle cat finding a patch of sun. "You're doing great," he panted.

"She is, isn't she?" Ella could hear the pride and admiration in her own voice, but she couldn't help it any more than she could stop herself from combing her fingers through the mare's coarse, tangled forelock.

Turning his head to stare at her, Grady said, "Yeah, she is. But I meant you, actually. I know you're not exactly a horse person, but you're really helping her."

Heat flooded Ella's cheeks. "It shows, huh? No, Merry's the one whose horsey phase never really went away. I went through it when I was younger, like a lot of girls, but

I've never actually been around a real live horse until now. It's not how I thought it would be."

"Everything's messier in real life."

Ella nodded, conceding the point. "But that's not really what I meant. Seeing this whole thing, being a part of it . . . I don't know how to explain it. I haven't felt anything like this in a long time. Maybe ever."

He locked eyes with her as a smile spread across his tired face. "I'm glad you're here."

Her heart did a slow roll in her chest, and Ella smiled back. "So am I," she said, and meant it.

The mare lifted her weary head from Ella's lap and shifted restlessly.

"Okay, break's over," Grady announced, curling back up to his knees.

After that, everything seemed to unfold in a blur. Unbelievably quickly, almost between one heartbeat and the next: one moment there were the three of them, Grady bent over and swearing under his breath and Ella's shoulder muscles coiled in sympathetic pain and the mare pushing with her last ounce of strength . . . and then there were four.

Gasping for air and trembling with the aftermath of exertion, Ella couldn't take her eyes off the tiny, spindle-legged creature shivering on the gritty sand a few feet from its mother.

"Try to keep her still," Grady whispered thickly, moving slowly back. "If she stands up too soon, it'll break the umbilical cord, which is still doing some important stuff."

Ella nodded, unable to speak through a throat clogged with emotion. For long, long moments, the small group on the beach worked to catch its breath and come down from the adrenaline rush of the past hour.

Within minutes of entering the world, the foal had hitched itself over onto its stomach with its legs folded under it. The foal was dark, its fur matted with fluid and roughed up all over its skinny, awkward body. Ella had never seen anything more glorious.

"What happens now?"

Ella stared up at him, and Grady saw silvery tear tracks streaking through the smudges of sand and sweat on her red cheeks. She didn't seem to know she was crying. Her eyes shone with more than the tears.

Something rushed through him like a torrent, a wave of emotion strong enough to knock him off his feet.

Through sheer force of will, he kept his balance. "They need to stay connected for about an hour, and then sometime in the first six hours, the foal should stand and try to nurse."

Ella cooed a little, deep in her throat, a softness around her eyes that Grady loved.

In the distance, Grady caught the sound of a faulty engine stalling out and turning over. He didn't need to look back toward the road to know Ben had finally arrived.

The veterinarian's approach through the tall grass was slow and cautious, but when he was only halfway across the meadow, the mare spooked. Pulling her head out of Ella's lap, she heaved herself to her feet in a weary scramble of long legs and snorting to stand over the foal.

Grady gave the new mother and baby a wide berth, circling around to help Ella up. He felt the way she stiffened when she finally unfolded her legs, but even when he looked at her sharply, he didn't detect much more pain than the pins and needles of blood flowing back to her extremities.

"Thanks," she said. She was a beautiful, breathless mess, her dark hair damp with perspiration at the temples. One long strand stuck to her cheek, and without thinking, he reached toward her face to smooth it back behind her ear.

The sight of his ugly, scarred hand next to her flawless skin sent a shock of wrongness through him. He faltered, clenching that hand into a loose fist, but Ella's gaze never wavered. She put her hand on his wrist, her touch landing as delicately as a butterfly, and pressed his fingers to her cheek.

Grady felt the fine-grained texture of her skin against the pads of his fingertips like a solid hit to the gut.

The moment was quiet and suspended, a blossom drifting to the surface of a lake. Grady's mind was nothing but static, dizzy white noise pulsing with a single thought.

Want.

"The cavalry's here!"

Ben's gruff voice startled them apart. Grady dropped his hand from her face, closing his fingers to preserve the lingering sensation of human contact against his palm. Tugging his gloves out of the back pocket of his jeans, he slid them on with a sense of mingled relief and suffocation as he faced his closest friend.

"You're late."

Ben smirked and shrugged his backpack full of medical instruments off his shoulder. "That's the cavalry for you—always swooping in at the last minute to do the cleanup and take all the glory."

His hands were busy sifting through his tool kit, but he indicated the mother and baby with his chin. "Looks like you two managed just fine without me. Gonna introduce me to your lovely assistant?"

"Sorry." Grady stuck his hands in his pockets, not sure where to look. "Ella, this is Dr. Ben Fairfax. Ben, Ella."

"You're Jo's other daughter." Ben was still crouched over his open backpack, but Grady noted the way the back of his neck flushed red. "I just had the pleasure of giving your sister a tour of the barn."

Ella laughed, the sweet, husky sound rolling through Grady like thunder. "I can't believe she didn't demand to come out here with you. This is right up her alley."

Ben stood up, clutching a pair of latex surgical gloves and a cup of something Grady didn't recognize. "She didn't ask. But I wouldn't have brought her, anyway. Don't need the distraction of a civilian fluttering around over how adorable the widdle baby horse is. No offense."

The quirk of Ella's lips made Grady want to kiss her. "None taken. And if Merry had asked to come along, I'm pretty sure we wouldn't be having this conversation. She's hard to say no to."

"Yeah," Grady commented. "I don't get the sense that she's the shy, retiring type."

Ella snorted. "Merry? Shy? Right. I think she was born without the inhibition gene."

Mouth twisting in a mockery of a grin, Ben shrugged. "Hey, maybe she just didn't like me. Wouldn't be the first person, won't be the last."

A glance at Ella's thoughtful expression told Grady she hadn't missed the dark thundercloud over Ben's head when he talked about Miss Merry Preston.

Grady decided to do Ben a solid and practice a little deflection. "So you're good here, right? I think I'd better get Ella home. Jo will kill me if I let her daughter keel over from exhaustion on her first full day."

"Do we have to leave? I want to see the baby take its first steps!" Ella wobbled as she said it, though.

Grady gentled his voice, but not enough so she'd feel like he was handling her. "It could be dinnertime before he figures out what his legs are for. Don't worry, the horses are in good hands with Ben, and if you want, I'll bring you back out to check on them tomorrow."

God knew, Grady wouldn't be able to stay away.

As if eavesdropping on his thoughts, Ben jabbed an accusing finger in Grady's general direction. "Don't get too close, if you do come back. These two need to bond. And they're not domesticated barn animals—that foal doesn't need to imprint on a human or get used to humans being around."

"Killjoy," Grady grumped with a sideways look at the pout Ella was working, but he knew Ben was right.

Ben waved them off, turning the full force of his attention on the shivering foal, and with a last look over her shoulder, Ella began the long trudge back to the car.

Grady almost started after her, but sighed and turned back, defeated by his need to make sure his friend was all right.

He didn't have so many friends that he could afford to ignore any of them.

Clasping Ben's shoulder, Grady gave him a gentle shake. "Hey, man. You doing okay?"

Ben snorted without looking up from his careful inspection of the umbilical cord. The deft motions of Ben's long fingers reminded Grady that before his friend got his large-animal vet certifications, he'd actually trained as a surgeon. A people surgeon.

"Not as okay as some I could name," Ben said with a sardonic lilt. "You dog, you."

Damn it. This was what happened when Grady tried to do the manly heart-to-heart thing. He hedged with, "What do you mean?"

And there went Ben's left eyebrow. He must have extra facial muscles to be able to make it stick up like that. "Only you, Grady. Only you would think a dangerous, problematic foaling on an open beach was the perfect way to seduce a mainlander into loving Sanctuary."

"Hey, it's not like I planned this! I thought we'd check out some scenery, then take a hike up Wanderer's Point, maybe go cliff diving."

Ben appeared to be biting the inside of his cheek to hold back a snicker. "And instead, she ended up sweating through an hour of equine labor. Not that cliff diving would've been better—I honestly don't know why Jo asked you and your death wish to play tour guide. Which reminds me, you know I was with Jo when I got your call?"

"I don't have a death wish. I have a life wish! And life is better when you take some risks, get your blood pumping." He paused, fiddled with the hem of his filthy shirt. "Was Jo mad?"

"Expect to hear from her." Ben spared him a sympathetic grimace. "Jo's daughters . . . they're not what I expected."

"No." Grady thought about the way Ella had pitched in and helped, even though she was clearly afraid of the horse at first. "They're full of surprises. Like true Hollister women."

Ben's mouth flattened into a straight line. "I hate surprises."

"Hate. That's what we're going with, huh? Because when you talked about Merry before, I got the distinct impression—"

"Leave it. Merry Preston wouldn't look twice at someone like me—and I wouldn't want her to. Sweetness and light give me hives." Ben nodded at Ella's retreating back. "Now get going, before that city girl decides to steal your Jeep and drive herself home."

Grady started walking backward, keeping his friend pinned with a grin. "Surprises are good for the soul, man. Don't knock 'em."

Ben waved him away irritably, and Grady took off after Ella with the word "home" echoing through his brain.

He wondered what Ella would say if he invited her back to his house—aka the Fortress of Solitude, as Taylor called it, since he never invited anyone over. The little shingled cottage was his refuge. The silence and peace he found there were his reward for recovering enough to leave his uncle's house and buy a place of his own.

So what if Grady didn't like a lot of company? His friends knew who they were—they didn't need dinner parties and invitations to watch the game in his living room.

But now that Ben had inadvertently injected the idea into Grady's head, when he closed his eyes, he didn't have any trouble picturing Ella there.

His steps slowed, as if his body knew his startled brain needed a few more seconds to catch up.

At that moment, Ella looked over her shoulder, probably to see what the heck was taking him so long. The sun sparked off the deep red highlights in her dark hair as the wind caught it and whipped it across her neck.

Her smile was slow, questioning, as if she wasn't sure she had the right to be happy, but she couldn't help it.

And with a sinking sensation in the pit of his stomach, Grady knew he wouldn't mind seeing that smile across the breakfast table in the sunny nook next to his kitchen window.

As nerve-racking as the past couple of hours had been, as exposed as he'd felt and as worried about accidentally damaging that foal or hurting the mare rather than help-ing her . . . none of it had terrified Grady as much as this moment.

He'd promised Jo he'd make her daughter fall in love with Sanctuary Island. He'd never imagined how much he might come to depend on the magic of Sanctuary to make Ella Preston want to stick around.

Because Grady had done the unthinkable.

He'd let himself care.

CHAPTER 14

After a few hours Ella had intended to use for work, but instead spent Googling info about bed-and-breakfasts and the origins of the horse in North America, she realized she'd skipped lunch.

Wandering downstairs, she found Merry in the dusk-darkened kitchen, her face illuminated by the glow from the open refrigerator door.

"Grazing?" Ella felt a surge of gratitude for the way even the sight of her little sister made her smile. Merry was a guaranteed mood lifter, and with all the thoughts and worries swirling through Ella's exhausted brain, she could use a shot of Merry's patented brand of sunshine.

"Oh hey!" Merry stood up quickly, almost guiltily, as if she felt bad about the fact that she was hungry pretty much all the time these days. "I didn't know you were back. Is Grady with you?"

Just the mention of Grady Wilkes brought a tingle of warmth to Ella's cheeks. "No, he dropped me off this afternoon while you were napping. I didn't want to wake you."

"You should've invited him for dinner." Merry's eyes took on a mischievous twinkle.

"Grady had a family thing tonight," Ella said firmly. "Something with his uncle and cousin."

"Guess that's the place to be," Merry said. There was an odd note in her voice, a wistfulness that made Ella frown as she joined her sister at the fridge. "Jo's there, too. She left us cold chicken and something she called 'a mess of collards,' which doesn't sound too appetizing. I didn't want to tell her I had no idea what she was talking about. And oh my gosh, what is that?"

Ella sniffed suspiciously at the bowl full of dark braised greens studded with slivers of ham and bits of red onion. "Smells better than it looks," she decided, setting the big ceramic bowl on the kitchen table.

"I think there's a microwave in the pantry closet," Merry said, swaying over to the table with her hands full of a platter of chicken pieces.

Ella collapsed into one of the straight-backed kitchen chairs as if all her strings had been cut. "This looks pretty good as is. I don't have the energy to figure out how to heat anything up. But if you want it hot, I'll—"

Before she could heave herself out of the chair, Merry was shaking her head, mouth turned down at the corners. "Nah. Let's just dig in and then go to bed."

So much for sunshine.

"What's wrong?" Ella braced herself. She wasn't sure how many more revelations—about herself or the people she loved or the ones she'd just met—she could handle.

Merry fidgeted with the tines of the ancient silver fork that had belonged to their great-aunt Dottie, and sighed. "Nothing. I'm being dumb. Let's just eat."

Ella's heart ached at the lost look in Merry's downcast

eyes. "Kiddo. Nothing about you is dumb. Okay," she amended when Merry shot her a raised brow, "maybe your choices sometimes. A little bit. And your taste in men, because, wow. But if something's wrong, I hope you know you can tell me."

Squirming in her chair as if having a hard time finding a comfortable position on the hard wooden seat, Merry said, "I do know that. I just . . . doesn't it bother you that Mom is off with her new friends, her island family, and we're here?"

Swallowing the question that wanted to pop out—*oh, we're calling Jo Ellen mom now?*—Ella forced herself to take a calm bite of the collard greens. "I don't really care what Jo Ellen does. I mean, you're my family. You're all I need."

Merry's pursed mouth softened. "I love you, too." Picking up a chicken leg, she took a bite out of it before gesturing with the drumstick. "But be honest. You're not the slightest bit bugged? I mean, even Mom was worried about it, I could tell when she left. She wanted to invite us along, I think, but then she said that she needed to spend some time with Taylor, so I said it was fine, and of course we'd be okay on our own tonight. But secretly?"

"You're not fine," Ella guessed.

"Mom" again.

She shook it off, but a lingering sense of unease prickled over her skin as Merry scowled down at her plate.

"Not so much. Because hey, family. That's why we're here, right? And if we want to be part of Mom's life, we should get to know the people who are important to her here and now."

"That makes sense," Ella said cautiously, sensing a dangerous undertow. "But keep in mind, this is only temporary. We're leaving in twelve days. Give yourself a break, it's okay not to fully integrate into Jo's life."

Good advice, which she could do a better job of remembering herself. Ella cringed at how much time she'd
spent researching business plans for turning the old house
into a small inn.

"I know, but—" Merry began unhappily, but Ella cut
her off. She needed to nip this in the bud, for both of
them.

"No. You got what you wanted—you made a connection. Does it make sense to get completely enmeshed here
when we don't even know when, or if, we'll be coming
back to the island?"

As soon as the words were out of her mouth, Ella was
conscious of a pang of something sharp poking through
her breastbone. She didn't want to put a name to it, but
when she blinked, the image of Grady's rough-jawed,
handsome face swam to the surface of her closed eyes.

"Right." Merry waggled her eyebrows suggestively.
"Because you haven't been building any relationships on
the island."

"Shut up!" Ella aimed a gentle smack at Merry's arm,
but she dodged it with more agility than anyone in her
third trimester ought to possess.

"Out there on the beach all alone with Grady Wilkes.
Must have been romantic."

Ella snorted. "Oh sure, what with all the amniotic fluid
and horse sweat, I could barely keep my panties on."

"Sounds amazing." Merry pouted. "I still can't believe
you didn't call me the second you realized there was
about to be a baby foal wandering around the beach!"

That stupid blush prickled Ella's cheeks again. "It all
happened so fast! There was barely time to breathe, much
less to call everyone on the island to come down and
watch. Besides, I don't think someone in your delicate

condition should be exposed to the rigors of horse birth. It might give you nightmares!"

Merry rolled her eyes in her patented my-big-sister-is-dumb way. "You're the one with all the issues about having kids, not me. Seriously, though. Be honest. You wouldn't be sad to never see Grady again? Because I think you would. I think you'd be the saddest sad sack ever to weep bitter tears of regret if you left Sanctuary Island before you figure out where it's going with him."

Ella couldn't help but laugh, even though her throat was oddly tight and aching. "Come on back to reality, kiddo. It's not going anywhere with Grady."

No matter how tempting he is.

"Why not?"

"A million reasons! Like, for instance, our lives are completely different, we have different goals, and . . . oh yeah, we live in different places."

"Exactly." Merry leaned back in her chair with an air of having made her point.

Ella shook her head in confusion, feeling as if she'd missed some crucial part of the conversation. "What are you saying?"

Merry licked her lips, fingers drumming a staccato rhythm on the edge of the table. "I'm saying . . . let's stay here."

A chill raised every hair on Ella's arms. "You mean you want to extend our visit?"

Merry pressed her lips together for a moment, as if she were steeling herself for something, then said decisively, "No. I mean I'm thinking about staying. Indefinitely. As in, I'm considering moving to Sanctuary Island."

White noise like waves breaking on a stormy shore rushed through Ella's ears as Merry kept talking. Ella only caught a phrase here and there . . . not enough time . . . get to know . . . want a connection . . . not just about Mom . . .

All Ella could really process was an overwhelming, instinctive "No."

"Hey, I know this isn't what you planned on." Merry laid a concerned hand on Ella's arm. "And I know how much you hate to deviate from The Plan, but you look like I just told you I wanted to do something crazy. This wouldn't be that crazy."

That jolted Ella back into the conversation. "Not that crazy?" she sputtered, barely recognizing her own voice at that pitch of freak-out. "You're talking about moving to an island that doesn't even have a bridge back to the mainland. There's no hospital! When you go into labor, you'll have to hop the ferry to get to a real doctor! How is that not insane? Have you thought this through at all?"

Merry's face went stubborn, and Ella's heart sank. She knew that look. "In fact, Miss Bossypants, I have thought this through."

The plates and silverware rattled as Ella banged her hands down on the surface of the table, making both women jump. "When? We've only been here a couple of days!"

"I've been thinking about leaving D.C. for a lot longer than that," Merry said quietly, pushing away from the table. "And as for the rest of it, you and your control issues might need six months and pro-con lists filled out in triplicate to make a decision about anything, but I don't. I like it here. I think I could be happy on Sanctuary Island, and I want to raise Baby someplace where I'm actually happy."

Painful memories reverberated through Merry's low voice, tearing at Ella's heart. She drew in a shuddering breath. "That's not fair. Dad did his best."

"I know that. And I'm not blaming Dad for being sad and distant for most of our childhoods—he had a lot of tough breaks. But did he do everything he could to change that? Did he give himself the best possible chance at happiness? Because I don't think staying in a go-nowhere job he hated, in a city where he had no family or friends outside of the two kids he was raising on his own, was the best way for him to be happy."

"He did it for us!" Ella pushed back from the table, feeling trapped. "He left Jo for us. He went to that office every day to keep food on our plates and clothes on our backs."

"He could've done that somewhere else," Merry argued. "But he gave up. He was afraid to try. And this isn't about Dad, anyway, it's about me. I can't believe you're pitching a fit about this. I thought you'd be more supportive."

Ella ran both hands through her hair, pulling slightly to try and ground herself. "I can't support every nutso thought you ever . . . God, Merry, why are you doing this?"

"Because I have to try," Merry countered. "I don't want Baby to grow up feeling like I did . . . like there was some vague, undefined thing wrong all the time, every minute. And like maybe it was my fault and if I could just figure out how to change, how to be better, we'd be a normal family."

Ella's cheeks were cold. It wasn't until she brushed at them with her fingertips and felt wetness that she realized she was crying. "It wasn't your fault. If it was anyone's fault, it was Jo's. She's the one who broke our family into pieces . . . and now she's the one you're running to?"

Merry set her jaw. "One day, you're going to have to quit blaming everything that goes wrong in your life on Mom. She's a person, too, with her own problems—I promise, not everything is about her trying to mess up your life. From what I can tell, you're doing a fine job of that on your own."

It was a solid hit, a punch to the gut. Ella stared at her sister and saw a fierce-eyed, stubborn-jawed stranger. Suddenly, their father's bitter warnings about how far Jo would go to get what she wanted exploded through Ella's mind.

"Did she put you up to this?" Ella barely recognized her own voice, so low and flat with suppressed rage.

Merry's eyes widened incredulously. "Who, Mom?"

"She showed you the letter, didn't she? She played on your sympathies." Ella's analytical brain sped in circles, drawing lines and making connections. "Problems of her own . . . sure, like the fact that she's so far in debt, she's about to lose this death trap of a house? How did she get you—did she cry, or did she put on a brave face and say she'd get by, somehow . . . ? God, it makes me sick."

"Stop it," Merry cried, putting her hands over her ears. "Just shut up for a second, oh my gosh. What are you even talking about?"

Ella panted through her nose. Her insides were so cold and shaky, she had a momentary terror that she might throw up all over the tabletop. "You mean . . . you didn't know?"

"Mom never said a word." Merry stared, accusation clear in the crystalline depths of her eyes. "And neither did you."

Ella felt the water closing over her head and kicked desperately to try to get back to the surface. "I don't really know much, just saw a letter in Jo's room. It might be nothing."

Merry's gaze narrowed, and Ella slumped. This was a nightmare. "It's not nothing. Tell me everything you know, right now."

That was it. Game over. As soon as Ella had haltingly

laid out the few facts she was sure of, Merry stood up from the table. Her face was frozen, set in lines of anger and betrayal.

"If I wasn't sure about staying on Sanctuary before, I am now. You were right—if Mom had told me all that stuff, it would've been a no-brainer. Because now that I know she's in trouble, I want to do everything I can to help. Maybe you can't forgive her, and that's your choice. Personally, I can't live with that much negativity weighing me down—I have to let it go."

"Sweep it under the carpet and pretend it never happened," Ella translated. "Merry, ignoring an issue and hoping it'll never come back to bite you is not the same as letting it go."

But Merry didn't want to hear it—and like everything she didn't want to hear or deal with, she ignored it. "She's our mother."

She's not our mother, Ella wanted to say. *Not in any way that matters.*

But years of negotiations had trained her to hold back anything that wouldn't help her cause—and to look for the weak spots in an opponent's argument.

"So," Ella said slowly, her mind spinning like the wheels on a race car. "How about we make a deal."

Merry stopped in the doorway. "What deal?"

Ella took a deep breath and gambled everything on her one chance to save her sister from the biggest mistake of her life.

"If I can figure out a way to save Jo Ellen and Windy Corner, you'll come back to D.C. with me."

Ella held her breath as best she could while meeting her sister's stare head-on.

"And if I say no . . . ?"

Doing her best to appear casual, Ella shrugged one shoulder. "Then I guess Jo Ellen better start looking for a new home, because I won't lift a finger to help her."

No matter how wrong it felt to let Windy Corner leave the Hollister family—Merry was more important.

Despite herself, Merry looked impressed. "I always knew you could be ruthless, but this is the first time I've seen the Ella Shark in action."

"Commercial real estate is a cutthroat business." Ella smiled thinly. "And I'm good at it. Which is how you know when I say I can come up with a plan to save Jo Ellen, I'm telling the truth."

Merry nodded, her lashes sweeping down to hide her expression. "You win," she said, her voice small and tired. "Figure out a way to save Windy Corner, and Baby and I won't move to Sanctuary. But for the rest of the time we're here, you don't interfere in my relationship with Mom. We get to spend as much time together as I want, and you stay out of it. Deal?"

"Deal."

Merry nodded and slipped out of the kitchen before Ella could do more than draw in another breath to tell her it would be okay.

And it would be. All she had to do was structure a business proposal with enough projected income to get a bank to extend Jo a loan. Of course, certain people on the island might object, but Ella couldn't worry about that. Her first priority—her only priority—had to be Merry.

She tried not to think about the blank resignation tugging her sister's mouth into an unhappy curve when she had said, "You win."

Funny. Ella had never felt more defeated.

CHAPTER 15

The knock on his door startled Grady so much, he flailed
hard enough to roll out of bed and land on the hardwood
floor. He lay blinking up at the rafters for a long, breathless moment with the quilt tangled around his legs before
the old shoulder injury pinched painfully. Groaning, he
sat up and shook his head to clear away the fog of sleep.
Had he dreamed that knock on the front door?

No. There it was again.

It was probably Ben, maybe with an update about the
foal. The prospect was enough to have Grady dragging
himself to his feet. He wrapped the quilt around his naked shoulders and made his way down the stairs to the
front door.

"Awright, awright. Geez, what time is it?" he complained, swinging the door open on a jaw-cracking yawn.

"I'm sorry!" Ella exclaimed. "I didn't mean to wake
you up."

Grady's eyes popped wide, all vestiges of sleep clearing

away under the shock of Ella Preston on his doorstep at oh-dark-hundred.

"Hey, no," he said, hitching up the quilt awkwardly, hyper-aware of the stretch of scars over his shoulder and hoping like hell they were covered. "You didn't. I mean. What are you doing here?"

Her cheeks had been paler than usual when he first opened the door. Grady noticed mostly because now they flushed a prettier pink than the sunrise lighting up the sky over the tops of the pine trees circling his cottage. "I should go, let you get back to bed . . ."

She trailed off as her gaze slipped down his nearly naked body, and when both her eyes and her flush brightened, Grady felt his mood lift. It turned out, one embarrassed ogle from Ella Preston was better than a hot cup of joe.

And in spite of the fact that he'd spent many hours the night before tossing and turning under the weight of the revelation he'd had after the foaling, now that it came to the point, it was surprisingly easy to step back and reach out a hand to hold open the door. "Don't worry about it. Come on inside."

Ducking her head, Ella brushed past him in a cloud of soapy, sweet-smelling warmth. She paused in the entryway, her curious stare taking in everything from the hand-carved wooden furniture to the multicolored rag rug covering the hearth.

"This is . . . beautiful," she said, sounding surprised.

Now Grady was the one who was embarrassed. He shrugged off the compliment, not wanting to make a big deal out of how much the praise for his hideaway pleased him. "It's home."

"Was this your family's summer cottage?"

Surprised she remembered what he'd told her about his history with the island, Grady was a beat too slow in replying. "Ah, no. When I was a kid, we'd come and stay with my aunt and uncle. We stopped coming when my aunt Carol got sick."

"But you never forgot the island."

There was something in her voice, something wistful and a little yearning as she took in the simple charcoal drawing over the mantel. In a few fluid lines, the artist had rendered the sense of movement and freedom of a band of wild horses sweeping across a meadow, tall grass rippling in the breeze like waves on the shore.

"This place tends to get into your blood," he said quietly. "At least, that's how it was for me. When I got out of the hospital, all I could think about was coming here."

Drawing close enough to study the framed photograph on the mantelpiece, Ella said, "Is that you?"

Grady nodded, grinning a little as he remembered the day that picture was taken. "In my first boat. My uncle took up sailing and gave me his little powerboat. He even paid for a slip at the public dock for whenever I came to visit."

"It's so beautiful," Ella said, eyes wide and interested. "And you couldn't be more than . . . what, fifteen in the photo?"

"Sixteen." Sixteen, gangly, towheaded, and grinning a mouthful of braces from ear to ear as he took his pride and joy out for the first time as her captain.

"Do you still have that boat?" Ella asked.

"Yep, tied up down at the dock. A '98 Stingray 200LS. I work on her every now and then, keep her in good shape. She's a bit of a collector's item now."

"Maybe we should plan a boat tour around the island

sometime," Ella suggested, her gaze lingering on the image of the happy boy.

Grady felt the grin drop off his face. "I don't take her out anymore."

Startled, Ella looked up at him. "What, never?"

"That's right." He clenched his jaw, uncomfortable and wishing she'd just drop it.

As if she'd heard his unspoken wish, Ella turned a bright smile on him. "So, I guess you're wondering what I'm doing here!"

Something about the abrupt subject change grated on him, pinging his finely honed something's-not-right instinct.

No one should be that perky this early in the morning.

"Honestly?" He relaxed enough to feel another yawn threatening. "I'm wondering what the odds are that I have time to put on a pot of coffee before we head out to check on the foal."

Her eyes lit up. "Oh, can we?"

Grady hiked up the quilt again, taking the opportunity to make sure it was tucked securely under his more heavily scarred left arm, and headed for the eat-in kitchen. "Sure. I mean, I thought that's why you were here."

"Actually, I had a different request. But I'd really, really like to see the foal again. Please."

He hid his grin by busying himself with his coffee-maker. "Shouldn't be a problem."

"I just . . ." She fidgeted in his peripheral vision, her hands making graceful circles as she groped for the right words. "I've never seen anything quite like that before."

Grady laughed. "Who knew the miracle of life involved so many bodily fluids, huh?"

But that wasn't what she meant, and he knew it.

"Don't make fun of me." Her voice was quiet, intense enough to stop Grady in the middle of scooping coffee grounds into the paper filter.

"I'm not," he told her, focusing on what his hands were doing to avoid having to face her. "I've never been involved in anything like that before, either."

Silence stretched between them for a long moment, broken only by the gurgling rush of coffee perking.

Grady managed not to tense up when Ella stepped closer and turned to lean against the counter beside him.

"And here I thought you were the original Horse Whisperer," she said.

He shot her a look, but the half smile quirking her lips told him she was teasing. "Nah, not really. Your mom's the one with the magic touch. I just . . . care about the horses, is all."

He didn't know how else to say it, how to explain the need he had to keep tabs on the wild horse herd. No one on Sanctuary acted like it was that big a deal, or weird, but saying it out loud to someone new, like Ella, made him uncomfortably aware that Protector of the Island wasn't exactly an official title, with a salary and benefits and a career path.

He cleared his throat. "If you didn't come over because you wanted to check on the foal, what did you have in mind?"

"Oh. I was hoping you'd be willing . . ." Ella trailed off, her gaze glancing off him and slipping away to the side.

Grady was having a hard time imagining something he wouldn't be willing to do with Ella Preston. "What?"

"I made a promise to get to know Sanctuary," Ella said, her gaze sliding off to the side. "Can I get the rest of that guided tour?"

Grady blinked down at her, blood rushing in his ears. He'd been right—she looked good in his kitchen. Her trim, slender form slipped into the corners of his life as if there'd been an Ella-shaped hole at his side, waiting for her.

I am in so much trouble.

But she wanted to see Sanctuary. That had to be a good sign. He breathed in and felt something sharp and clean pierce through the clutter in his brain.

It had been a long time since he'd felt anything like it, but Grady was pretty sure he remembered and recognized it, from before the accident.

Hope.

Ella was very careful not to fidget.

There was so much riding on Grady's response—she needed his help to scout the island as a potential property for development. But she was pretty sure if she told him that, he'd refuse to listen to anything more.

She comforted herself with the knowledge that once he realized how much her ideas would help the island, in general—and his very good friend Jo Ellen Hollister, in particular—he'd understand.

In the meantime, she had to push through her worries and fears about Merry and the thorny prickle of guilt that she was using Grady's knowledge of Sanctuary for a purpose he wouldn't approve of. This was all business. It had to be.

But as she stood there, so close to him, every square inch of her skin began to tingle. Her lungs opened up, every breath filling her entire body with the rich scent of coffee beans and the sleep-warm spice of Grady's skin.

A lot of skin, barely covered by that beautiful, hand-worked quilt, although he was clearly trying to conceal the rest of his scars.

Ella tried not to stare. The last thing she wanted was to make Grady feel awkward, on display in his own home.

"What do you want to see?" Grady's deep voice startled Ella.

Resisting the urge to say "your naked torso," she determinedly met his gaze and said, "Everything. The wild horses, the town square, the best restaurant in town . . . whatever you want to show me."

The slow smile that spread over his face took her breath away. It changed his harsh, closed features, softened and illuminated them into something she wanted to keep looking at for a long, long time.

As she stared up at him now, it was hard to remember she'd only met him a few days ago. The hard line of his jaw, shadowed with the dark gold beginnings of a beard, was already familiar to her.

His cheeks burned red for a brief instant before he busied himself pouring coffee into his mug without spilling or dropping his grip on the blanket over his shoulders.

"I can do that. I did promise Jo I'd try to give you a sense of your heritage. Believe it or not, there's more to the island than pregnant mares."

"Maybe," Ella conceded. "But I wouldn't mind finding a few other things on the island that gave me the same feeling I got around those horses yesterday."

Without taking his eyes off the coffee mug, Grady mumbled, "How did you feel?"

Ella paused. Feelings were slippery things, in her experience.

After years of therapy, she didn't have any problem analyzing or talking about her feelings. But she'd also noticed that feelings weren't concrete. They didn't get set in stone. They were defined, in large part, by the ways people reacted to them. And the story a person told about the emotion later on was every bit as important and meaningful as the experience of that emotion in the moment.

So it was with a certain amount of deliberation and purpose that Ella said, "I felt at peace."

"And that's something you don't get a lot of, in your life."

It wasn't phrased as a question, but Ella shrugged anyway. "Not a lot of time for meditation and yoga, in my line of work. I tried a couple of different religion courses in college. Modern dance and avant-garde theater exercises that involved lying on my back on the floor and visualizing numbers in my head."

He took a sip of hot coffee, hiding his mouth, but his moss-green eyes over the rim of his mug were bright and curious.

"It was all interesting." She laughed a little. "But honestly? The closest I came to true happiness was exam time. I know. I'm a nerd. But that feeling of studying hard—absorbing information, spilling it back out for the professors to give a high grade—that made me feel good."

"I bet you were a straight-A student all through school."

Her smile faded. "Oh, there were a few rocky years."

The year her mom spiraled down into the depths of alcoholism, for instance. The year after, when her parents split up and her dad moved them across the city to that tiny apartment on the depressed, crime-ridden north side.

She shook her head to jog the bad memories loose and gave him a smile. "But mostly, yes. I was always working hard to fit in, to keep anyone from noticing there was something very wrong at home. It made me a bit of an overachiever."

Grady frowned, and she held up her hands. "Hey, it turned out okay, because doing well in school meant I had my pick of colleges, and later, careers. Maybe I owe Jo Ellen a thank-you."

Grady winced a little, and Ella bit her lip, regretting the sour twist of bitterness that lingered on her tongue.

"Sounds like you've given a lot of thought to how you got where you are," he said quietly.

"That's what thousands of dollars' worth of therapy will get you," she quipped. "No, seriously. It's important to me to understand myself, what drives me. I never understood that about Jo, and part of me—" Ella stopped short, surprised at what she'd been about to reveal.

Grady didn't pressure her, though. He simply watched her with those deep, soft eyes, his body a solid wall of strength keeping the real world at bay.

"Part of me is scared that if I don't figure out what went wrong with Jo and our family . . . it could happen to me, too. And I don't want to ever be like her." She paused for breath, feeling as if a weight she'd been carrying around for a long time had just slid off her shoulders.

Neither of them spoke, but the silence was perfectly comfortable.

Soon she realized that if she stood here much longer, staring up into his focused, interested, intense eyes, she was going to do something crazy.

Suddenly needing to move, she pushed away from the kitchen counter and found a smile. "So are you ready to head out?"

"Well, now, city mouse. We might be a touch more

casual out here on the island, but I still probably need to put some real clothes on."

He spread his arms out to the sides, holding the quilt at his back like a superhero cape, and Ella's gaze dropped as if magnetized.

The chiseled lines of his bare chest were shadowed and mysterious in the dim morning light filtering through the window above the kitchen sink. A narrowing V of crisp, dark gold hair drew her eye down his flat, hard stomach, disappearing into his pants.

He'd obviously been in a hurry when he pulled on the faded pair of jeans, which hung low, exposing the cut of his lean hip bones. They were zipped, but he hadn't bothered to do up the button at the top of the fly, and Ella felt all the blood in her body pooling low down in a languid, honeyed rush.

She didn't even know she was planning to speak before she said, "Do you have to?"

Grady stilled, alert tension entering his big, rangy frame, like a stallion scenting the wind for danger.

Swaying toward him, Ella felt the core of herself warming to his nearness. Her body knew what it wanted and her mind . . . her mind was telling her she'd never felt this level of connection with another living soul. His quiet stillness called to her, made her feel safe and crazy and brave enough to take a huge risk, all at the same time.

The knowledge that this was every bit as big a risk for him pushed her forward.

She took a step toward him, holding her breath against the moment when Grady would take a step back. But he didn't. He stood his ground, every muscle and sinew tensed, practically vibrating with stress—but he didn't move.

He wasn't wearing his gloves. But she'd seen him without the gloves already—felt the gentle scrape of his scar-roughened fingers along the back of her hand, the curve of her cheek—and Ella wanted more.

She wanted to see everything, to know all of him. On a level deeper than rational thought, she understood how difficult it would be for him to expose himself that way.

Baby steps, she decided, capturing Grady's left hand, the one with the deeper scars, between both of her smaller, smoother hands. He didn't resist, but he didn't take over, either, as she cradled his hand and brought it up to her face.

Staring up into his set, expressionless face, Ella pressed his hard palm to her cheek.

The simple touch unleashed a shiver that coursed over the surface of her skin, and something flared hot and fierce in the depths of Grady's eyes.

Light-headed, giddy, no thought in her brain except for him, Ella turned her face far enough to press a kiss to the center of his palm. The scarred skin was raised under her lips, a strange mix of smooth and rough.

"Do you feel that?"

His throat clicked when he swallowed. "The scars themselves are pretty numb. But the edges can be sensitive. Hard to tell pain from pleasure."

That sounded like a challenge.

CHAPTER 16

Ella let go of his hand, satisfaction roaring through her when he didn't pull away.

Nestling her cheek more firmly into the cup of his palm, she touched the part of his body that had been tugging at her attention since he'd first opened his door to her.

Her hands skimmed his lean waist, the taut flesh under her fingertips hot and silky, before her grip settled gently on the jut of his hip bones above the line of denim. She didn't even try to stop her thumbs from finding the divots of his hips, the gorgeous planes of his muscular body drawing her in.

Grady shifted his weight under her touch. The muscles in his outstretched arm went tight, corded with trembling tension, but his touch on her face stayed soft and warm. Almost tender.

Keeping the caress light, she traced her way up over the bellows of his rib cage. His chest expanded and contracted under her hands as he sucked in an audible breath. "Ella, what are you . . . ?"

"Shhh," she hummed, the way she'd calmed the mare yesterday, and like magic, she felt some of the tension melt out of Grady's body.

"I thought you wanted to get going," he tried, his voice strangling on the rush of words. "Pour yourself some coffee and I'll put on a shirt."

Ella shook her head, skimming her fingers up, up, feeling the broad slabs of powerful muscle under her hands. "I like you like this."

"Come on, quit playing around. I have to get dressed." With a bitter twist to his mouth, he dropped his hand from her face and stepped away from her, hitching the quilt higher over his left shoulder. "I'm not going out like this—I don't want to scare anybody."

"Stop." The sharpness of her voice startled Ella. Grady, too, if the way he paused and stared at her was any indication. "I mean it," she insisted, her palms already aching with emptiness, the buzz of desire demanding that she get her hands back on him right now, immediately, if not sooner.

"Stop what?"

The genuine confusion on his face struck at Ella's heart. It was a long moment before she could speak.

The words felt huge, too big to force out of her throat, but she managed it. "Nothing about you is ugly. I don't know how you got those scars, but they're part of you. I'm starting to know you, a little bit, and I promise—anyone who'd be turned off by any part of you isn't worth your time."

Grady stopped, eyes wide and intense on her face, and Ella lifted her chin. She meant every word, and she wouldn't back down.

She saw the moment when his control evaporated. And as his lips brushed against her mouth, like a whisper, like a dream, his arms slid around her shoulders and Ella felt the whoosh as the quilt dropped to the floor.

Once, during location training in the Colorado mountains, Grady and his partner had gotten lost in a sudden fog so intense that it had turned the familiar forest training grounds into a thick, damp cloud full of hidden obstacles.

Trees and branches loomed out of nowhere to bash them in the face; rocks and gnarled tree roots leaped up from the ground to trip them. It had taken Grady and Tom seven hours of fumbling through the forest—the forest they would've sworn they knew like the back of their hands, the forest they had extensive maps of in their packs—before the fog finally lifted.

The moment when the fading afternoon sunlight finally speared through the dense gray and burned it away in a burst of blinding glory was etched into his memory for all time.

When Grady kissed Ella Preston in his kitchen, he felt his heart expand exactly the way it had that day in the forest.

She opened her mouth, inviting him in, and every thought was wiped from Grady's mind in a blast of hunger.

For long moments, all he knew was the clean taste of her mouth, the soft heat of her body leaning into his chest, the silk of her hair tumbling over his hands—the thunder of blood through his veins, and the heavy throb between his thighs.

But then she wrapped her arms around his back and

her fingers found the slashing edges of his worst scar, and it was like a bucket of cold water cascading over Grady's head.

He jerked back, stumbling a little as his heel caught in the folds of the blanket at his feet.

"Don't." Grady swallowed, wishing his voice weren't so wrecked. But there was nothing he could do about it.

Ella pressed her kiss-swollen lips into a brief line before making an obvious effort at a smile. "You're right, I was pushing. I do that, sorry."

Busy slowing down his heartbeat and getting his lungs under control, Grady didn't have a lot of strength to spare for regulating his tone. "It's fine. Let's just go."

She flinched a little, but caught herself before Grady could do more than drag in a breath to apologize. "No problem! Take all the time you need, if you want a shower or something . . . not that I'm saying you need one!"

"A shower might not be a terrible idea—preferably freezing cold."

Grady watched as hectic pink flushed up her neck and into her cheeks. Squeezing her eyes shut tight, Ella said in a stifled voice, "I'll wait in the car. I really am sorry."

"You don't need to apologize." He was starting to feel stupid about overreacting to a simple kiss. So she touched his shoulder. Big deal. Not like plenty of doctors and nurses and physical therapists hadn't touched it after the accident. Granted, it had been a while.

And not one of those medical professionals had made him feel the way Ella Preston did.

She huffed out a frustrated breath, face drawn and tight. "Oh really? I invited myself over, forced my way into your house while you were half asleep, and then climbed you like a tree. Seems pretty apologyworthy to me."

When she put it like that, Grady felt embarrassment scorching the tips of his own ears. "I'm not mad about any of that. Promise. You can climb me anytime."

She cut her eyes at him as she tucked a lock of hair behind her ear. "So long as I don't touch you. Right?"

Grady froze, not sure what to say. Before he could figure it out, Ella smacked a hand to her forehead and grimaced. "There I go again! Seriously, do you have a muzzle lying around anywhere? I'm an idiot. We barely know each other. I don't have any right to pressure you about anything."

Okay, they hadn't known each other very long, but it had been an intense few days. Still, as dedicated as Grady was to living like today was the last day of his life, he wasn't completely ready to strip himself bare for Ella.

Some adrenaline junkie he turned out to be. But he felt splayed open and raw; it was taking everything he had to stand in front of her with no shirt, no blanket, nothing to cover up the visible marks of his past.

But he already wanted to punch himself in the face for shying away from her touch.

"It's fine," he repeated firmly. "You startled me, but it's not a problem."

Ella sighed, looking away. "Yes it is. This was a mistake. My mistake."

Suddenly, a cold shower seemed way less necessary. "A mistake," he muttered, hearing the echo of her words after their first kiss, back on Jo Ellen's front porch. "Let me guess. It didn't mean anything, either."

A spasm of memory crossed her pretty face. She looked like she wanted to duck her head, but instead, she met his glare with eyes wide open. A trickle of respect dripped through Grady's anger.

"No." Ella swallowed visibly. "This time . . . I didn't mean for that kiss to happen, but I won't pretend it meant nothing to me."

His frozen heart kicked back to life. Nerves fired sporadically down his spine, making his skin buzz with awareness like the electricity in the air before a thunderstorm.

He wanted to tell her how long it had been for him—how long it had been since he believed he'd ever even want this again.

Closeness with another human being.

Throat working, heart hammering, all he could bite out was, "It meant something to me, too."

She swayed toward him for one brief, charged moment, her hungry gaze dropping to his mouth. Grady's fingers itched with the need to touch her, to wrap around her arms and pull her in close.

But instead of falling into him, Ella stepped back. Shaking her head, she said, "I can't," in this scratchy voice. "Grady. It's not that I don't want to—at this point, it would be stupid to pretend I'm not incredibly attracted to you. But my sister and I are leaving Sanctuary Island in a week and a half. If this meant nothing, then maybe I could go ahead with it, have some fun, and head back to Washington without a second thought."

"I understand," he told her. And he did.

Grady wondered when he'd turned into a naïve schoolgirl. He knew she was leaving. She'd never so much as hinted that she might stay. How had he let himself forget that this whole visit was nothing more than a reluctant vacation from her regularly scheduled life? None of this was real to her.

Trouble was, Ella was just about the most real thing Grady had seen in years.

"But I still need your help." She turned pleading eyes on him, trying on a tremulous smile that only made him want to kiss her more. "Can you show me your Sanctuary, if I swear to keep my hands to myself?"

Grady did himself the favor of taking a moment to actually think about it. Being near Ella, showing her his island—that was going to be damn difficult, knowing that she had no intention of pursuing the simmering attraction between them.

Then again, he mused as he watched her nervously tuck a lock of hair behind the delicate pink shell of her ear, *intentions change.*

He'd defy anyone to spend time on Sanctuary Island without falling in love with the place.

Grady didn't question exactly why it was so important to him that Ella fall for the island. But it was—and showing off the place he loved most on earth to her wasn't exactly going to be a chore.

As for being forced into close contact with her for days on end . . . well, maybe his original plan of counting on the magic of Sanctuary wasn't such a crazy one, after all.

"Of course I'll show you around the island." The grin came easily, his heart lightening now that he had a plan. "I promised, didn't I? Although your meddling mother gave me a talking-to about what kinds of things to show you. She won't let me take you cliff jumping! Can you believe it?"

Ella's eyes glazed over. "Cliff jumping," she echoed faintly. "Dear Lord. Is that what you do for fun?"

Grady shrugged. "If you know the right spots, it's safe

enough. And what a rush! Okay, let me grab a shirt. You go on, get some coffee—we've got a lot to see before lunch."

Ella smiled at him, face lit up like he'd handed her the moon, and Grady had to turn and almost bolt up the stairs to keep from grabbing her again.

The plan was to make her fall for the island, to let her come to him, like a wild yearling. He could be patient. He'd been trained to move carefully, with deliberation, keeping his senses alert for danger and mapping out trouble areas beforehand.

He could do this. He'd wait for her to come to him.

And in the meantime, he'd let Sanctuary Island work its magic.

CHAPTER 17

Ella yelped out a laugh and chased the cold dribble of ice cream that dripped from the cone onto her wrist.

Sweet, tart, creamy—she couldn't help but moan appreciatively as the flavor of wild strawberries burst across her tongue.

She licked up the stray droplets of melting ice cream and wished she'd been smart enough to grab a paper napkin from the counter of the roadside stand.

"You really need to quit doing that."

Grady's rough voice broke into her haze of enjoyment. She blinked her eyes open to see him staring at her across the picnic table, his own forgotten ice-cream cone tilting precariously in his big hand.

Whoops.

Guilt—Ella's constant companion, after four days of touring the island with Grady—tugged sharply at her, reminding her that she'd promised herself she wouldn't do anything to make this harder on Grady than it had to be.

Licking herself right in front of him definitely counted.

"Sorry," she said, feeling a blush heat the back of her neck. Or maybe that was the afternoon sun beating down through the shifting branches of the trees lining the road where Miss Ruth's Homemade Ice Cream stand had stood for decades.

Forty-two years, to be exact, according to Miss Ruth herself, who scooped up the ice cream with a practiced twist of her wrist and packed it into a couple of cake cones without spilling a drop.

A trim, petite woman in her sixties, Miss Ruth moved slowly, with precision. She was a woman who took pride in doing things perfectly. Ella could relate.

Miss Ruth had winked at Ella when Grady turned to lead them across the grass to the weathered red picnic table set up under the trees beside the stand.

"Be patient with that one," Miss Ruth whispered, tilting her head so her bobbed ash-blond hair swung against her pointed chin. "He's sweeter than he looks. Trust me, I know about sweet things."

Unsure how to answer, Ella had smiled back before hurrying after Grady.

Now, with Miss Ruth's signature ice cream melting in her mouth, all Ella could think was that the ice-cream lady was right.

Grady was sweet. He was a good man. And merciful heavens, was he ever sexy. She looked at him, the heat in his gaze as she lapped up ice cream, and felt fire flash through her entire body.

She really, really wanted to lean across the table and lick the taste of strawberries off his lips.

But she couldn't. Knowing what she knew, that this whirlwind tour of Sanctuary Island had only confirmed her decision to present Jo with a proposal to turn the Windy Corner house into a small inn. Knowing how much Grady would hate that idea, she couldn't allow herself to kiss him.

Even though they both wanted it.

Swallowing hard against the surge of desire, Ella got up and hustled over to the stand to fetch a handful of paper napkins. Luckily, Miss Ruth was busy with other customers, a family with two little kids, so it was easy to avoid her avid, inquisitive eyes.

Ella used one napkin to clean up the rest of the dribbles from her cone as she walked back to the table. Tossing the wad of paper onto the table, she said, "You're a mess, Wilkes."

He muttered something that sounded like, "You have no idea," switching his cone to his left hand and shaking sticky drops off his right with a grimace. The pale pink ice cream was stark and obvious against the brown leather of his gloves.

"Here, you're going to ruin those gloves." Ella reached for him. "Let me just—"

"No," Grady said sharply, pulling away with an instinctive flinch that Ella felt like a punch in the gut.

They stared at each other, tension mounting until Ella was honestly afraid she might suffocate.

Making a big deal out of this was the worst thing she could do. Going back to her ice cream, she said, "I've seen them already."

"I know." Grady was gruff, defensive, but his eyes gave him away. When his gaze darted to the young family still chatting with Miss Ruth, who was leaning both her elbows on her scuffed wooden counter, Ella knew exactly what was bothering him.

"Those people are not going to care. They won't even notice."

He pressed his lips together grimly. "They might."

"Well." Ella concentrated on finishing off her cone, barely tasting it. Which was a shame. "So what if they do? What's the worst thing that can happen?"

She watched the struggle play out on his face, all the fear and shame he'd built up around his scars. And suddenly, she couldn't stand it for another moment.

Ella met Grady's worried eyes and took his free hand in both of hers. Moving slowly enough to give him plenty of time to pull away, she tugged at the fingertips of the glove and loosened it, bit by bit.

Grady's breath came in quick, shallow pants and his entire frame was rigid—but he didn't stop her.

Trying to telegraph that it was all going to be okay, Ella set her jaw and pulled the glove off his right hand.

They stared at each other, wide-eyed, his naked hand clasped in hers. Sunlight flickered through the gently swaying branches overhead, dappling the paler skin of his right hand with spots of gold. Somewhere nearby, a child laughed, high-pitched and happy, but Ella was only vaguely aware that there was a world outside of the two of them.

A soft breeze ruffled Grady's dark gold hair, sending a few stray tendrils to catch in his eyelashes. He blinked, swayed toward her.

Ella couldn't deny him. She couldn't deny either of them. Lifting his ungloved hand to her lips, she pressed a gentle kiss to the backs of his nicked, scarred knuckles.

She would've been tempted to do more, but the rest of the world was coming back into focus. The little family was still standing over by the counter, the mother talking to Miss Ruth while the kids, covered in the sticky remnants of their ice-cream treats, played in the grass in front of the stand.

Following her gaze, Grady glanced over at the family. He watched them for a long, tense moment. The husband, a nice-looking guy with thinning brown hair and glasses, noticed them and lifted a hand in greeting.

Grady hesitated, then pulled his naked hand from Ella's grasp and lifted it in a silent wave.

Pride and tenderness swamped Ella, forming an aching knot in the back of her throat.

Careful, she reminded herself. *Let it seem normal, ordinary.*

Even though she felt like she could cry at being witness to Grady's breakthrough moment.

"Come on," she said thickly, standing up. "Let's let that nice family have our table."

Grady finished off what was left of his cone in two big bites, then got to his feet. He looked at Ella, who was still holding his right glove, and down at his own hands. A half smile pulled up one corner of his mouth. "Might as well go all the way."

Without another word, he stripped the glove off his left hand and gave it to her. Ella closed her fingers around both gloves and worked up a smile. Her throat was almost too tight for words, but she managed to say, "What's the next stop on the tour?"

In one week on Sanctuary Island, they'd seen the tiny, one-room jailhouse, exclaimed over the well-preserved architecture of the small public library, listened to the local high school conduct a band camp practice on the steps of the gazebo, and gone to the square after dark to sit on blankets alongside what seemed like the entire population of the island to watch *The African Queen* projected on the blank white wall of the bank.

Grady thought about it for a second. "We could check out Wanderer's Point."

Ella narrowed her eyes in suspicion. "Isn't that where you planned to take me cliff jumping? Because I'm telling you right now, Grady—"

He held up his hands in surrender, laughing. "You don't have to jump. But we should drive up there anyway. It's the highest point on the island."

"So it's got a great view, I bet." Ella started walking toward the Jeep, needing movement and time to get herself under control. "Let's go."

Grady got in the driver's seat and curled his fingers around the leather steering wheel, flexing his hands.

As he drove up the narrow country road, Ella cleared her throat. It didn't help. There were words stuck in there that she had to get out, or she'd choke on them. "Thank you. That was . . . amazing."

He took his eyes off the road for a brief moment, and there was a flicker of answering gratitude in the green-gold depths before he said, "Yeah, it's good ice cream, huh?"

Grady shifted gears and put his attention back on the road in front of them, and Ella smiled to herself.

"The best."

They rode the fifteen minutes across the island and up the tall, pine-studded hill in silence, each locked in their own thoughts.

The Jeep bumped over the rocky single-lane road and crested the hill. The sky opened up over their heads, gossamer white clouds wisping softly across the blue expanse. Grady parked at the edge of the tree line and got out.

Slamming the Jeep door behind her, Ella turned her face up to the sky. The sun beat down on her cheeks, warm and bright, and when she opened her dazzled eyes, she had to blink a few times before the beauty of the vista in front of her really registered.

"Wow," she breathed as Grady shut his door and rounded the Jeep to stand beside her. "I asked for a view, but I didn't expect you to give me a peek into heaven."

Grady stood shoulder to shoulder with her, his long legs bracing both of them against the wind buffeting the rocky bluff where they'd parked. "This is one of my favorite spots on the whole island."

His voice was full of quiet satisfaction and pride. Ella edged as close as she dared to the side of the cliff. "It's glorious."

Below their feet, the rocky hillside sheared away to a fifty-foot drop, straight down to the white-capped waves crashing into the cliff face. The air smelled of salt and honeysuckle, a beachy perfume rushing into Ella's lungs and filling her with a sense of freedom and serenity as she stared out over the endless blue horizon.

Part of her mind couldn't help but note that this would make an excellent end to a nature trail. The B and B wouldn't attract serious hikers—Sanctuary was too small to provide long, challenging trails—but there were lots of nature walkers out there who'd pay plenty for the chance at a view like this.

Ella sighed. It seemed like no matter which way she turned, she found some new aspect of the island that she could envision as part of a marketing proposal to tempt investors to develop Sanctuary.

Which was a good thing. Of course it was.

"Most people, when they get up here and see that view, they don't scowl. What are you thinking about?"

Grady's voice shattered her train of thought. Hurriedly smoothing out her features, she dredged up a smile for him. "Nothing, really. Just . . . wishing I had a little more time here."

With a few more weeks, she might be able to come up with an alternate plan for Jo Ellen, something that would let her keep the house without turning it into an inn.

"You could stay longer," Grady pointed out.

And as he shifted behind her, the hard length of his rock-solid body brushing against her, Ella closed her eyes and admitted that she was worried about just what might happen to her heart if she spent too many more afternoons like this one.

"No. I really can't."

King Sanderson and Pete Cloudough spent most summer days playing checkers in front of the hardware store and arguing about whether this particular vista was the most beautiful place on Sanctuary Island or not.

Personally, Grady had always agreed with the island's unofficial royal highness that no swan-speckled pond or wide field of waving reed grass and blooming mallow could compare to the view from Wanderer's Point.

It was one of his foolproof ways to quiet the rumblings of nightmares in his brain, to calm himself down and even himself out. Usually, one look out over the ocean and he was transfixed. He'd sat up here for three and a half hours once, without even realizing how long it had been until the sun kissed the far horizon in an explosion of orange and red splendor.

And then he'd taken a running leap off the side of the hill, letting the endless seconds of free fall and the shock of the cold water jump-start his heart. There was nothing better.

But today, the view he couldn't take his eyes off was the woman at his side.

A week on Sanctuary Island had been good for Ella. The prim, buttoned-up beauty he'd rescued from a hole in Jo's front porch stood on the rough rock outcropping over the water in jeans and a blue tank top that bared her smooth shoulders and the upper swells of her small breasts. Her dark brown hair was pulled back in a messy ponytail, but the wind up here caught at the flyaway tendrils and lashed them against her flushed cheeks.

Grady decided he deserved a reward for taking off his gloves in public. He reached up and swept his fingers through the small, loose curls at her temples.

Soft. Her hair, her skin, her eyes when she tilted her head and gave him a look from underneath her sooty lashes.

So unbearably soft, softer than anything Grady was used to in his life—but there was a core of steel running through her, too.

"It's nice," she murmured. "Without the gloves. I like your hands."

A warm wash of satisfaction poured through him, even when she pressed her lips together as if frustrated with herself, and turned away.

"Still trying to keep your distance," he observed, letting himself grin a little. "No problem. I'm wearing you down, I can tell. Funny that of everything I've tried, it's these ugly paws of mine that have come the closest."

"They're not ugly!" The protest was immediate, almost annoyed, and Grady's grin widened.

"Well, they're not going to win any beauty contests." He studied his ravaged hands as impartially as he could, finger by finger, scar by scar. "But I guess they're not going to make any little kids run away in terror, either. You were right—they're part of me now. They're only as big a deal as I make them. I might as well get used to them."

A shudder of memory sucked him under for a second—darkness, heat, the poisonous stench of burning natural gas—but he shook himself free of it in time to meet Ella's watchful gaze.

"Can I ask . . ." She stopped, uncertain, and he realized it had been a while since he'd seen her so hesitant. He didn't like it.

"You want to know how I got the scars," he said, breaking her stare to look out over the water.

He hadn't told this story to anyone in years. The island gossip machine was well oiled, and ensured he'd never had to have this conversation with anyone who lived here. The last person he'd told had been his physical therapist in the hospital, and then he'd only talked about it because she needed all the details to be able to plot out the best course of treatment.

But what had hiding the scars for five years gotten him?

Ella slipped her warm, slender hand into his and curled their fingers together. Their linked hands felt like an unbreakable bond, a solemn vow, a promise for the future.

Grady closed his eyes and jumped.

CHAPTER 18

"It's not a pretty story, but it's not some deep, dark secret, either." Grady tried to laugh, but it sounded kind of choked. "You sure you want to ruin our afternoon with this?"

Determination hardened the lines of her jaw and sharpened her eyes to navy blue. "I'm sure."

"Come on, we might as well get comfortable." Heart hammering, Grady led her over to the large slanted boulder that served as a convenient backrest when he wanted to lose himself for a few hours in the infinite horizon.

This time, he took comfort in the familiarity of the view while he braced himself to go spelunking in the darkest corner of his own mind.

"I told you I was with Texas Task Force One." Even now, he could hear the immediate surge of pride in his own voice. "Do you know what that is?"

She settled on the ground next to him, pulling her raised knees into her chest and wrapping her arms around them. "Not really, sorry."

He shrugged. "It's okay. We—*they* are an elite urban

search-and-rescue team that operates out of Dallas. But we used to get sent all over the country, and even abroad sometimes, whenever there were disasters—man-made or natural. The force was there to sift through the rubble in the aftermath of September eleventh, and we went into New Orleans after Katrina hit."

Every bit of Ella was intent on his story, her entire body inclined toward him and her eyes fixed, unblinking, on his face. "Search and rescue," she said. "Tell me what you did, exactly."

He rolled his shoulders, remembering the weight of his gear. "We did it all. Whatever it took, when people were in trouble, we went in and got them out. Floods, collapsed buildings, earthquakes, train derailments, you name it, Texas Task Force One has dealt with it."

"It sounds like worthwhile work. You must have done a ton of training to prepare you for such a variety of situations."

"More than ninety hours of training a year, in addition to the cross-training for the specialist position I held on the structural engineering team."

Ella's gaze flickered and went transparent. For a moment, Grady imagined he could read the thoughts spooling out into her active mind.

"So." He took a stab at it. "How did a guy who trained with the best and worked a job like that for years wind up a handyman on a tiny island, rescuing nobody but the occasional wild horse that gets caught in a bramble patch?"

Red scorched up her neck and into her cheeks. "I'm not judging you," she said hurriedly. "Really. But the task force sounds like a job that requires a level of dedication and commitment that, honestly, I can barely even imagine . . . and I've literally been diagnosed as a workaholic by a mental health professional!"

"You needed a professional to tell you that? I pegged it the minute I met you."

That got her to quirk a smile and slug him in the shoulder.

Grady grinned, feeling a little easier in his skin. "I get it, though. You love your job. SAR . . ." He paused when she drew her brows together bemusedly. "That stands for 'search and rescue.' Anyway, SAR teams tend to be made up of . . . I guess, true believers. For lack of a better term. It's insanely difficult, strenuous, exhausting, stressful work. You're always on call. Middle of the night, Thanksgiving Day, whenever. And when you get called out, you never know exactly what you'll be facing. All you know is that it will be dangerous. Potentially deadly, in fact, or they wouldn't have called you. It's a rough life."

Ella leaned her chin on her folded arms and studied his expression. "You miss it, don't you?"

Grady blew out a breath and let himself confront the truth. "Every day."

"So why did you quit?"

"I didn't." And boy, wasn't that still a bitter pill? "They asked me to leave. After . . ." He flexed his hands into fists and felt the pull of scar tissue all the way up to his shoulder.

For the space of four heartbeats . . . five . . . there was no sound but the clash of wave against rock at the base of the bluff and the rustle of a cool breeze through the stands of bayberry bushes.

"If you don't want to talk about it," Ella said, "it's fine. No pressure."

He forced himself to smile. "I appreciate that. But it's okay, I want to tell you. It's just . . . I need a minute to work up to it."

"Take your time."

A whipcord of self-disgust lashed through him. "This shouldn't be so hard," he snarled. "Empty words, memories of stuff that's over and done with. That's nothing compared to what my buddies on the force are dealing with right this minute, or any of the other minutes since I left."

"Grady." Her worried tone and the concern in her eyes grated over his raw nerves. When she put a light hand on his arm, he jerked away from her and spoke in a harsh monotone.

"It was a natural-gas explosion. A five-story apartment building in Richardson, outside Dallas, came down. We were called in to search for survivors. I found some in an air pocket, in what used to be the building's elevator shaft. SAR teams work on the buddy system. My partner was a guy named Tom Caldwell. Our captain sent us into the elevator shaft on a rope-and-pulley system we rigged up to help us lift out the victims. Some of them were in medical distress."

Bile rose up in the back of his throat, sour and acidic with adrenaline, as his body remembered how it had felt to peer up into the impenetrable, windowless blackness of that shaft and see the elevator suspended by its frayed cables only twenty-five feet above his head.

"It was my turn to be the pivot point, the anchor at the top of the rope, but I wanted to go down. I loved the hard ones—the challenge and the satisfaction of coming out on top. And this one was hard because we had wounded civilians, which meant we were working against the clock, trying to get them out before they went into shock or fell unconscious, or their condition deteriorated to the point where even if we got them to the hospital it would be too late. And there was that dangling elevator, let's not forget that. We were all aware that if those cables snapped, if those emergency brakes went, we were in a lot of trouble."

Ella's eyes were huge and round. "But you volunteered to go down and rescue those people."

"I was an idiot. A cocky idiot. Sure, I aced all the tests about spotting potential risks—but deep down, I never truly believed anything bad could happen to me. And up until that day, I'd lived a pretty charmed life. But that's skipping ahead."

Ella looked sick. "Oh, Grady."

"No, you wanted the whole story. You're getting it."

She subsided, but she didn't look happy. That was fine; he wasn't happy, either. But now that he'd started, he couldn't seem to stop.

"So, the wounded disaster victims. We had a middle-aged man, overweight, with chest pains. A young woman and her two kids—one of the kids wouldn't stop crying, and the other one never made a sound. The mom had a broken arm, but she wouldn't put the crying kid down. We got her and the crier out first, then the silent kid, then the fat guy. I sent them up on the litter, then prepared to head back up the shaft myself. And that's when it happened."

She sat up straight, pale and riveted. "The elevator?"

"Nope." Grady closed his eyes and breathed through the memory, tasting nothing but ash. "A second explosion. I found out later that a second natural-gas pipe burst before they could contain the fire from the first explosion.

But I didn't know that at the time, because the second explosion brought the rest of that building down on my head. I was knocked unconscious, and when I came to, they told me every bone in my left hand had been broken. A piece of foundation wall crumbled and pinned me at the left shoulder, half in and half out of the elevator shaft. My legs were fine—they were stuck out in the shaft."

He paused. "That damn elevator never did come down."

Silence. Ella had buried her head in her arms—all he could see were the knobs of her knees, sharp through the thin denim of her jeans, and the golden tan of her arms and shoulders. She shuddered once, then again, and Grady braced himself for a storm of tears or—worse—an outpouring of sympathetic pity.

But Ella never seemed to do what he expected.

"You idiot." Her furious voice jerked his head around like she'd snapped a leash on his collar. "Have you honestly been beating yourself up for five years over the fact that you left the task force after that?"

He blinked. "It's not like I was the first guy to ever get injured on a rescue, or even like I was hurt the worst on *that* rescue."

Narrowing her eyes, Ella placed a hand on his shoulder. "And how long did the physio take? We're not talking a few weeks here, or even a couple of months. Grady, it sounds like they basically had to rebuild your arm from scratch. That's not a simple injury—that's a life-changing event."

The uncompromising edge to her voice was a weird contrast with the gentleness of her touch, and it confused Grady enough that he almost wanted to shrug her off. "Maybe that's true. Maybe I'm being dumb. But it's not just about the task force."

"What do you mean?"

He felt a strange compulsion to tell her everything, to lay it all out for her, all the ugliness inside him. That would be the end of it, he knew—if she got how truly messed up he was, Ella would leave. She'd stop looking at him like that, with expectation in her eyes.

And that would be better. For her, obviously. But for him, too, because then he could stop this ridiculous hoping and wishing for something he could never have.

Mostly so he wouldn't have to see Ella's reaction, Grady looked out over the ocean at the blurred, distant edge of the world.

"I didn't leave the task force," he ground out. "I was drummed out. Officially marked down as unfit for duty, so no other SAR team in the country would have me. After that, I tucked tail and ran to the most isolated place I could find, and I never left."

Unbearably soft wisps of hair brushed his arm as Ella shook her head. "There's no shame in being afraid, after brushing so close to death."

Be a man. Face up to it.

If he couldn't be the man she deserved, the least he could do was look her in the eyes when he told her.

Grady steeled himself, shutting down as much as he could to get through the next few minutes. He met Ella's concerned gaze and said, "I wasn't afraid. At least it wasn't the kind of fear where I lost my nerve. But after I got out of the hospital, I felt . . . 'invincible' isn't the right word. It was more like I didn't even see the risks—I was always an adrenaline junkie, but after the accident, I started taking insane chances, doing all the things they trained us not to do."

"I don't understand."

"I became a danger, to myself and the other guys on my team, even to the people we rescued. I lost the job I trained my whole life for. I committed everything to the task force—it was the most important thing I've ever done. The adrenaline rush, the focus, the direction, helping people . . . I'll never be the same without it."

"That's why you do the cliff jumping thing." Ella gestured toward the rocky ledge that stretched out over the water.

"It's a piss-poor substitute, because I know the depth below the cliff, I know there are no dangerous rocks, and nothing that can truly hurt me," he said. "But it makes me feel alive. And it reminds me of what it was like to be brave."

"You're one of the bravest people I've ever met," Ella said, a fierce light in her eyes.

She needed to hear the rest of it. Grady swallowed his shame and self-loathing. "You're wrong. I'm a coward. Since the day I moved here, I haven't left Sanctuary Island. Not once in the last five years. I can't. Panic attacks. At this point, I'm pretty sure I'll die here without ever seeing the mainland again."

CHAPTER 19

Ella stared at the man beside her. Grady's body was like a carved wooden statue. The only part of him that looked alive was his eyes, which burned with a dark fever that Ella recognized, deep down.

There was nothing quite as toxic as hating yourself for your own inability to cope with what life threw at you. Her heart was a giant bruise, tenderized and sore from too many blows to count.

"That boat in the photograph in your living room," she realized. "The one you're so proud of, but you don't go out in it anymore."

"I can't," he confirmed in a monotone. "Can't force myself to cast off and pull away from the dock."

The way Grady sat there beside her, impervious and stoic, she knew he was waiting for her to get up and walk away from him. Or maybe for her to laugh and tell him he needed to suck it up and get over it. But Ella had worked too hard and for too many years to conquer her own demons to ever minimize someone else's.

Not that she was completely demon-free yet, but it was okay to be a work in progress.

Treading carefully, Ella said, "And you think that makes you a coward."

His face twisted up for the space of a breath, but in the next instant, he'd smoothed his expression into an impassive mask. "Can't change the facts."

"No. But you can allow for nuance."

Arching a single sardonic brow, Grady sneered. "That sounds like touchy-feely shrink-speak for 'love yourself,' or some crap like that."

"Would that be such an impossible concept?"

"It's pretty hard to love myself when I've turned into a man my old teammates wouldn't even recognize."

Ella shuffled around in the dirt to get her knees under her so she could lean into Grady's space. She wanted to make sure he heard what she was telling him. "If you don't like who you are, change."

Anger sparked in his green eyes, and his mouth turned hard and a little mean. "I know you don't believe that people can change."

She sat back, surprised. "Of course I do!"

"Oh yeah? Let's talk about your mom, then. I assume that applies to her, too."

Direct hit.

Ella swallowed back an answering surge of temper. It shocked her a little, how easily he pushed her buttons.

She lifted her chin, determined to prove her point even if it might actually choke her to get the words out. "In fact, yes. Jo Ellen has changed; I can certainly see and acknowledge that."

Grady shut up, surprised out of his defensive attack. "Really. You're ready to admit you were wrong about her."

"Not exactly. Let me say it once again: nuance." Ella stood up and dusted off her dirty knees and backside. "Learn it, live it, love it, baby."

"More dancing around." Grady sounded disgruntled, as if Ella's refusal to admit that life was a study in black-and-white offended him personally. "Just say what you mean."

"It's not that easy," Ella protested, staring down at the thick, windblown waves of his dark blond hair. "In the last few days, I've had a chance to watch how Jo Ellen interacts with people on the island. With Merry, with you, with your cousin Taylor."

Grady tipped his head back to rest against the rock. Even with the wide expanse of the ocean at her back, Ella felt consumed by Grady's presence, as if he sucked all the air out of the world just by sprawling at her feet and breathing.

"She and Taylor have always been close," he observed, watching her intently.

Ella felt his scrutiny like a caress along her cheekbones. Schooling her face to show nothing, she said, "I can tell. And from everything I've seen, Jo has been a mostly positive presence in Taylor's life. Jo appears to truly love and care for her, and Taylor trusts her to continue in that vein indefinitely."

She paused. "But I can't extend Jo a similar trust, because no matter how wonderful a mother figure she's been for Taylor, she was nothing like that for me. Maybe it's my own failing—I'll cop to that. But I don't think I'll ever be able to trust Jo not to turn back into that frightening, selfish . . ."

Grady appeared to pause and really take in what Ella was saying. His golden brows drew down, wrinkling his forehead into a frown. "Ella. When you were little—did she hurt you?"

"Now who's dancing around? The question you want to ask is, Did she hit me? And the answer to that is no. Not really. But that was mostly because I learned early on to stay out of her way when she was in one of her moods." Ella smiled faintly. "That's what we called it when she drank. A mood. It made sense at the time, because you never knew from one day to the next what you were going to get—happy, bubbly, frenetically energetic Mom who'd insist on taking you to the park but would get distracted and leave you there for hours?"

"God. Ella." Grady stood up and reached for her, tugging her against his chest.

Ella pushed her face into the sun-warmed cotton of his shirt and sniffled. She wasn't crying. She hated crying—it always felt like emotional manipulation to her.

"Or there was sad, sobbing Mom," Ella said, her voice muffled. "She didn't leave her room for days, not even to kiss you good-night. And sometimes—when Dad was home instead of traveling, and he tried to talk to her about her drinking—we got angry Mom. When they fought, the whole rest of the world fell away. I used to think the house could burn down around their ears, and they'd just keep screaming at each other. It felt like nothing mattered but the fight. Not Merry, not me—and the fact was, Jo cared more about drinking, about herself, than she cared about any of us. She didn't say it in so many words, but she proved it over and over again. Every time she made a humiliating public spectacle of our family or forgot a birthday, she proved we didn't matter to her."

One of Grady's broad palms cupped the back of her

head gently. It was indescribably comforting, but Ella pulled back to get a better look at his face. She had to know if he understood.

His eyes were dark green, filled with shadows. "How old were you when they split up?"

"I was eleven when Dad finally got us out of there. Merry was eight."

Understanding lit his face. "So young. I bet Merry barely remembers what it was like to live with Jo back then."

"Little kids absorb more than you think." Ella sighed. "But I believe she's blocked a lot of it. What memories she does have, she's choosing to ignore. Merry's never been great at learning from the past—she tends to make the same mistakes over and over."

A wintry smile stretched Grady's lips, but never reached his eyes. He dropped his arms and stepped back. "See? People don't change."

The distance between them could be measured in inches, but it felt like miles. Shivering in the breeze that had felt warm and friendly with Grady's arms around her, Ella stared up at the harsh lines of his face, and suddenly, she couldn't stand it.

"People can change," she said. "And I'll prove it to you."

Before she could overthink it, Ella toed off her sneakers and ran for the rocky ledge over the open water.

Air pumped into her lungs, salty and bracing. The sun was hot on her skin. A gull flew from the clump of bushes clinging to the ledge, buffeted by the breeze and spreading its wings.

A deep thrill of fear sang through her blood, but she was running, her body taking over for her brain, for once, and with Grady's shout of "Ella!" ringing in her ears and the rocks at the edge of the cliff scraping her bare feet, Ella bent her knees and soared into the air.

Heart in his throat, Grady had his boots off before the dark banner of Ella's wind-whipped hair had disappeared below the edge. The splash got him moving. He skidded to a stop and peered over, terrified of what he'd see, even though he knew there was nothing down there for Ella to hit.

That had always seemed like enough before, when it was him doing the jumping—but when it was Ella?

He scanned the water frantically, terror punching straight to his gut when she didn't appear.

The surface of the ocean was smooth, the only movement the white-capped waves breaking on the cliff face.

"Ella!" he shouted, the wind snatching the word right out of his mouth.

He didn't waste another second. His brain clicked over into rescue mode as he backed up a few steps to get a running start.

Feet pounding the hard-packed earth, Grady raced for the edge and hurtled off, the familiar surge of adrenaline spiking his bloodstream. He plunged into the icy water, but he didn't have time to give in to the shock of it. Kicking hard for the surface, Grady shook his head like a dog and gasped for air.

Blinking the salt water from his stinging eyes, the first thing he saw was Ella's radiant smile.

"That was amazing," she panted, paddling gamely toward him. She wasn't the strongest swimmer he'd ever seen, a fact that sent another spurt of belated adrenaline coursing through his system.

"Ella! You're okay."

"Better than okay!" Her eyes were wide and full of joy.

His heart squeezed hard enough to burst. Getting his hands on the chilled flesh of her upper arms and feeling her flailing legs tangle with his helped a lot.

She clung enthusiastically, forcing Grady to tread water powerfully enough to keep them both afloat.

"I've never done anything like that." She was bubbling over, her lips so close to his ear that he felt every word as much as heard it. "It's like the foal all over again. Oh my gosh."

"Are you warm enough?" He folded her in to his chest, reveling in the slip of her skin against his where his T-shirt had ridden up with the jump.

"I'm too excited to feel anything." Ella laughed, her arms winding around his neck as she wriggled distractingly.

Even half submerged in cold water, Grady couldn't say the same. He felt it all—every movement of her body, the friction of her movements, and, even through her jeans, the heat where she was splayed open against his belly.

Unable and unwilling to resist, Grady rasped, "Let's see what we can do about that."

And he dipped his head to take Ella's laughing mouth in a deep, hungry kiss.

CHAPTER 20

Ella shuffled her stack of projections, location reports, and graphs charting the potential for Sanctuary Island, and tried to convince herself there was no reason to be nervous.

A truck engine rumbled loudly out front as Jo drove up the driveway. Ella fumbled her papers and dropped them in a fluttering cascade.

So much for not being nervous.

When Jo walked in, Ella was scrambling under the table for the last elusive page of her prospectus.

"What on earth?" Jo sounded mystified.

Cheeks flaming hot, Ella snatched the final page and backed up on her knees. She got to her feet as gracefully as she could under the circumstances, meeting Jo's amused gaze with a self-conscious smile.

"It never fails." Ella shook her head. "Ever since I set foot on Sanctuary Island, I can't seem to stop finding new ways to make a fool of myself."

The amusement in Jo's eyes faded to unhappiness..

"I'm sorry you haven't found anything on the island to enjoy."

An echo of the exhilaration she'd felt while free-falling fifty feet into open water shivered down her arms and legs. All she could think about was the warm passion of Grady's mouth against hers, and the way they'd smiled at each other afterward, even as Ella realized she'd broken every promise she'd made to herself about keeping her distance from Grady Wilkes.

Not helpful to think about that now. Focus!

"Oh, not at all!" Ella pasted on a broad smile, fingers carefully riffling the pages of her proposal back into order. "I think Sanctuary has a lot of potential. That's actually what I wanted to talk to you about."

Jo pulled out a chair with a slow scrape of wooden legs against the hardwood floor. "Really? What kind of potential?"

Ella let out a surreptitious breath and felt herself settle into the familiar rhythm of pitching an idea to a prospective client.

"With its natural beauty, hiking trails, and the unique attraction of the free-range wild horse herds, I think Sanctuary Island could draw a fair bit of tourist trade." She spread a chart she'd printed out from her laptop on the table in front of Jo, who leaned over it as if fascinated. "But the problem is that once they're here, there's no place on the island to stay. Not even a campground. Winter Harbor has some nice inns, but the ferry schedule is erratic, making day trips to the island inconvenient."

Jo glanced up at her, blue eyes unreadable. "True enough. We don't get a lot of day-trippers."

"That's not where the money is, anyway," Ella told her.

"What Sanctuary needs is to be able to attract tourists to stay overnight and spend their dollars over the course of a weekend, or longer. Sanctuary needs an inn."

The chair creaked as Jo sat back to study Ella's face. "And where are you envisioning this inn?"

Ella produced another page, the jewel of her proposal, and the one she'd spent the most time on.

It was a large photograph she'd printed out of Jo's house. She'd gone into a photo manipulation program and touched up the paint in the image, carefully erased the signs of wear and tear, and added some flowering bushes out front—along with a sign that read WINDY CORNER BED & BREAKFAST.

She placed the photo in front of Jo. "Right here."

Silence stretched between them, long enough for Ella to get uncomfortable. She was used to getting a big reaction from clients—most of them weren't able to visualize the possibilities for themselves, but once she showed them images of how the place could look, she usually got gasps and interest. Something. Anything!

"It's not the most professional mock-up in the world, but you get the idea," Ella said, hating the nerves she could hear in her own voice. "Normally, I would've used glossy paper for the photo, but I couldn't find any. I wasn't expecting to need to come up with a prospectus on the fly while I was here."

"Why did you?" Still fingering the edges of the B and B photo, Jo lifted her head to pin Ella with a sharp gaze.

"What do you mean?" Ella tried to sidestep the question, but Jo wasn't having any of it.

"You've been more than clear about your feelings for the island—and for me. I think you know I'm willing to do whatever it takes to be a part of your life. But I know that doesn't go both ways. What possessed you to spend so much time and energy coming up with this?"

Ella's defensive shields slammed into place. "This is what I do for a living," she reminded Jo. "I look at properties and see their potential, then I work to develop it. I'm very good at what I do—I've made a lot of money for my clients and my firm. And from what I can see, you need an infusion of cash just to keep this place from falling down around your ears."

Jo stiffened. "The upkeep of a house this old is expensive. But I'm doing all right."

Sensing weakness, Ella leaned in. "Are you? Because I've done my homework. I know about the lien. I also know you won't be able to pay it off without a major loan from a bank. And no bank is going to fork over any cash unless you can show a way that you'll be able to use part of that loan to turn a profit and pay them back."

"I have the stables!" Jo protested, before narrowing her eyes. "And how do you know about the debt? Does Merry know?"

Time for another sidestep. "The stables aren't making money," Ella said bluntly. "And according to my projections, giving riding lessons and boarding other people's horses aren't likely to provide a huge income. Unless you have connections in the horse racing or champion breeding worlds that I don't know about?"

Jo looked away, and Ella read her answer in the tight, slumped line of the older woman's shoulders.

Too bad. That would have been an elegant, simple solution. One that would have allowed Ella to avoid suggesting something she knew Grady would hate. Setting her jaw, she said what Jo needed to hear—and silently acknowledged that they were words Ella could stand to remember, as well.

"You have to be realistic about this. Banks don't hand out loans for the fun of it. They need collateral. Even the expectation of future earnings isn't usually enough." She paused delicately, then dropped the bomb she'd been saving. "That's where your boyfriend comes in."

Jo's head shot up as if a high-voltage electric current had just zapped through her seat. "What? How—"

Ella had expected to feel smug. Pleased. But sitting at the table across from her mother, she couldn't find that familiar pleasant sense of having gathered the exact piece of hidden information guaranteed to serve as the perfect pressure point in a tricky negotiation.

All she felt was angry. And tired—tired of being angry, of fighting. Tired of realizing that no matter how often she lectured herself about the foolishness of having expectations, she was still surprised when all of Jo's platitudes about opening her life to them and getting to know each other turned out to be so much bull.

"Harrison McNamara." Ella didn't bother to keep the thread of bitterness out of her voice. "Taylor's dad. Grady's uncle. The man you've been seeing for who knows how long . . . but certainly long enough to be a maternal figure for Taylor. It wasn't exactly a huge leap, especially once Merry told me about the man who came to see you at the stables that first day."

Red filtered into Jo's shocked face. Her wide eyes were like two holes burned through a white sheet. "Do you want to hear my explanation or are you so sure you've got everything figured out?"

"Not quite everything." Ella crossed her arms over her chest. "The one thing I don't understand is why you lied.

You're an alcoholic. I'd think telling the truth would be important for you."

It took everything Jo had not to flinch from the knife edge of her older daughter's voice.

"You're right." Jo carefully flattened both hands on the tabletop, palms down to stop the tremor in her fingers. "Living an honest life is a big part of the recovery process. But I didn't lie to you and your sister. I just didn't tell you everything."

Ella snorted. "So much for opening your house and your heart to us."

Frustration sizzled under Jo's skin. "And what about you? How open have you been—to Sanctuary, to your family history?"

To me.

But Ella only shook her head, her lips a stubborn line. "I never promised you anything. You're the one who offered, who wanted a chance to get to know each other. You and Merry. I'm only here for her."

Ignoring the stab of Ella's rejection, Jo leaned forward across the table, resting her weight on her forearms. "Harrison and me—it's a complicated situation. We've known each other a long time, cared about each other for years, but we're not always on the same page about what our relationship should be."

If that wasn't the understatement of the century, Jo didn't know what was. Especially considering how up in the air everything with Harrison was at the moment.

He asked me to marry him.

She shook her head to clear it of the extremely distracting thought, along with the even more distracting fact that she'd turned him down. Again.

Ella's face was hard, but there was a soft blur of pain at the corners of her downturned mouth. "Spare me the incredibly vague nondetails. I'm not concerned about your relationship beyond the fact that having an in with the local bank manager will help me achieve my goal."

"What goal is that, exactly?" Jo zeroed in on the heart of this conversation. "I know you haven't forgiven me— and that's fine. That's your choice, and I'm not going to say I deserve any better. But given that, I can't see why you're working so hard to help me."

Ella struggled visibly, her mouth working silently as she tried to decide how much to say.

"Cards on the table," Jo said. "If I promise to be honest from here on out, same goes for you."

Ella lifted her chin at the challenge. "I'm helping because you're in trouble. And if you lose this house, Merry is going to want to come back here and be supportive. She's got enough problems of her own, along with an overactive empathy gland; she doesn't need to be saddled with any down-on-their-luck family members. She needs to focus on herself and her baby."

Understanding began to dawn, like a match flaring to light in the darkness of Jo's mind. "And you think if I'm set for life, running your B and B, then Merry will never feel a need to come back here?"

Ella shrugged, glanced away. "It's a start."

"Oh, sweet girl." That got her a sharp look, but Jo couldn't help it. She ached for both her daughters—but at least Merry knew something about love. The ability to love, the desire for love, glowed all around her. But Ella . . . The young woman sitting in front of Jo was all folded in on herself like a locked puzzle box without any key, and the knowledge that Ella was paying for the sins of Jo's past and the mistakes Jo made . . . it was enough to make her determined to call her sponsor later.

"What?" Ella demanded.

"I don't know what you've convinced yourself of," Jo said, picking her way softly. "But I'm not giving up on you or Merry. And I'm pretty sure your sister feels the same way."

"So?"

"So even if things are going well with me here, even if you remove all the logical, rational reasons you can think of for Merry to want to come back and visit—there will still be the illogical, irrational ones. Nonsense concepts like love and family and wanting to be a part of something bigger."

Guilt squeezed a tight knot into Jo's throat at the spasm of fear that flashed across her daughter's face.

Faster than thought, Jo reached out to Ella, the impulse to comfort and care for her overriding everything else. But it was the wrong move, as Ella proved by jerking away.

The fear in her eyes shifted, darkened to anger. "You've got a lot of nerve, talking to me about family, when you're the reason our whole family fell apart. And if I have anything to say about it, Merry's going to realize she's only setting herself up to get hurt."

It would be easy, so easy, to give in to the defeat of knowing that Ella was right. But Jo refused to surrender—there was more at stake here than indulging her own guilt.

Gaze steady on Ella's flushed cheeks, her glittering eyes, Jo said, "But you don't have anything to say about it. Merry is an adult, Ella. She can make her own decisions about what's right for her. That's not your job."

Ella stood up from the table so quickly, she knocked over her chair. It fell to the hardwood floor with a clatter, but she didn't even spare it a glance. All her attention was on Jo. "Yes, it damn well is my job to look out for Merry. It always has been, since the day she was born. Who else was going to take care of her? You? Please. You weren't fit to be her mother then, and you're not fit to be around her now. She deserves more."

Jo couldn't suppress her flinch, but before she could say anything else, a quiet voice from the doorway froze both Jo and Ella in their places, like wax figures in an ugly tableau.

"Stop it. Both of you, just stop."

Jo caught the minute flicker of that same, sick fear in Ella's gaze before they both turned to face Merry.

Fists clenched, Merry hunched over her big belly, lines of tension and strain bracketing her mouth.

"Merry! Are you okay?"

"I'm fine," she grated out, panting a little. "I want to know what the hell is going on in here."

Still looking worried, Ella said, "We were talking about my proposal."

"We had a deal, Ella." There was steel in Merry's voice, a strength Jo hadn't been sure her younger daughter possessed. In spite of the awfulness of this moment, Jo couldn't help but be a little bit glad to see it.

"What deal?" Jo asked, glancing between her girls.

Ella straightened her spine defiantly, her gaze touching on the papers scattered across the table. "A proposal that will get you a bank loan in return for Merry doing the smart thing and coming back to D.C. with me."

A frisson of awareness shivered up Jo's spine. So there had been the possibility of Merry staying longer, then.

Even if it didn't happen, it meant something to her that Merry had wanted to. It meant a lot.

"But there was a condition," Merry reminded her sister coolly, straightening her back with a grimace. "No interference from you in my relationship with Mom. And I think getting into a screaming fight about how she's not fit to be around me counts as interference."

Jo couldn't take any of this in. "Wait, girls. I don't completely understand what's going on here, but please don't fight because of me. The last thing I'd ever want to do is come between you."

"Too late," Ella choked out, her eyes shining brilliant blue with unshed tears as she stared at her sister's stubborn expression. "This is a mistake, Merry. The worst you've ever made, and that's saying something."

Merry shrugged. "Maybe. But at least it'll be *my* mistake." The mask of her face crumpled a little, then, and Jo's breath caught at the soft, bruised look of hurt in the depths of her eyes. "If that makes you feel bad, I'm sorry."

"All I feel is tired. This is going to blow up in your face," Ella warned, gathering up her sheaf of papers, the proposal she'd worked so hard on, with shaking hands. "And when it does, I'll be the one cleaning up the mess, as usual."

"Not this time." Merry squared her shoulders. "Whatever happens, you're absolved of the responsibility of rescuing me. I won't call you in tears, you won't have to come back out here, since you hate it so much."

Ella blinked, a horrible blankness covering her face like a white sheet. "Fine," she said, her voice sounding odd and distant. "I hope you're happy. I really do."

Before Jo could gather herself to protest, to demand an explanation for what the hell was happening, Ella had dropped the proposal on the floor and walked out of the kitchen without a backward glance.

The moment she was gone, Merry's face crinkled up like tissue paper. She brought up a hand to hide her tears, but the shaking of her shoulders gave her away. Faster than thought, Jo was on her feet with her arms around her daughter.

"So. Maybe I should have asked this before. But can I stay?"

The words were muffled against Jo's shoulder, where a patch of her cotton sweater was getting damp with Merry's tears. The rush of love and protectiveness was so sudden and overwhelming, it stole Jo's voice.

Misinterpreting the pause, Merry pulled back to swipe at her cheeks. She gave a tremulous smile. "Sorry, I shouldn't have sprung that on you. But I've been living in Ella's apartment for the last few months, and now I'm pretty sure I've burned that bridge. I don't really have anywhere else to go."

Clearing her throat, Jo tugged her daughter back into a hug. Closing her eyes at the perfection of feeling Merry relax against her, Jo said, "Of course you can stay. As long as you want—you're always welcome, I told you that. But you haven't burned any bridges with Ella. I don't know either of you as well as I hope to, but I'm sure about this. Ella loves you. You'll always have a place with her."

Merry shuddered out another sob and clenched her fists in Jo's sweater. Jo shushed her and petted her dark magenta-streaked curls, cherishing every heartbeat of this moment.

But even in the midst of the heady rush of comforting her baby girl, Jo couldn't stop worrying about her older daughter.

Ella's the one who has nowhere to go, she thought with a pang. Jo had to fix this. But how?

Whatever she came up with, it wouldn't happen tonight. Merry sagged against her chest, unsteady with exhaustion. She needed a glass of water, then sleep.

Before she got them both moving in the direction of bed, though, Jo took one last moment to cuddle her near. And, closing her eyes, Jo sent up a silent prayer that the magic of Sanctuary would guide Ella's footsteps and keep her safe until morning.

CHAPTER 21

Grady parked his truck next to the little beige rental car and let himself smile in the darkness.

In the week since Ella had first pushed her way into his house and deeper into his life, he'd seen her car in his driveway many times. But the sight never failed to send a thrill through his chest.

And usually it was a little earlier in the day than this, Ella showing up with two cups of coffee and some rolls from Mitchell's gas station—or a grease-stained paper bag full of their truly awesome fried chicken, if it was close to lunchtime—all ready to get her jeans dirty on a trek around the island or to check on the foal they'd nick-named Tough Guy.

There hadn't been any more kissing since that searing liplock in the water below Wanderer's Point, but Grady hadn't given up hope.

In fact, as he wondered what Ella was doing here so late, his pulse sped up and he felt anticipation pool hotly in his belly. Grady stepped down from the truck cab and peered into the rental car.

"Finished with your nightly rounds?"

Her voice came from behind him, and Grady twisted to find her sitting on his front steps, arms wrapped around her knees and a tight, tremulous expression pulling at her face.

Grady nodded, studying her in the golden glow of his porch light. "You're up late."

She pressed her nose to her raised knees for a second, then lifted her head with a determined smile. "How's our boy doing?"

Warmth washed through him. "Tough Guy's doing great."

Grady had spent a good portion of his nightly rounds watching the new colt frolicking around the older members of his family band, all knobbly knees and exuberance.

"Looking at him," he said, walking over to fold himself down on the steps beside Ella, "you could never tell that he had such a dangerous, difficult start in life. And you wouldn't be able to predict all the crap he'll be facing when he's grown, either."

"What do you mean?"

The worry creasing Ella's brow made Grady wish he could call the words back. "Oh, you know. Life is uncertain out there in the wild. A summer drought, a bad ice next winter . . . hell, sometimes we even catch the edges of hurricanes and tropical storms."

She cocked her head, gaze intent on his face. "Yeah, but you meant something else. Didn't you?"

Grady sighed. Not for the first time, he wished Ella were a little less perceptive. "Well, you've seen the horse bands. One stallion plus a bunch of mares—that's pretty much how it goes, and they generally stick close together like a family. But if you see a lone wild horse, that's a male yearling who got kicked out of his band by a more dominant stallion."

"That's sad." Ella propped her chin on her crossed arms. "But if his family ditches him, can't he just start his own band?"

"Sure, if he can steal a mare. And sometimes a few stallions will join together and form a bachelor band."

Silence spread between them, punctuated by the hoot of an owl in the pine trees overhead. When she spoke, her voice was soft and muffled.

"What if he can't? He'd be fine on his own, right? I mean, being alone isn't the worst thing in the world."

Grady chose his words carefully, aware that there were undercurrents to this conversation that he didn't fully understand.

"Horses are pack animals. They don't deal well with loneliness. If that lone stallion doesn't find or make a new family, he'll . . . well, if we don't get to him in time and bring him into the barn, try to tame him—he'll go down to the cove where Tough Guy was born, he'll lie down, and wait to die. That's why they call it Heartbreak Cove."

Ella breathed through the bolt of electricity stiffening her every limb. Everything was all tangled up in her head— her confused feelings for Grady, the fight with Jo, and oh God, Merry . . . and now this.

The possible fate of the foal she'd helped bring into the world was like the final tap of the hammer to the crack in her heart, the last blow needed to break her in two.

"Hey, don't look like that." Grady sounded alarmed enough to make Ella wonder just how pale she'd gotten.

"I'm not pronouncing a death sentence on our little man, here. Who knows, maybe he'll grow up and fight the dominant male, take over the band, and become the leader of his own family. Or maybe he'll get kicked out and take up with a buddy, and be fine, just the two of them. There's a lone stallion out there whose best friend is a feral kitten from one of Jo's barn cats' litters. You never see one without the other."

"Great." Ella laughed, but it sounded damp and wobbly, even to her. "So what you're saying is, I'm destined to become a crazy cat lady?"

Confusion drew Grady's dark gold brows down into a line. "I don't know what—"

"Nothing, ignore me," Ella said, waving it away. She felt incredibly tired, all of a sudden. "Thanks for trying to put a good spin on it. I hate the idea of leaving Sanctuary and then hearing about Tough Guy wandering the marshes all alone, dying of loneliness."

Grady got that look on his face, the closed-off look he got lately whenever she mentioned her impending departure, but when he spoke, his voice was threaded through with firm promise. "I won't let that happen. If his band kicks him out, I'll bring him into the barn myself, and I'll work with him until he's happy in the paddock. You don't have to worry about him."

Ella bit back a sigh. It was too late for that. It had been too late before she'd heard anything specific about the dangers that could befall the foal. But she appreciated Grady's solemn vow more than she could express. "Thank you. That means a lot to me."

He studied her. "Did something happen tonight? You seem upset."

"Nothing much. Except my sister is making the biggest mistake of her life."

Grady's brows climbed toward his hairline. "What now?"

"When I leave in a few days, I'll be the only one on the ferry back to the mainland." It hurt to even form the words in her brain, but Ella forced them out. "Merry's staying here. She's quitting her job and moving to Sanctuary Island."

"Is she?" Grady's gaze was wary, watchful. "Jo must be happy."

"Well, as long as Jo's happy." Anger coated the back of Ella's tongue with bitterness.

He shook his head. "I can't say I'm sorry—not when I wish you'd stay longer, too."

Ella fisted her hands against the slap of truth. "I wish we'd never come to this stupid island," she whispered.

The solid heat of his body along her side went statue still, coiled tension and power tightening his jean-clad thighs as Grady moved to stand.

Ella grabbed for his hand just as he pushed off the steps, her heart in her mouth. "I'm sorry," she cried, feeling wretched as he stared down at her, eyes burning like molten jade on his frozen face. "I didn't mean that."

"Sure you did." His jaw ticked once. "You've been up front about it from the beginning. Don't start lying to spare my feelings now."

"I'm not!"

He tugged away from her. Ella launched herself off the steps to follow him as he paced down the driveway before turning on her.

"Grady, please." Ella kept her voice as steady as she

could when it felt like everything inside her was twisted into knots.

He looked away from her, his jaw like granite. "Why did you come here tonight?"

The straightforward, uncompromising question rocked Ella back onto her heels. "I guess . . . because I couldn't stay in that house. I needed to get out before I broke down and said something Merry and I can't come back from."

That brought his stare back to her, and the banked fires in his gaze set Ella's blood ablaze. "No. That's not why. And you're not upset about Merry making a mistake, either."

Ella blinked. "What?"

"You . . ." He struggled for a moment, his throat working as he swallowed around the words that tried to escape. "Merry is your family. You're mad at Jo for stealing Merry away, but she didn't. They're both still there. They're still your family."

It hit her like a dash of cold water in the face. She shook her head to clear it, but Grady wasn't done.

"You're not afraid she's making a mistake—you're afraid of being alone. You think if you're alone, you'll wither away and die."

The truth rang like a bell inside her. He was right.

All the breath left her body. He was so fierce and gorgeous in his righteous anger. She blinked, dazzled and dazed. It felt as if she were waking up from a deep sleep.

"Take a look around." Grady spread his arms out at his sides. *"You're not alone."*

"I know," Ella whispered. She must have swallowed some kind of truth serum. "I think I always knew—that's why I came here tonight. Not to get away from Merry and Jo, but because I needed you. Needed to see you."

His strong brown throat moved as he swallowed convulsively, knocked sideways by her confession.

Excitement rolled around her chest, warm and tingly. Ella silently vowed to open up and spill her innermost thoughts and feelings more often if it got this kind of response from him.

"I'm right here," Grady said, low and steady.

Ella looked every bit as wrecked as Grady felt, her eyes huge and shocked in a face as white as a gull's wing.

Her pale pink mouth worked silently for a second before she let out a muffled little sound and leaned up on her toes, both arms going around his neck.

Grady caught her more by instinct than any sort of romantic smoothness, his mind still churning over the revelations of the past few minutes, but the moment her lips touched his, all thought beyond pure, animal desire flew out of his head.

She was soft and smooth against him, a bundle of nerves and tension that wound tighter and tighter the longer they kissed. Waves of sound crashed and broke in his ears as the blood rushed through his body.

They stumbled into the house, knocking elbows on the door frame and scraping shins on their way up the stairs. Grady was so caught up, lost in the honeysuckle scent of Ella's hair, the salt-sweet savor of her skin, he couldn't bring himself to stop touching her long enough to get their clothes off.

In the end, it was Ella who disengaged with a tremulous smile, shuddering breaths heaving her chest against his, and said, "Can I . . . is it okay if I take your shirt off?"

The ingrained instant of denial was followed quickly by a trickle of warmth. He liked the fact that she'd asked, that she'd seen his scars before and hadn't run. Maybe it was time for *him* to stop running, let someone catch him.

Gripping the hem of his shirt, Grady held his breath and pulled it off over his head. The cool air of the room hit his skin in a ripple of goose bumps.

He felt naked, even though his pants were definitely still on. He could tell because of the painful constriction around his cramped erection, which hadn't subsided at all. Apparently, his dick was completely fearless when it came to Ella Preston.

Grady looked down at the first slow, tender touch of Ella's fingers. She brushed timid fingertips along the lines of his chest, her hand warm and heavy enough not to tickle as it drifted down his side. And the look on her face . . . Grady had to close his eyes again to avoid climaxing on the spot at the frank, honest desire in Ella's eyes.

"We've been here before," she murmured. "This time I want to see it all. Show me?"

He tensed, understanding at once. She wanted him to turn around, display the worst of his scars for her, and trust that she wouldn't be scared off.

"I don't know if I can yet." The aching words ground out of him like gravel under truck tires, but Ella only nodded.

"It's my turn, anyway." She gave him a particularly female smile, one of those mysterious lady smiles that hinted at secret knowledge, and slowly unbuttoned her black cotton shirt.

The smooth, subtle curves she revealed dried out

Grady's mouth. He found himself licking his lips and staring, as if he could pierce through the scalloped edges of her black bra with the power of X-ray vision.

But he didn't need to, because Ella twisted an arm behind her back and deftly unhooked the bra, letting it fall to the floor in a flutter of filmy lace seduction.

All of a sudden, Grady could breathe easier.

Okay, he was still breathing pretty hard, but it no longer felt like a boulder was sitting on his chest, crushing his lungs.

They were both naked from the waist up, their skin glowing pale in the yellow light of his ancient bedside lamp, and Grady couldn't think about the scars that had dominated a corner of his mind since he first woke up in that hospital covered in white bandages.

He could only look at Ella and appreciate the pure, perfect symmetry of her form. The lean, uncomplicated lines of her body, the slope of her ribs and the roundness of her breasts, topped with dark pink nipples that tightened under his gaze.

It wasn't that the scars no longer mattered—if he blinked, he still pictured them like neon glaring through the darkness—but devouring Ella with his eyes mattered more.

The longer he stared, the more pink she became as a flush spread from the tops of her breasts all the way up her neck and onto her cheeks. Grady's fingers itched to discover the heat of that blush, the silken grain of her skin.

But before he could touch her, Ella backed up a step with a shaky smile and uncertain eyes. "Your turn."

Grady froze, and Ella's eyes went soft and understanding.

"It's okay," she said. "You don't have to. We can just . . ."

"No." Grady cut her off with a firm shake of his head. He might not be a daredevil anymore, but he was still a man. He was doing this. They were doing this. Ella had stripped herself bare for him, in more ways than one. He could return the favor. On impulse, he leaned down and stole a quick kiss for luck.

Her lips parted easily beneath his, welcoming him in, and Grady took heart.

With fingers that were remarkably steady, Grady unbuttoned and unzipped his jeans and pushed them down his legs, along with his underwear. His erection was so hard it slapped against his stomach as he straightened up. Ella's bright eyes went straight to it, hot and needy, but the tough part was still to come.

Pushing out a strengthening breath, Grady turned around and let Ella look her fill.

The muffled gasp from behind him made Grady close his eyes. He knew what she was seeing—an ugly tapestry of red, pink, and white lines scoring up over the left side of his back and hips, ending in a concentrated mass on his left shoulder blade.

It took everything he had, every ounce of the courage he used to take for granted, to stand there in front of her.

Ella sucked in a breath as if she wanted to say something, but no words came. Grady spoke to the blank white wall in front of him, picturing the compassion and empathy on Ella's beautiful face.

"You were right—they basically had to build me a new shoulder. I'm like Darth Vader, more machine than man, at least on that side."

"Oh, Grady," Ella said, sounding as if she'd swallowed something that made her throat hurt.

He shrugged, vividly aware of how the movement tightened and stretched the scars across his shoulders.

The first tentative brush of her warm fingers against his back startled him. No one but doctors, nurses, and physical therapists had touched him there in years. Summoning all his self-discipline, Grady planted his feet and braced himself to endure—but to his shock, the way Ella traced slow lines across the scars seemed to uncoil something inside him, a knot he'd been clutching tightly to himself for a long time.

"I'm glad you got out of that building alive."

"You know, we didn't manage to rescue everyone that night. There were casualties from the first explosion, even more from the second. Not everyone made it out alive."

Grady struggled for a breathless moment, but the thought that was always with him, running under every moment and through every action, spilled out of his mouth.

"Some days, I'm not so sure I made it, either."

"You did." Conviction filled her voice, her words hitting his skin like a cleansing rain. "You're right here, like you said. With me."

She didn't say anything more, but her gentle touch said everything Grady could've hoped to hear.

Ella was still there. He'd showed her a glimpse of the deepest, darkest part of himself and it hadn't scared her away.

Facing her was one of the hardest things he'd ever done, but the moment his eyes met Ella's, he forgot the struggle. He forgot everything but the quiet strength of her, the complete acceptance in her deep blue eyes.

Grady raised his hand and cupped the delicate line of

her cheek. His thumb nestled into the hinge of her jaw as his fingers slid into the dark waves of her hair. The shape of her skull under his hand was impossibly fragile, but when she lifted up on her toes and wrapped her arms around his shoulders, she was the opposite of weak or breakable. She was a force of nature, a storm breaking over him, and he rode the storm down to the expanse of the mattress.

Laying her out on his sheets, Grady worshipped her with his hands and mouth, every gasp and high, thready sound entering his bloodstream like a drug. And Ella gave it all back to him with unstinting generosity, tumbling across the bed with him until they were so wrapped in each other, Grady didn't know if he'd ever untangle the mess they'd made of his sheets. Or his life.

Much less his heart.

CHAPTER 22

Ella stretched luxuriously, feeling the satisfying twinge of muscles she hadn't used in a while. The unfamiliar lines of dark wooden rafters slashed across the white ceiling above the bed, and some part of her brain immediately started working on describing it: warm, cozy, elegant in its simplicity.

She could only imagine the way Grady would roll his eyes if she told him his house was a perfect example of "rustic chic."

Huh. She really *could* only imagine his reaction, because when she reached one bare arm out of the covers to pat the bed beside her, it was empty.

Flopping onto her back with a frown, Ella let the images from the night before wash over her in the early morning light.

Last night. Fighting with Jo and Merry. Almost fighting with Grady—and his startling, upsettingly correct insight into what was really bothering her.

She didn't want to think about that, so she turned her

mind to what came after: kissing Grady, touching him, the way he opened up . . . the way he'd opened her, making her feel everything, every touch, every glance, so acutely.

It was as if every other time she'd been with a man, she'd kept all her clothes on and been half asleep.

With Grady, she was wide awake and alarmingly, deliciously naked.

The way he looked at her, the intensity in every caress, made Ella feel as necessary as sunlight, as air. She smiled, touching one fingertip to sensitized lips that were swollen by kisses. Last night, she and Grady had needed each other.

So where was he now?

The mattress next to her was empty, but he couldn't have gone far. It was his house, after all.

Fighting disappointment, Ella swung her legs over the side of the bed and started feeling around for her underwear. When she was decent, or decentish, since she never did manage to locate her bra, she made her way down the creaking hardwood stairs with her shoes in one hand and the other combing through her hair in a futile attempt to tame the morning mess.

"Um, hello?" she called out, disliking the tentative question in her tone but unable to suppress it.

All her usual defenses had been obliterated last night, and now in the bright light of morning, she felt as awkward as a newborn colt, shivery and vulnerable.

"In here!'

Grady's shout from the kitchen warmed her and brought a smile to her face. He was at the stove, which was starting to become a wonderfully familiar sight, but he spared her a quick smile and a coffee-flavored kiss when she sidled up to him.

"Your timing sucks," he told her. "I was going to bring you breakfast in bed, if you'd waited a little longer."

Ella raised her brows, but inside, she'd gone as mushy as the oatmeal he was stirring on the stovetop. "Should I go back upstairs?"

She made as if to leave, then laughed in delight when he snagged her around the waist, his big bare hands hot even through the cotton of her shirt.

"I ought to say yes," he growled, "since that's the image I've been holding in my head all morning. You, in my bed, with your hair all spread out on my pillows."

Ella caught her breath at the heat in his gaze, before it slid to the side and he set her gently back on her feet.

"But it's probably good that you're dressed. Less distracting."

She tried not to pout, but she wasn't sure how successful it was. "Oh, come on. That oatmeal can wait an hour, I bet."

Grady's mouth twitched into a reluctant smile. "An hour, huh? I must have done something right last night to give you that high an opinion of my stamina."

"Mmm." Ella grabbed for Grady's hand and tugged, giving him her best flirty, fluttering lashes. "Let's go test your stamina."

But he set his heels and resisted her pull. "Ella. We need to talk."

Her smile wanted to fade, but Ella kept it in place even though her cheeks ached stiffly. "Do we? I don't think so. Wouldn't you rather take me upstairs and . . . get distracted?"

She waggled her brows suggestively, but instead of laughing, Grady closed his eyes tightly for a brief moment, as if gathering his strength. "Hot damn, yes. I'd rather, and if you still want to in a minute, I'll be the first one up the stairs. But first, I need to say this."

Suppressing a sigh, Ella dropped his hand and ran frustrated, fidgety fingers through her messy hair. She had zero desire to stand here and try to define this thing between them.

"Fine. But I feel compelled to point out that you're messing with a lot of gender norms here." She shrugged. "I've read all the self-help books."

Irritation sparked in his shadowed eyes. "Let me guess—those books say men are supposed to be strong and silent, and never want to talk about things? Well, tough. Because the way I was raised, real men aren't afraid to speak up when they've got something to say."

Ella was sure the stubborn, dogged clench of his jaw shouldn't be so appealing. Pulling out one of the kitchen chairs, she sank into it and gestured to the seat across the table. "Believe me, after last night, I'm the last person on the planet who'd have doubts about your masculinity. So go ahead, talk."

With movements jerky enough to make her realize how uncommonly graceful he usually was, especially for such a big guy, Grady hooked a hand through the ladder back of the chair and flipped it around to straddle it backward. He rested his strong forearms on the top wooden slat and regarded her so solemnly, Ella had to fight the urge to squirm.

"I need to make sure," he began, "that last night happened because you wanted it."

Ella felt her eyebrows shoot up. "Grady. I don't know

how long it's been since you were with a woman, but here's a hint: I pretty much could not have wanted it—or enjoyed it—more."

Red scorched his cheekbones, but he didn't break her gaze. "It's been a while," he admitted baldly. "But that's not what I meant. When I found you here waiting for me, you were very upset. There are rules about that. I need to know that I didn't take advantage of you."

"Is that something else you learned about how to be a man?" Ella propped her elbow on the table and rested her chin on her palm, almost unbearably charmed. "I'd like to meet your dad sometime."

A smile ghosted over Grady's lips. "He'd love you. But I can't help noticing you haven't answered the question."

Choosing her words carefully, Ella said, "Look. While I very much appreciate the Southern-gentleman routine— believe me, it's a welcome change from most of the guys I've dated—you don't need to worry about me. I'm an adult, I make my own, usually very rational, choices. I don't do anything I don't want to do."

It was Grady's turn to arch a brow. "Right. Because you were just dying to use your vacation days to come out here to Sanctuary Island."

"That's different," Ella objected, and Grady held up a hand.

"Yeah. It was about Merry. And you'd do anything for your sister. She's your soft underbelly."

There was no judgment in his tone or expression, but Ella still shifted in her chair. "Look. I know you think I'm borderline psychotic when it comes to Merry—and, trust me, my friend Adrienne Voss, my ex-therapist, is more on your side than mine there—but Merry's my family. My whole family, really."

Grady sat back, his eyes soft and searching. "What about your father? He's still around, isn't he?"

She wrestled with herself for a moment, then confessed, "He did his best for us when we were kids. But once we got old enough . . . there's definitely some distance, on both sides. I think it's hard for him to be around us. And he still works a lot, so he's busy."

All Grady did was nod, but as Ella heard the echo of her own words, she slumped forward to rest both elbows on the table. "I know," she said. "I make a lot of excuses for him, and I never give Jo a break. It's been pointed out to me that this is a double standard."

"Not by me." Grady held up his hands in surrender. "Families are complicated. Jo's my friend, and I hope you'll give her a chance to be good to you—but maybe some scars are too deep to ever really disappear."

"I don't believe that." Ella's denial was instantaneous, instinctive, in the face of Grady's quiet shrug, the pain in his eyes.

"At least," she amended ruefully, reaching across the table to clasp his scarred right hand. "I don't want to believe that."

He turned his hand palm up and curled his fingers over hers, warm and solid. Giving her one of his slow smiles, Grady said, "Come riding with me."

Up until now, Ella had resisted all efforts to get her into a saddle. As much as she'd loved seeing their little foal through the first moments of his life, and had felt strangely empowered by helping Tough Guy's dam through the birth, Ella was still nervous at the thought of perching on the back of that much pure muscle and animal instinct.

Plus, when she'd asked Grady where he kept the gelding he'd been riding when she met him, he'd told her he boarded Voyager out at Windy Corner Stables. Which meant that any horseback riding they did would involve a trip to Jo's barn.

As if reading her mind, Grady said, "You're going to have to see her eventually. Might as well get it over with."

He was right. Ella squeezed his hand and tried on a smile. "I'd rather do it with you at my side. Thanks."

Another thought occurred to her as Grady stood up and walked over to the stovetop to stir the oatmeal—a thought that almost wiped the smile off her face.

It took sheer determination to keep her voice light as she said, "I really shouldn't pass up this opportunity, since I'm leaving in three days. Who knows when I'll be around horses again."

Grady's long-handled spoon paused for a moment before he resumed stirring. "You never know. Maybe you'll fall in love with it and never want to leave."

Ella shivered. Were they still talking about horseback riding? She opened her mouth, but couldn't think of a sensible reply. Of course she was leaving in three days. She had a job, a life, back in D.C. There was no way she could even consider staying.

But as Grady pulled two rough, hand-thrown earthenware bowls from his cupboard and started dishing up oatmeal, Ella couldn't stop thinking that for two people who hated change so much, she and Grady were building something between them that could change everything.

Three days. He had three days to convince her to uproot her entire life and move to Sanctuary Island.

For the first time in years, he wondered if he'd ever be able to bring himself to leave the island. It was completely unfair to ask Ella to be the one making all the sacrifices here—but when he even considered the trip across the bay to Winter Harbor, a cold sweat broke out along his hairline and the tips of his fingers went numb.

He could lose her, he realized, despair like bile in his throat. And all because he was too much of a coward to take a damn ferry ride.

It was an impossible situation, but a voice in Grady's head kept repeating that he had to "stay positive, man." The voice sounded a lot like Tom, his ex-partner back on the task force.

Grady wasn't sure what it meant that after five years of not thinking or talking about his time on the team, he was suddenly hearing Tom's relentlessly cheery, upbeat nagging in his head.

He suspected it had something to do with the woman in the passenger seat of his Jeep.

Stealing a glance at Ella, who had her arm propped on the open window so she could ride the air currents with one hand while they drove deeper inland toward Windy Corner, Grady felt his body stir and heat with the memories of the night before.

He had to admit, if only to himself, that he'd been more than halfway certain he'd convinced Ella to stay. Which was stupid, of course. So she went to bed with him—that didn't mean she was in love with him. God knew, he hadn't been in love with every single woman he'd ever slept with.

Still, he hadn't been able to suppress a sharp pang of disappointment when she made it clear that her plans hadn't altered.

Because nearly everything was different for him since he met her.

Grady downshifted as the paved road turned to gravel, the Jeep grinding across the ruts from last week's storm.

"Gosh," Ella said, pitching her voice to be heard over the engine. "If only Jo Ellen had a handyman to help her smooth this driveway out."

Her teasing grin was infectious. Grady found himself smiling back. "Once we officially hit summer, closer to the end of June. But we're likely to get a few more serious rainshowers and windstorms between now and then. It's not worth it yet."

"I was kidding." Her eyes were round and surprised. "But you really do everything around here, don't you?"

He shrugged. "Whatever I can do to help Jo, I'll do it."

Ella looked away for a moment, wind blowing her hair into her face. "How did she earn so much loyalty?"

"I told you before—she saved my life when I came home to Sanctuary."

"But how?" Ella made a frustrated noise in the back of her throat.

"It's hard to explain." Grady pulled the Jeep around the final bend. The barn rose up in front of them, sturdy and solid with its clean, fresh coat of dark green paint and its white doors thrown wide open.

He parked the truck on the grass next to Jo's pickup and lifted Ella's fist from her lap, kissed her curled fingers until they relaxed. She met his eyes, and Grady smiled. Time to play his last, best card.

"Let me show you."

CHAPTER 23

Jo stood in the cool, dusty darkness just inside the barn and watched the Jeep take the gravel drive that led to Windy Corner Stables.

Grady's call had come through just as Jo and Merry finished up the morning feeding. He hadn't been specific about what they were hoping to do, what Ella wanted, and Jo had been too thrown and thrilled by the idea that Ella might want anything from her to quiz him.

After last night, she'd been doing her best to prepare for the possibility that Ella might cut her visit short and leave the island today.

As she watched her older daughter hop down from the high seat of Grady's Jeep, Jo sent up a prayer of thanks for the magic of Sanctuary. She had another shot at Ella, a chance to stitch up the rift she'd inadvertently caused between her daughters, and she couldn't screw it up.

Putting on a determined smile, she propped her elbow on the handle of the pitchfork she'd been using to muck out the stalls. "Welcome to Windy Corner Stables."

Grady slammed his door and came around to stand beside Ella, who was shading her eyes and scanning the spread with clear surprise.

"Wow," she said, blinking. "I wasn't expecting this much gorgeousness."

Jo's eyebrows climbed toward her hairline when Grady poked her daughter in the ribs, getting a tiny, sheepish grin out of Ella.

Very interesting. She'd never seen Grady voluntarily touch anyone other than one of the few people he considered family. And even then, it was usually more of a quick slap on the back or an awkward one-armed hug— not such a casually intimate touch.

Looked like she owed her thanks for Ella's turnaround to something more specific than the magic of Sanctuary.

Jo gave Grady a short, grateful nod to thank him for bringing Ella out here. "Do you want the full tour? Merry's around somewhere—at this point, she probably knows more about this place than I do. I swear she's had her nose in every corner of this barn in the last week and a half."

She was watching for it, so she saw the way Ella stiffened a bit at the mention of her sister's name before walking over to get a better look at the big outdoor paddock to the left of the barn. Two geldings, Jeb and Buckwheat, made their curious way over to the fence to check her out.

"No, thanks," Ella said. "I'm not here to . . . I mean, there's no need to bother Merry."

Jo's fingers tightened around the shovel handle. She hated being the cause of her girls' unhappiness—she'd already made so many mistakes, hurt them so badly . . .

Lord, grant me the serenity to accept the things I cannot change, the courage to change the things I can, and the wisdom to know the difference.

The familiar prayer calmed her fretting, as it almost always did, and Jo tugged off her filthy, battered work gloves. "I don't think showing you the horses would be a bother to Merry."

Ella turned away from her contemplation of Buckwheat's shameless begging for a handful of the juicy green clover beyond the fence line. She smiled slightly, her eyes shadowed. "She never did grow out of her horsey phase."

That wasn't really what Jo had been getting at, but she allowed Ella to shift the subject a bit. "Neither did I, I guess. Does that mean you went through a horsey phase at some point?"

Ella shrugged. "Oh, sure. When I was about fifteen, I had toy horses and watched *National Velvet* about a zillion times. I could probably still quote you whole passages from *Black Beauty*. But that was as far as it went."

Jo wondered why. Maybe because Neil and the girls had lived in D.C.? Riding lessons would've been expensive and inconvenient.

Jo tried to imagine Ella pleading with Neil for riding lessons, asking Santa for a pony, and couldn't quite picture it. Remembering the tiny, quiet, serious-faced little girl she'd been, Jo realized with a pang that it was possible her elder daughter had never in her life asked or hoped for something unrealistic. Something unattainable and crazy and out of reach.

A smart way to live, probably. But even in the worst throes of her struggle with addiction, Jo had never been able to cure herself of the urge to dream big. And now, fourteen years sober, she was glad.

Looking back, she didn't think there was any way

she'd have made it through if she hadn't been a bit of a dreamer.

Dream big, Jo reminded herself, and the thought made it easier to smile. "Merry's in the tack room, cleaning the bridles. Come on, I'll show you where . . ."

"Actually," said Ella, reaching out with loosely curled fingers to let Buckwheat snuffle at her fist. "I'm here for a ride. Grady says you've got a sweet, gentle old mare who's exactly my speed."

Delighted, Jo leaned the shovel against the barn door and dusted off her hands. "That would be Peony. Hold on just a quick sec, I'll get her saddled up. Grady, I assume you want Voyager?"

He sauntered into the barn with a tip of his chin. "If you get Miss P going, I'll do Voyager."

That was when Jo noticed he wasn't wearing his gloves.

She was so shocked by that, blinking away dust motes to make sure her eyes were working right, that it barely startled her when Ella's hand shot out and grabbed her by the wrist.

"Can I have a quick word?" Ella's gaze flickered after Grady before settling on her mother.

Jo fought down the impulse to tell Ella she could have anything it was in Jo's power to give. "Of course."

Ella dropped her hand to smooth the wrinkles from the hem of her trim black button-down shirt. Quite a few wrinkles, Jo couldn't help noticing, especially considering how put together and perfect Ella usually looked.

"I guess you probably figured out I went to Grady's house last night. We . . . talked, and he made some good points. There's more going on here than my leftover childhood issues, and if I ever want to be happy, I know

I've got to start coming up with ways to get over them. Which is what this trip should have been all about, really. Merry knew that." She blew out a breath that fluttered the wispy dark hairs on her forehead. "Whatever she likes to tell people, she's always been the smart one. I forget that sometimes."

Ella looked like she needed a hug, and Jo ached to give it to her. But, wary of pushing, she simply said, "You're both smart, but about different things."

An arrested look came into Ella's eyes. "I like that. I'm going to think about it more, and I'll be thinking about what Grady said, too—but in the meantime, I have a favor to ask you."

"Name it."

"I don't know what you're thinking about the preliminary proposal I put to you last night." She lowered her voice even further until it was almost a whisper. "The bed-and-breakfast idea."

It was a good idea, Jo knew that much from studying the pages she'd picked up from the kitchen floor after Ella ran out. In fact, it could be enough to save Aunt Dottie's house—but she wasn't completely sold on it yet. "I don't know, Ella. The thought of renovating the old place for guests, putting in en suite bathrooms, and opening the house up to strangers . . . something about it doesn't set right."

"Okay." Ella nodded firmly, not the least bit discouraged. "I get that. But it's a start. Let me keep working on the proposal, and I'll give you a revised plan to take to the bank before I leave."

Jo bit down on her lower lip. "Not that I don't appreciate the effort you're putting into this thing, but you know Merry's got her mind made up. Even if the plan works and the bank gives me a loan and we pay off our debt, I think Merry's got it in her head to stay on Sanctuary. At least for a while."

The joy brimming in Jo's chest was tempered by the flash of pain in Ella's eyes, but her older daughter merely nodded again. "I know. This time it's not for Merry. It's for me. I need to let go of some of this bitterness and anger." She glanced over Jo's shoulder into the interior of the barn, where Jo could hear the low, rough sound of Grady's laugh as he wrestled with Voyager's cinch strap. "If I can do something to help keep Windy Corner in the family, I want to do it."

Jo's throat closed up, so hard she had to swallow twice to be able to speak. "Well, I thank you. And if your great-aunt Dottie were still here, she'd be thanking you, too."

"Don't thank me yet," Ella warned. "I haven't gotten to the part where I'm asking for a favor."

This time, Jo didn't hesitate. She'd already gotten more from Ella this morning than she'd dared to hope for—whatever Ella wanted, Jo would give it to her. "Anything."

From deep inside the barn came the soothing rumble of Grady's voice, and Ella smiled faintly. There was a shadow over her pretty face, a sadness Jo read all too clearly.

"Don't say anything to Grady about the proposal," Ella said. "Let me do it."

Oh, sweet girl. Jo pressed the fingers of one hand to her mouth, thinking about the way Grady was likely to react to the idea of establishing a B and B specifically intended to draw tourists to his beloved private sanctuary.

"Are you sure?" The urge to spare Ella pain was huge and undeniable. "I could wait until after you head back to D.C. to tell him."

But Ella was already shaking her head. "No. I want to tell—I mean, I don't want to. He's going to hate it. Hate me. But I have to be the one to tell him."

It was one of the hardest promises Jo had ever made, but in the end, all she could say was, "I understand. And it's your call."

So many secrets. Jo pressed her mouth into a tight line and held herself as straight as she could. Grady didn't know about the B and B, Merry and Ella didn't know about Harrison's proposal, Harrison and Taylor didn't know how much Jo had wanted to say yes.

She sighed and pointed Ella around the barn to the paddock before heading down the dim hallway to the tack room to grab Peony's gear. Secrets made her head hurt.

The tack room was small and windowless, lit only by a dusty table lamp with a green shade. Merry was sacked out on the sagging love seat that crouched opposite the rows of saddles hanging from one wall.

Jo stopped in the doorway, wincing at the loud echo of her boot heels on the concrete floor, but it was too late. Shifting her bulk with a slight wince and a hand against the side of her belly, Merry sat up and yawned.

"Sorry, I don't know what's the matter with me. Guess I didn't sleep all that well last night."

Because of the fight with Ella, Jo thought, but all she said was, "No problem. Go back to sleep—you can nap as much as you like. How are you feeling?"

She watched sharply to see if Merry winced again. The girl had been doing that all morning, pressing a hand to her abdomen as if easing a cramp.

"Fine. And no more napping for me, I'm up." Rubbing her eyes, Merry watched as Jo selected Peony's brown leather saddle and lifted it down from its post on the wall. "Are you going out for a ride?"

"Not me. Your sister is, though."

Merry heaved herself off the couch. "She's afraid of horses. Did you know that? It's not fair." She pursed her lips a little, and Jo tried not to think about how helpless she was in the face of that pout. "I'd give anything to be able to ride, and Ella, who probably won't even like it, gets to."

They'd decided days ago that horseback riding wasn't the safest pastime for a woman solidly in her third trimester. But something was tickling at the back of Jo's brain—a plan to get Merry and Ella talking again, give Ella more confidence with the horses, and let Merry enjoy some time with them, as well.

Switching out the bridle she'd grabbed for a soft rope halter and lead, Jo shoved the heavy saddle back onto its post. "Come on. I need your help with something."

Grady laid the leather reins against the left side of Voyager's neck and clucked softly. The big gelding responded at once, pacing a slow, wide circle around the fenced-in paddock.

Voyager had to lift his hooves high to step over the white-painted wooden poles scattered around the sawdust-covered ground. Grady tested himself by closing his eyes and guiding Voyager's footwork using only the pressure of his knees against the gelding's sides.

"How are you doing that?" Ella asked from outside the paddock. She crossed her arms on the top rail of the fence and hooked one foot through the bottom rung.

Grady smiled slowly. "Magic."

"Don't let him fool you," Jo called as she led Peony out

of the barn and down the dirt track to the paddock gate. "Anyone can learn how to do it."

He turned Voyager's nose away from the gate when Jo went to open it. No sense giving him the idea it was time to head back to his stall.

"I don't know," Ella was saying, and he looked over his shoulder to see her leaning away from the bay mare as she passed. "Maybe this isn't such a good idea. And where's her saddle? You're not expecting me to ride her bareback, are you?"

There was a slight tinge of panic coloring Ella's tone, enough to make Grady wheel Voyager around and walk the gelding over to her section of fence.

"You don't have to do anything you don't want to," he assured her, not missing the way she seemed to hold her breath before letting it out gently and reaching a tentative hand to rub Voyager's soft gray muzzle.

The gelding snorted happily, flicking her with his whiskers, and Ella smiled, relaxed. Until she glanced back and saw who had followed Jo and Peony out of the barn.

Merry moved slowly, placing her feet carefully on the uneven slope down to the paddock. She didn't look at her sister, didn't acknowledge her with so much as a flutter of an eyelash, and Grady only realized he'd squeezed Voyager too tightly with his knees when the gelding backed up a few restless steps.

Calming the horse and settling more firmly into the saddle, Grady watched as Jo led Peony into the center of the paddock by the long lead attached to a simple halter.

He had a pretty good idea of what she was up to, and it was a damn smart thought.

"Come on in here, Ella," he said, jerking his chin in the direction of the mare.

"Really?" she squeaked.

"Both of you," Jo said, with a glance at Merry, who appeared simultaneously eager to get as close to the horses as possible, while staying as far away from her sister as she could.

"I don't know," Ella said again, rubbing her palms against the front of her thighs.

"Hey," he said quietly. "You wanted to know how Jo helped me when I came to the island. Well, this is how it starts."

CHAPTER 24

Ella stared in dismay at the stolid mare in front of her. "This is impossible. Merry, stay back."

"It's not impossible." The horse's long ears twitched in the direction of Merry's voice as she stepped forward to ruffle a confident hand through the mare's mane. "Just because you don't know how to do something doesn't mean it can't be done."

Peony snorted and sidestepped away from Merry and into Ella, nearly knocking her off her feet. Recovering her balance, Ella lifted her chin at her sister. "I don't think she likes it when you snark at me."

"She doesn't," Grady confirmed from his seat atop his giant gray gelding. He leaned forward over the pommel of the saddle, as easy and comfortable as if he were sitting in a lounge chair instead of straddling a thousand pounds of pure muscle.

Ella swallowed hard and inched backward, away from Peony, who gave her a look out of one of her chocolate-dark eyes.

"In the wild, horses are prey animals. They've evolved to be amazingly attuned to their surroundings, the emotions and intentions of every creature around them."

It was easy for Jo to lecture from the safety of her position leaning against the paddock's rail fence.

"So Peony knows you're angry, Merry," Jo pointed out. "And Ella, she can tell you're afraid, but she doesn't know of what. The two of you together are making her nervous."

"That's fair," Ella muttered. "Since she's making me plenty nervous. Hey! No, not this way, you're supposed to be going that way!"

Peony ignored Ella's tentative arm waving, shooing her toward the obstacle course of rails and barrels Jo had set up in the center of the paddock. Instead, Peony seemed intent on walking over to check out Voyager, and maybe to snatch a mouthful of the grass growing by the gate.

"If you'd put the halter back on her," Merry complained, "we could get her over to the obstacle course easily. Or I could ride her!"

Ella's immediate "No!" was actually a chorus of voices, with Jo and Grady both weighing in and sharing Merry's scowl among them equally.

Jo hitched herself up to sit on the top rail of the fence. "The obstacle course isn't the point."

"Easy isn't the point, either," Grady added.

Wondering when everyone around her had turned into Yoda, Ella gritted her teeth and stood her ground, arms spread out like a goalie blocking a trick shot. Part of her wanted to put her hands on the horse's shoulder and just push.

It had been a lot easier to dive in and help that wild

mare out at Heartbreak Cove, she reflected. A horse on the ground, focused on one thing and one thing only—giving birth—was a lot less nervous-making than a fully ambulatory mare who wanted to flirt with the handsome gelding on the other side of the paddock.

She and Merry had been tasked with leading the unhaltered, unbridled, unsaddled, uninterested mare through the obstacle course. And, as Ella had quickly realized, it was less about leading and more about persuading.

Clucking gently to get Peony's attention, Merry smiled and began walking backward when the mare's large head swung in her direction. Ella bit her lip, but Merry was being careful, placing her feet with deliberate attention to the uneven floor of the paddock.

Keeping one ear swiveled toward Ella, Peony took a few slow steps after Merry. Admiration and pride glowed in Ella's chest. "You're doing it! That's amazing, keep it up."

Merry walked the mare to the center of the paddock, clucking whenever it seemed Peony might be losing focus on her. Ella followed a few feet behind, feeling utterly useless.

Until they hit the obstacle course, which began with a white-painted wooden pole laid flat in the sawdust between two overturned barrels. Despite the fact that there was a good five feet of space between the barrels, Peony balked.

No amount of clucking could get her moving again. She planted her hooves in front of the pole and refused to step forward, tail swishing and hide twitching as if she were being annoyed by flies.

"Any hints?" Ella called, after five long minutes of coaxing got them no closer to starting the actual obstacle course.

"You're doing great." There was a smile in Jo's voice, but nothing more helpful than that.

Thanks a lot.

"Try some different things," Grady advised, his drawl slow and patient. "If you keep doing what you always do, you're going to get what you've always got."

Seriously, Ella thought. *It's like Yoda and Oprah had a love child.*

Pretty clearly, something had to give, or they'd be here until Merry went into labor. Ella was the queen of negotiating! How could it be so difficult to convince one dumb animal to do what she wanted?

The hot curl of aggravation and failure in Ella's belly overrode her nerves. Lifting her hands, she put them on the mare's warm side.

Short, straight hairs tickled against her fingers before she pressed in, leaning her weight against the horse. Ella gasped, pushing hard enough that her boots slipped and slid in the loose sawdust floor of the paddock—but, other than a curious glance over her shoulder, Peony never budged.

"You can't force her," Merry said. "I love you, but it's your default to try and make everyone around you do whatever you think is best. That's not going to work on her. She's bigger than you . . . and she doesn't have years of love and gratitude for everything you've done for her in the back of her mind at all times. You can't just push her."

Eyes burning, Ella dropped her hands and panted. "Merry, you don't have to be grateful to me. You're my sister. You and me against the world, right?"

Over Peony's back, Merry shot her a tremulous smile. "Always. And I am grateful—you've taken care of me for a long time. But now that I'm going to be a mom, I think it's time I started trying to take care of myself."

They were going to be okay. Ella felt her spirits lift. Merry's smile had always had that effect on her, since they were kids. She took a cleansing breath, inhaling the warm, clean scents of hay and leather.

Time to take a step back to survey the situation.

Ella cocked her head. "What if I go in front?"

Lifting her booted foot in a big, exaggerated step, Ella hopped over the pole and walked between the two barrels. She turned to look back at Peony, and jumped in surprise to find the horse right behind her, almost breathing over her shoulder.

"She followed you!" Merry clapped her hands together. "Okay, good, keep going."

Borne upward on the wings of accomplishment, Ella headed off toward the next obstacle, four hula hoops laid flat on the ground and spaced diagonally. But Peony hadn't moved.

Ella frowned. "Maybe if you do that clucking thing again."

The quiet, encouraging chirrup from Merry got Peony walking forward. Working together, Ella and Merry coaxed the mare through the rest of the obstacle course. There were some stops and starts, and a major stumbling block at the low jump Jo had set up—no more than a foot off the ground, but it required Peony to pick up her hooves farther than was natural, and all she wanted in the world was to walk around it.

But with every obstacle successfully passed, Ella felt her confidence grow. She could look at Merry and know what her sister was thinking, how they should move together to encourage the mare in the right direction.

By the time they reached the final obstacle, Ella and Merry were both walking beside Peony, each with a guiding hand on the mare's gleaming reddish-brown neck.

Jo waited for them at the end of the course, ready to slip the worn red rope halter over Peony's patient head. Merry held out an insistent hand for the lead rope, and Jo handed it over with a grin. She hesitated only a moment before slinging an arm around Merry's shoulders and giving her a squeeze.

"Well done, both of you," Jo said.

For the first time since they'd hit the island, Ella watched her mother and sister together, and didn't feel like a puppy with her nose pressed up against the pet store window. Still so connected with Merry that she could feel her sister's pride and giddiness at impressing Jo Ellen like a warm lump in her own throat, Ella stroked her hand along Peony's back and smiled.

"That was harder than I thought it would be," she confessed as Grady rode up to their little group.

"The first time Jo told me I had to get Voyager over those hula hoops without a lead rope, I thought she was nuts," he said, leaning down to give his gray gelding a friendly slap on the shoulder. "But it was kind of amazing. Got me out of my head for the first time in what felt like forever."

"Where did you get the idea for the obstacle course?" Ella asked, glancing at Jo.

Jo Ellen's eyes flickered with shadows for a moment, but she answered easily enough. "In rehab, actually."

Ella controlled a wince. She really hadn't been trying to ruin the moment by bringing up such a sore subject.

But before she could apologize, Jo lifted her chin in an eerily familiar gesture.

"No, it's okay. I don't mind talking about it. The year after y'all left was the worst of my life, and I easily could've spiraled down. The clinic Aunt Dottie got me into changed all that."

If she were ruthlessly honest with herself, Ella had to admit she wasn't sure she'd be able to talk about her past mistakes so openly. Wanting to know more, she asked, "Where was the clinic?"

Jo's face took on a remembering cast. "Just outside Winter Harbor. The director had a deal with a young man who runs a horse rescue operation next door to the clinic. He takes in stallions from the racetrack, or horses that local authorities find suffering from neglect or abuse, and fosters them, retrains them and gets them healthy, until they can be adopted. It's a nonprofit deal, so he always needs volunteers, and in exchange for help around the barn, he lets the clinic's therapists and patients use some of the more stable horses in different therapies."

"Like the obstacle course." Merry curled her arm over Peony's withers as the mare stamped her hoof.

Jo nodded. "But even just being around them felt like therapy to me. Some of those horses had been starved, beaten—you'd think that would turn them violent or aggressive. And there were a couple of horses no one could get near except Sam, the man who runs the place. But most of them?" She paused, pressed her lips together, and Ella saw that her distant blue eyes were damp. "Most of them were so gentle. They knew they'd been rescued, and they were thankful. You could feel it, every time you put out a fresh bale of hay or ran a currycomb over their hides."

Ella felt the sting of unshed tears behind her eyes. The

connection Jo had felt with those horses was obvious. Even more obvious was that the entire experience had truly altered the course of her life.

It couldn't have been easy to share all that, Ella knew. Especially considering that Jo was well aware of Ella's bitterness and lingering anger . . . but she didn't feel bitter or angry right now. She looked at her mother and saw a woman with deep flaws who'd made terrible choices and damaging mistakes—but who'd worked hard to overcome them.

"I think I get it," she said, as clearly and honestly as she could. "Thank you for showing me this. I'll never forget it."

Merry reached over Peony's back to squeeze her shoulder, and Jo's hopeful smile was like dawn breaking after a bad storm, almost too bright to look at directly. Scrambling for distance, Ella plastered on a grin and stepped back.

She caught Grady's gaze and swallowed hard at the expression of peace relaxing his handsome face.

Suddenly, an idea percolated in her brain, fizzing and popping with enough possibilities to make her dizzy.

She needed more information, needed to do more research—and she was almost out of time. The reality of her looming departure hit her hard, and to cover, she gave Grady her best smile.

"So now that we made it through the obstacle course, have I earned the chance to try actually getting up on a horse?"

CHAPTER 25

Progress, Grady decided, ducking as the trail Voyager
followed took them under a low-hanging branch. They'd
definitely made progress.

He twisted in the saddle to check on Ella. She and
Peony followed along behind Voyager, nose to tail. Grady
was glad to see that her white-knuckled grasp on the reins
had eased up. Instead of staring fixedly at the ground far
beneath her booted heels, she was relaxed enough now to
take in the scenery with bright, curious eyes.

As if sensing his stare, she turned her head and caught
him. "Hey, watch the road!"

Just to wind her up, Grady cocked a brow and leaned
a casual hand on Voyager's rump. "Don't need to. This
guy's watching it for me."

She struggled with that for a moment—he could practically feel her desire to argue that if he wasn't in complete control of his mount at all times, Voyager might
mindlessly wander off the trail and fall over a cliff or
something.

Finally, she settled for, "How far are we going?"

Grady frowned. "Not having fun?"

She sounded surprised when she replied, "Actually, I am. Trail riding is easier than I expected. Way easier than the obstacle course."

"Sure." Grady shrugged and cracked his back with a mighty torque of his ab muscles before facing front again. Tilting his face enough for the breeze to carry his words back to her, he called, "Out on the trail, all Peony wants to do is keep up with Voyager. She'll follow him anywhere. And all *he* wants is to get back to his stall and a nice handful of oats. So while we head away from the barn, our pace is going to be slow and easy. The real fun comes when we turn back—because Voyager will know, trust me. And I'll be holding his head the whole way home, fighting to keep him from galloping flat out."

"Don't they like trail riding?" He could hear the worry in her voice, and it made him want to smile. She was a lot more tenderhearted than she liked to let on.

"They don't mind it," he assured her. "Some horses like being out and about more than others. This big guy's used to going out in the mornings and evenings—an extra hike in the middle of the day feels like work to him. He'd rather be lazing around the barn, rubbing up against the mares and snoozing."

Grady gave Voyager an affectionate scratch along the crest of his mane. "But he's my boy. He's never turned me down for a ride yet."

"You seem like you make a good team," Ella said, pausing delicately. Expectation thrummed in the air between them.

After watching Ella work with her sister and Peony

earlier, and hearing Jo's story again, it wasn't as hard to talk about this as he would've thought.

"Maybe it sounds corny, but Voyager healed me. Working with him, being around him, it's like we're partners." Grady shook his head. "After the accident, part of me thought I'd never have that again. That maybe I didn't deserve it. But Voyager doesn't give a crap about any of that. He trusts me, whether I deserve it or not."

During the short silence that followed, Grady tipped his head back and enjoyed the warmth of the sun on his face as they passed through the copse of trees and out into the open marsh. They passed a snowy egret, startling it into ungainly flight.

"I've never been much of an animal person," Ella said. "I don't hate them or anything, but I didn't really get it. After this morning, though . . ."

Her voice was so soft and thoughtful, he could barely hear her over the thrush of wind through the prickly pear plants topped with their showy yellow flowers, the distant lap of waves against the shore. Grady checked to see where they were.

Oh, perfect.

Clicking his tongue against his teeth in a signal Voyager knew well, Grady guided them off the well-trodden path and around the back side of the pond that served as one of the wild horse bands' favorite watering holes. He led them to a sandy rise of land just above the pond and dismounted, looping Voyager's reins over the pommel of his saddle. Unfazed, Voyager lowered his head to dig into his favorite snack of salt marsh cordgrass.

"Don't you need to tie him up?" Ella asked, pulling nervously at the reins and causing Peony to shake her head and back up.

Grady grabbed the mare's bridle smoothly and nodded at Ella to drop the reins. "Nah. As long as the supply of grass holds out, he won't wander far. Need a hand down?"

She held her arms out to him in answer, and Grady felt something tighten in his chest at the implicit trust. He could be wrong, but he was pretty sure when she first came to Sanctuary, a question like that would've resulted in a short, polite refusal—a refusal to be touched, to admit she needed help, that she wasn't perfectly in control at every moment.

And now, nearly two weeks later, Ella Preston was a soft, supple weight in his arms, sliding down his body and laughing a little breathlessly when her legs wobbled.

"Oof! Who knew sitting around while the horse did all the work could be so tiring? My thigh muscles are like jelly."

"It's one of the big misconceptions about horseback riding," Grady said, enjoying the feel of her slim hips in his palms. He wasn't letting go until she made him, and from the way she grasped at his shoulders, he didn't think that was going to be anytime soon.

"I guess I was squeezing my legs pretty hard to stay on. Probably harder than I needed to."

"No, that's good," he told her. "Lots of beginners try to keep their balance by hanging on to the horse's mane, or sawing at the reins, which brutalizes the poor horse's mouth. You've got a very natural seat."

Ella lifted a brow, made a show of looking over her own shoulder. "What, this old thing? I'm so glad you like it."

He adored her this way, bright and laughing, the lines of tension and stress relaxed right out of her body. And what a body, slender and curved in all the right places, warm and sexy where they pressed together.

"I love it," he growled as heat shot through him in a throbbing wave. Pulling her even closer, until her denim-clad thighs parted around one of his legs, Grady hitched her high against his chest and stole a sun-sweet kiss from that smiling mouth.

And, of course, he slid his hands around to get a better grip on the seat in question.

Ella's surprised laugh turned into a soft moan at the way their bodies slotted together.

He wanted her with the sun beating down on them, turning her city-pale skin to gold. Keeping his arms tight around her, he executed a controlled fall that ended with him hitting the ground beneath her. The soft give of the sandy hillside cradled his back as he steadied her.

Ella rose over him like a goddess emerging from the sea. The naked desire in her gaze fired Grady's blood. She bent to take a kiss, and he tangled them together in the sand, wishing he could wrap her up so completely that she'd never even think of leaving him.

Breaking away with a gasp, Ella blinked dazedly. "Really? Here?"

"It's just us and the horses. No one ever comes out here except me. This is one of my best spots for checking on the wild horses."

"It's nice," she said, without ever taking her eyes off him. "I like what you've done with the place."

"There's a view directly down to the watering hole," he pointed out.

"Mm-hm." Ella's gaze had drifted down to his mouth. She licked her plump bottom lip, so pink and shiny, and it was all over.

Enough talking.

The next time Ella raised her head to blink up at the

darkening sky, it was quite a bit later. She still seemed dazed, but this time Grady felt a caveman kind of satisfaction about it.

I did that to her.

She lifted one languid hand to push her tangled curls over her shoulder, and he caught sight of a livid red love bite on the side of her neck where she was extra succulent.

He grinned.

I did that, too.

"I really do like this place," she said, her voice a little rough. "You're probably getting tired of me gushing about how beautiful it is here, but I can't help it. D.C. is nothing like this—not only the landscape and the scenery, which is obviously gorgeous. But there's something about this island."

"I'll never get tired of hearing what you have to say. Especially about the island."

With a wry twist to her lips, she settled back against his chest and pulled one of his arms around her shoulders like tugging a blanket up to her chin. "Mm. You'll especially enjoy this bit. You were right. This place, Sanctuary Island . . . it gets under your skin."

Curling up in exaggerated shock, Grady made his eyes wide and joked to hide the ecstatic thump of his heart. "What? I think you're going to need to say that again."

She rolled her eyes. "You were right. Okay? Don't get sassy about it—you weren't even the first person who said it to me, now that I think about it."

"Who else has been filling your head with Sanctuary propaganda?"

"That older gentleman who sits in the guardhouse by the dock." She propped her chin on her hand. "The one who's a little . . . I don't like to use the word 'crazy.' My friend Adrienne definitely would not approve."

Grady laughed. "You must mean old King."

She sat up in a rush. "Don't tell me he's actually the king of something!"

"Not exactly." Grady crossed his arms underneath his head and enjoyed the view. Ella's shirt was still tossed over a nearby marsh elder bush. "His first name is King."

Ella blinked. "Why does he wear a crown?"

"He likes it? He's embracing his inner royalty?" Grady stretched into a shrug, loving the way Ella's gaze dropped to track the play of muscles in his shoulders. "Why does anyone do anything?"

"You say that like you think there aren't reasons behind why we do what we do," Ella argued. "But there are. If I learned anything at all during therapy, it was that."

"I'm not trying to talk down the work you did in therapy—but that's not really what we're all about here on the island."

A stubborn light kindled in her eyes, and Grady suppressed a smile. So much for afterglow. But he wouldn't want her any other way.

"I know lots of people think there's something shameful about therapy." Ella shook her head. "As if admitting you've seen a mental health professional means you need to be fitted for a straitjacket immediately. But I don't think I've ever met anyone, in my whole life, who was so well adjusted that they couldn't benefit from a calm, supportive, impartial ear."

This conversation called for pants. Hitching up his jeans, Grady arched his back and did up the buttons while he talked. "I'm not arguing that. I know it works for lots of people—but it didn't work for me, after the accident.

The therapist the hospital assigned was nice and every-thing, but those sessions were torture. Sitting around, talk-ing about my feelings while I knew the guys from my team were out there, risking their lives, doing real work, helping people?"

Even the memory of Dr. Lipshultz's bland, round-cheeked patience set up a feeling like fire ants crawling under his skin, itching and painful and just plain wrong.

Ella nodded slowly. "That makes sense. Talk therapy isn't for everyone. You're an action guy, used to working with your hands, to moving around."

Grady sat up and propped his arms on his raised knees. He wasn't a big one for talking, but it was important to make her understand. "Everything changed for me when I started working with your mom's horses."

Ella moved in the direction of covering herself up. Grady was sad about it, but he could see where she might rather have a shirt on now that the conversation had pad-dled into more treacherous waters.

"Before this morning, I wouldn't have understood what you meant." Her face was contemplative as she but-toned up her blouse. "But there was something about the exercise that cut through all the usual noise in my head and forced me to focus. To be present in the moment. And now, thinking back on it, I can see some interesting pat-terns emerging about the way I approached the problem."

This, right here, was why Grady would never dispar-age Ella for having gone to therapy. She was so smart, so willing to examine her own behavior and learn from it. Which he knew, from his own experience, was a lot harder than most people wanted to admit. He helped out by prodding her forward. "What do you mean?"

She pressed her lips together and attempted to restore order to her tumbled, sand-speckled hair. "When Peony didn't want to move, the first thing I thought of was to try and force her. I'm not sure I like what that says about me."

At the mention of her name, the little bay mare left off her desultory grazing and paced over to Ella, nosing at her hand in a search for stray sugar cubes or her favorite treat of all, peppermints.

The awed, gentle smile that spread across Ella's face as she turned her palm up to Peony's snuffling nose filled Grady with quiet joy.

"What's that thing TV shrinks are always saying?" He put his hands on his hips. "Acknowledging the issue is the first step toward change."

"I'll try if you will," Ella said, slanting him a look.

Grady's hands dropped to swing at his sides. "Meaning . . ."

Ella answered his question with a question—an annoying trick she'd probably picked up from her shrink. "What did the obstacle-course exercise tell you, when you first did it?"

He relaxed a little. "That I missed working as part of a team, that I was still good at it, even if it didn't feel that way."

She concentrated on rubbing Peony's whiskery muzzle as if the mare's flared nostrils held the secrets of the universe. "So . . . nothing about forgiving yourself for what happened after the explosion? Or about maybe leaving the island someday?"

The uneven ground shifted under his bare feet. He stumbled, and that's how he knew he'd taken an instinctive step backward. Setting his jaw and bracing his stance,

Grady pulled it together. "I'm not wearing a hair shirt and lashing myself nightly, or anything. I'm fine about what happened, it's just not my favorite memory."

"And the island?" Ella turned those soft blue eyes on him, a wealth of compassion turning her voice scratchy like raw silk. "You can't really intend to never leave Sanctuary again. Jo says everyone here makes weekly or at least monthly trips to the mainland for groceries, doctor's visits, to go to the movies or a restaurant that isn't the Firefly Café."

Unwilling to face the plea on her face, Grady turned in a circle, throwing his arms wide to the sky and the ocean. "Why would I leave? I've got everything I need right here."

"I know this island is your refuge, the first place you felt safe enough to slow down after the accident. I can understand why it would be difficult to leave it, or to ever see it change."

"Then why are you pushing this?" Feeling hunted, Grady paced to the small stand of sea myrtle that screened his lookout spot from the rest of the marsh.

"Because I'm leaving in three days," Ella cried brokenly, "and I don't want to never see you again!"

Heart racing, Grady whirled to face her. Tousled and mussed, cheeks red and a little blotchy with the force of her emotions, eyes brimming with tears she was too stubborn to let fall—he'd never seen anything so gorgeous.

He crossed the few feet of sand between them in two long strides and gathered her into his arms. It was all he could do not to squeeze the life out of her, to press her so close that she'd meld with his ribs, his heart, and never be able to separate herself.

"I don't want that, either," he said into her soft, salt-sprayed hair. The wish he'd held on to for so long, kept secret and safe in his head, burst out of him in a rush of honesty. "We've just gotten started—I can't lose you yet. Don't leave. Stay here with me."

Ella pressed her face to the hot, smooth skin of Grady's bare chest and breathed in his complicated scent of leather and salt.

She wanted to ask if he meant it, but she didn't need to. He meant every word. She could feel it in the slam of his heart against hers, the corded strength of his arms around her.

It wasn't a real plan. Not in a long-term sort of way. The situation hadn't changed—he refused to leave this island, and her whole life was back in D.C.

As long as she ignored the fact that the bits of her life she really cared about, like her sister, the mother she was only beginning to understand, this new thing with Grady, and her burgeoning interest in and excitement about the renovation of Windy Corner, were all here on Sanctuary Island.

The desire to throw rationality to the wind and recklessly agree to stay was like a hook behind her belly button, tugging at her. But a lifetime of ingrained caution wouldn't let her. And as much as she'd come to appreciate Sanctuary, she didn't truly want to shrink her horizons to the edge of the island and never experience anything outside of it.

Although . . .

"I guess I don't have to go back to D.C. at the end of the week," she said, muffling the words against the wings of his collarbone.

She felt him draw in a breath. "But . . . your job. Do you have enough vacation days saved up to stay longer?"

Squirming slightly, Ella nudged his clavicle with her forehead and studied her own sandy toes. "Well. As it happens, I'm not actually on vacation, per se."

His fingers tightened, individual points of pressure on her back. "Tell me what that means."

Sighing out a breath, Ella turned her cheek to nuzzle into his chest and let her arms steal around his trim, hard waist. "I may have had a bit of a burnout issue. According to my boss. Who mandated that I take a leave of absence, which happened to coincide with Merry's decision to come down here for a visit."

"That's why you accepted the leave of absence," Grady guessed, with startling accuracy.

"I didn't want to admit that he was right, that the way I was going, I was heading for a nervous breakdown."

Grady ran a hand down her spine as if he were soothing a nervous cat, and Ella had to smile. "But now that you've had some time to take a break and catch your breath, you can see how stressed out you were back in the city."

"Right." Ella laughed. "Because reconnecting with my estranged mother, fighting with my sister, and starting a new relationship has been so relaxing!"

As soon as the words left her mouth, she cringed. She'd never been with a guy who wasn't, on some level, surprised to find out they were in a relationship, no matter how many dates they'd been on or how many times he'd slept over at her apartment.

Grady's hand never stopped in its slow, rhythmic stroking of her back, though, and after a long moment, Ella felt herself relax against him.

"I guess that's true." His voice was a deep rumble she felt through her whole body. "You've been through some rough stuff in the last couple of weeks. But hopefully a few good things have happened, too."

"More than a few," she managed through a throat gone suddenly tight. "Even the hard things. I wouldn't change any of it now if I could."

"So you'll stay." A wealth of satisfaction wrapped around his tone, like vines around a tree.

"At least for a little longer," Ella said, tilting her head back to get a look at his face.

Even the slow smile she loved couldn't erase all the darkness in his eyes, but Grady was happy. She could tell. And his happiness sent an answering thrill through her.

Hard on the heels of that thrill, however, was a cold shiver of doubt. Would he still be this happy, this interested in keeping her around, when he heard her plans for Jo's property?

CHAPTER 26

Jo happened to be out in front of the barn when Harrison McNamara's big black SUV emerged from the pine copse and parked in the patch of gravel by the doors.

Hands tightening on the back gate of her own truck, Jo did a quick head count. Merry was inside, determined to help the vet as he made his rounds, but since Dr. Ben Fairfax was no idiot, she wasn't getting any closer to the injured stallion in stall four than the hallway. Last Jo saw, Merry was fuming at Ben's restrictions and Ben was scowling inflexibly. It made Jo grin.

And Ella was out in the back paddock with Grady, running through the exercises Jo showed him when he first moved to Sanctuary.

Which was basically where she'd been for the last five days, ever since she asked if it would be possible to extend her visit—except for the time she'd spent on the phone and at her laptop, working on what Jo assumed was the revised proposal for the Windy Corner B and B.

The last few days had been idyllic, almost perfect. She

had both her girls at home, and there'd been a lot of warmth, a lot of storytelling about the history of the Hollisters on Sanctuary Island. Every hesitant smile and surprised laugh renewed Jo's hope for a real relationship with both Ella and Merry.

Relaxing her hands enough to work the finicky locking mechanism, Jo lowered the back gate and contemplated the stacks of fifty-pound bags of horse feed that represented the last of her budget for the month, and waited for Harrison.

After the way they'd left things, him showing up here wasn't likely to mean good news.

She heard his door slam and closed her eyes briefly, trying to prepare herself for the punch of regret and longing when she looked at him.

But nothing could prepare her for the tired set of his shoulders, the way his bearded cheeks seemed a little hollow, as if he'd skipped too many meals in favor of sitting at his desk. Her heart clenched tighter than a fist.

"Jo. How have you been?" His voice, though, was the same as ever—gruff and calm, steady as a rock.

She suppressed a shiver and gave him a nod. "Good."

"Are your girls here? I heard they didn't leave as planned last Friday."

She read nothing in his tone other than politeness, but Jo couldn't help but stiffen a bit. Which was unfair, because she wanted to feel only easy, uncomplicated joy at the chance to deepen her connection to both her daughters—but as she stared at Harrison, she was conscious of a deep pool of sadness.

Covering it up with a smile, she said, "You heard right. Merry's even talking about moving here for good."

His brown eyes went bleak for a bare instant before his polite mask descended once more. "I'm very happy for you."

Jo rushed to fill the well of silence between them. "How's Taylor? She hasn't come by the barn in almost a week."

"Fine. Well, mostly. You know Taylor—she really feels her feelings."

"She's still a teenager," Jo reminded him. "That's normal. I'll call her tonight and make sure she knows she's always welcome here, no matter what."

"That would mean a lot." Harrison glanced at his watch, and Jo swallowed hard. Time always seemed to be slipping away from them.

Searching around for another topic, she said, "Ella said she wanted to stay because she needs more time to research her proposal for how to turn Windy Corner into a moneymaking property."

Wry amusement warmed Harrison's expression. "Based on the hearts and stars and little bluebirds twittering around my nephew's head these days, I hope that's not her only motivation for sticking around."

Jo's smile widened, felt more real. "I'm not sure even Ella understands why she's having such a tough time leaving Sanctuary."

She and Harrison shared a smirk, the threads of history and understanding that wove them together tightening into solid knots. After a moment, though, his answering smile faded, his lips thinning down until they all but disappeared behind his salt-and-pepper beard.

"Unfortunately, I'm not here to gossip about young love," he said grimly. "Although I'd like to hear more about Ella's business proposition, because I got a call from Mr. Leeds's attorney this morning. Apparently, Mr. Leeds is getting impatient."

All of a sudden, it was there between them, as solid and impenetrable as a brick wall—Harrison's proposal.

Jo's refusal.

"I still have a couple of weeks on the grace period they promised," Jo said tightly. "Are they going back on that?"

"No. But I think the attorney was hoping to get an idea of what your plans are for coming up with the money." He raised his bushy brows. "I admit, I'm more than a little curious about that, myself."

Finding refuge in movement, Jo turned back to her truck. Those feed bags weren't going to unload themselves. "Well, I'm sorry you made the drive all the way out here for nothing, but you can tell Mr. Leeds and his attorney they'll have my plans by the end of May, as agreed."

"Jo." His quiet voice stopped her in the act of reaching for the first stack of bags. "That's not the only reason I drove out here. I miss you."

Oh, now that was just unfair. She'd never had any defense against him when he went all frank and honest on her.

Jo scrambled to get her legs back under her. She needed to find her footing in this conversation, or she'd end up agreeing to anything that might bring a smile back to Harrison McNamara's handsome, weathered face.

"I miss you, too. But my answer hasn't changed."

Frustration sharpened his tone. "You're not thinking this through."

She heaved one of the fifty-pound burlap sacks of feed over her shoulder and marched off toward the barn before she exploded. "No, you're the one who hasn't thought it through. Say I marry you, the debt gets paid off, my home and the stables are saved . . . then what?"

"Hmm, I don't know. Then we live happily ever after with our beautiful daughters, who all fall in love with good men like Grady and never leave Sanctuary Island?"

Tossing the bag to the ground, Jo rounded on him with fire rising in her face, hot enough to blow the top off her skull. "Listen to yourself! This isn't a fairy tale—this is real life. Can you honestly tell me you'd live happily ever after with me and never wonder if I'd only married you to get myself out of debt?"

Harrison planted his hands on his trim hips, pulling his black polo shirt tight across the barrel of his chest. He looked mad now, too, and some part of Jo heaved a sigh of relief.

Fighting, she could handle. It was when he broke out the vulnerability, let her see beneath the suave, charming banker to the decent, loyal, imperfect, struggling single dad underneath that Jo got into trouble.

The muscle below his left ear ticked, the way it always did when he ground his teeth. "Do you remember what you told me on our first date? You said you wanted to take it slow, and given your history—and mine, for that matter—I certainly understood. Things were good between us; at least, I thought so. You certainly helped me see that life was still worth something, that there could be joy in the world after Carol died. I'd like to think I did the same for you. But Jo, ten years isn't taking things slow—it's being stuck in the mud. And now you've come up with yet another excuse, the same way you do every time I try to take us to the next level."

"Now hold it right there. My daughters finally being

ready to reconcile with me was not an excuse!" Jo bit out. "It was my one chance to finally get everything I ever wanted, but it wasn't going to be handed to me on a silver platter. It was hard enough getting them to trust me and open their hearts to me—I couldn't risk how much harder it would've been to introduce them to a whole new ready-made family that didn't include them."

"I know." The lines around his whiskey-brown eyes softened and the line of his shoulders dropped. "I get it, Jo. And I'm glad that's working out for you. But it's hard to face the fact that there's no room for me—for Taylor and me—in the life you always wanted."

Jo's skin felt too tight, her body stiff and distant, like a cage around her heart. "That's not what . . . I never meant to hurt you. And Taylor will always be like a daughter to me."

"I believe you, and I appreciate it." He pulled his keys out of his pocket and jingled them restlessly, avoiding her eyes. "But I wish I could believe what we had together ever meant a damn thing to you."

She pushed out a shaky breath. "You know that it did. I love you, Harrison."

"Right." He smiled faintly, but his eyes were dark and distant again. "It's just our timing that needs some work, I guess. I'll wait to hear from you about the lien, if you want me to go with you to the meeting with Leeds and the lawyer."

"Thank you. I honestly don't know what I'd do without you."

So many more words crowded Jo's chest, fighting and kicking to get out. But what could she say, really? Nothing she could say would help this situation.

She couldn't do what he wanted. She refused to marry

him with the specter of this money between them. It would be like adding a third person onto the marriage license—one who wanted nothing more than to make trouble.

And her relationships with her girls were only now starting to get better—she was still afraid to risk rocking that boat, and Harrison knew it.

What he didn't know, and what she couldn't tell him as he turned and trudged off to his car without a backward glance, was how tempted she was to say yes.

Marrying Harrison McNamara would be a dream—but Jo would spend the rest of her life knowing that when it finally came time for her to stand on her own two feet, the way Aunt Dottie taught her, she'd stumbled and clutched for the nearest support.

No, there was no way a marriage between Jo and Harrison right now could work. And as he'd said, ten years was a long time to wait.

She could only hope that his patience held out a little longer.

Ella stood in the darkness just inside the barn and reflected that her coming-to-terms-with-stuff muscles were getting quite the workout this month.

She'd been looking for Jo to ask her a question about one of the exercises Grady couldn't recall with perfect clarity when she'd seen her mother facing off with that handsome older man.

The tension between them was palpable at fifty paces, and Ella was about to fade back and let them have it out when she heard her own name.

Even telling herself it was none of her business, and anyone who eavesdropped deserved whatever they ended up hearing about themselves, she couldn't stop herself from sliding back into the shadows behind the open barn door and listening in.

And what she heard changed everything, rearranged her preconceived notions as if someone had upended the box of puzzle pieces that made up her ideas about her mother, and shook them out all over the floor.

She waited until Harrison McNamara was in his big SUV and driving away down the gravel road before stepping out of the barn.

Ella watched Jo, whose shoulders had slumped the instant Harrison's truck disappeared into the pines, reach down to heft the bag she'd dropped in the midst of her argument.

The question beat at Ella's chest like a trapped bird.

"Was he right?"

At her voice, Jo dropped the bag again and pivoted, dismay written all over her face. "Ella!"

Unable to stay still, Ella paced closer, her hands clasped around her elbows, fingers digging in. "Harrison. I knew you'd been together, off and on, but . . . He asked you to marry him?"

Jo's eyes closed briefly, a spasm of pain tightening her mouth. But her gaze was clear when she met Ella's stare. "He did."

"And you turned him down, because of us." Ella could hardly take it in.

"There were a lot of factors," Jo hedged, as if she wanted to keep Ella from feeling guilty.

Ella shook her head. "But he said he'd asked you other times. Before the debt?"

She waited for Jo's reluctant nod before asking again,

"So was he right? Was it just an excuse? Were we your easy way out of a marriage proposal you didn't want?"

Shivers ran through her as she posed the question, and part of her couldn't believe how much the answer mattered to her. Especially when she was almost certain she knew what Jo was about to say.

Jo stood silent for a long beat. Ella saw the moment her mother decided to tell her the truth.

"No." Jo tipped up her chin. "I love him. I want to be with him. But sometimes that's not enough. And sometimes rushing to grab what you want means you lose out on what really matters."

Ella heard what Jo wasn't saying. She and Merry— they were what mattered to their mother. Them, and her own self-respect. And Jo was willing to deny herself what she wanted, even though Ella could see how deeply it hurt her.

"I told Grady I believe people can change." Ella had to force the words out of her tight, scratchy throat. "But the truth is, I didn't want to believe that about you, because that would mean I'd have to leave room for the possibility of forgiving you."

Jo's eyes went wide. "Honey, no. I'm not trying to guilt you into anything."

"I know that." Ella shook her head, a little amazed at herself. "I really know it. Which must mean . . ."

"What?"

Ella could feel the surprise on her own face as she gazed at the woman she'd sworn never to believe in again. "I think it means I want to forgive you."

Something fragile came into Jo's eyes, incongruous and wrong in that strong-boned face. "Ella. You don't have to.

I know what I was like. Your father . . ." Her throat worked. "He was right to take you away. Some things are unforgivable."

"Maybe," Ella said slowly. "But regardless, I don't want to be the kind of person who's so closed off and afraid of being hurt that I can't see what's right in front of me."

As if she couldn't help herself, Jo made a motion toward Ella, her tanned arms lifting slightly. But she stopped still, and Ella knew she'd have to be the one to make the first move.

It was harder than it should've been, after everything that had happened in the last few weeks, but as she stepped into the circle of her mother's arms and felt them close around her for the first time in fifteen years, Ella knew a moment like this couldn't be rushed.

Emotion clogged her throat, wanting to push out of her mouth as a sob, or maybe a laugh—everything was jumbled up inside her. But she forced herself to stay put, to let the feelings wash over her and through her, and to return her mother's hug until her heartbeat slowed back to something resembling normal.

She pulled away, and Jo let her go reluctantly. Sniffling, Ella gave her a watery smile and said, "About the rest of what you and Harrison were discussing."

Jo seemed to read the plea for a return to less emotional topics in Ella's eyes. "My debt to Mr. Leeds. You knew about that already."

"I've been working on some changes to the proposal I gave you before." Unaccountably nervous, Ella had to struggle not to fidget. "I'd like to go over it with you again. And maybe with Harrison, too, since he mentioned wanting to know the details?"

"He's really the one to convince," Jo agreed.

"That we have a viable enough moneymaking idea to warrant a loan," Ella said, nodding firmly. "To cover the lien and save Windy Corner."

Jo covered her eyes with one hand, mouth trembling.

Alarmed, Ella said, "Are you okay?"

Blowing out a breath, Jo lowered her hand to show blue eyes brimming with tears. "More than okay. You said 'we.' It's a little thing. I know it doesn't mean anything, but . . ."

Understanding warmed Ella all the way through to her bones. "No, it does mean something."

It still felt strange, but somehow right, to reach out and lay a hand on her mother's shoulder. "We're in this together. Windy Corner is part of my history, too, and Merry's. We're going to help you keep it."

The dawning joy on Jo's face bolstered Ella's courage. It almost made up for how nervous she was at the prospect of finally letting Grady in on her big idea. As soon as she got confirmation from the bank that her plan had merit, she'd figure out the right place and time to tell him.

But as she grabbed one of the feed bags from the back of Jo's truck and followed her mother into the barn with it, Ella realized she had hope.

She actually hoped she might have figured out a way to have it all.

CHAPTER 27

The knock on his front door had Grady cursing and fling-ing soapy water all over the kitchen counter before he unearthed a dish towel to dry off with.

The old Fortress of Solitude wasn't quite as impregna-ble as it used to be, pre-Ella, but it wasn't exactly Union Station.

Frowning, Grady ducked down the hallway, wonder-ing who it could be. Ella had told him she had a business meeting this morning, so he assumed she was still out at her mom's house. He grinned, picturing her on her little cell phone headset, wheeling and dealing long distance.

Heck, if that worked, if she could run her business from here—maybe she'd see her way clear to staying on Sanctuary for good. Things between them had been so amazing since she extended her trip, Grady couldn't help but want more.

He opened his door and felt his eyebrows shoot up at the sight of his young cousin bouncing on the balls of her sneaker-clad feet.

Taylor slapped a manila folder impatiently against the wooden door frame. "I know you don't like people to stop by without calling first," she said, pushing past him and into the living room. "But this is an emergency."

Grady watched her pace the perimeter of the striped rag rug he'd picked up at the craft fair in the square last summer. Taylor wasn't a calm, easy girl on the best of days—she registered at about a twelve out of ten on the overreaction scale, and she had a well-developed, if understandable, tendency toward melodrama.

Whatever had spun her up this morning must be a lulu, Grady mused, taking in the hectic flush on her cheeks and the haphazard mess of her dark blond hair. "What now?"

"Don't do that." She pointed at him, never stopping in her quest to wear a path around the rug. "Don't 'what now' me. Not until you hear what I just found out."

Grady kept his eyes from rolling through a heroic exertion of will. "So tell me."

After a thrilling pause, Taylor brandished the folder she'd brought with her like a lawyer in a movie presenting a winning closing argument. "Your little girlfriend is a bitch."

"Watch your mouth," he growled, feeling the hackles rise at the nape of his neck. Damn it, he knew Taylor was having a hard time of it lately, but he wasn't going to let anyone talk about Ella like that.

Righteous indignation burned in Taylor's narrowed glare. "Oh, she has everyone fooled. You're completely whipped and useless, and now she's got Jo walking around like she won the lottery, just because Miss Perfect Ella deigns to speak to her. But it's all a lie."

Anger spiked through his confusion and sharpened his voice. "No, it's not. You don't know Ella—you haven't even tried to get to know her or Merry. You don't understand how much it's cost Ella to be here, to give Jo a chance."

You don't understand what she's given me.

Taylor's mouth pulled down in a grimace, but it was the pity in her tone that roughed a chill down Grady's spine. "I hate to be the one to break it to you—I honestly do. But Ella's presence on the island is going to cost all of us, everyone who loves Sanctuary and wants to keep it the way it is."

"Explain."

"I don't have to." She held up the folder. "See for yourself."

Feeling stupidly as if he were asking for a punch in the face, Grady held out a hand. With an air of vindication, Taylor forked over the folder and crossed her arms over her chest.

Trying to convince himself this was going to turn out to be Taylor throwing a hissy fit, Grady opened the file.

His heart stopped.

A page fluttered free of the folder, and he bent slowly to pick it up off the rug. It was a color image, a picture of Jo's house all fixed up, looking remarkably similar to the vision he had in his head of how it would be after he finished the repairs. But out front, next to the paved circular drive, was a sign that spelled out WINDY CORNER BED & BREAKFAST in fancy curlicue letters.

"Jo called me last night, and we talked. I was ready to admit maybe I'd been a little sulky and unfriendly, whatever, so I went out to the barn this morning. But no one was there. And I found *that* in Jo's office," Taylor said, sounding more subdued. He could only imagine what the look on his face was telling her.

He didn't even know how he felt, what to do or say other than to look through the rest of the papers in the folder. Profit-and-loss projections, sample promotional materials, speculation on Sanctuary Island's potential as a tourist destination.

It was laid out in black and white, real and undeniable. Proof that Ella had come to the island looking to make money off her mother's recent inheritance.

Proof that she didn't understand anything he'd told her about what made Sanctuary so special—or that she didn't care.

Evidently, she didn't care about much beyond turning a profit.

Dropping the folder as if it were covered in manure, Grady moved blindly in the direction of the cabinet in the corner and found the bottle of bourbon collecting dust in the bottom cupboard.

Glass? No. The kitchen was too far away. Twisting the cap off, he took a slug, eyes watering at the burn.

"So you didn't know." Taylor's voice was muffled through the ringing in Grady's ears. "I wondered."

He snorted, took another drink. "No."

"I wanted to ask Jo about it—I actually went to the house to confront her," Taylor said, crouching to gather the pages back into the folder. "But she wasn't around."

A prickle of foreboding pierced through the fog of betrayal and disappointment clouding Grady's brain. "Did you see Merry when you were out at the barn or at the house?"

Taylor frowned up at him. "Nope."

Merry, Jo, and Ella were all missing—and Ella had

told him she had a business meeting. Wetting his suddenly dry mouth with another swallow of bourbon, Grady rasped, "Call your father. Right now."

Whatever Taylor saw on his face convinced her not to argue. Whipping out her cell phone, she pressed a button and held it up to her ear for several seconds. "No answer. Which is weird—he always picks up for me, unless he's in a bank meeting."

"It's Saturday." Grady's head was swimming. He told himself it was the bourbon, and set the bottle down on the coffee table. "Does he work on Saturdays, usually?"

Taylor shook her head. "Only for special clients."

Thunder grumbled in the distance as Grady cursed, low and vicious.

Taylor's eyes got big. "Oh crap," she faltered. "You don't think—"

"Get in the truck." He tossed her the keys. "I need you to drive me to the bank."

"Yes!" Taylor snatched the keys out of the air with a nimbleness Grady couldn't hope to match right now.

He felt gutted, split wide open and scoured raw. His head spun ceaselessly, a sickening whirl of *she wouldn't she did can't believe but I trusted her believed in her loved—*

Cutting the thought off with a savage snarl, Grady hurled himself into the passenger seat and hung on to the one thought that burned bright and clear in his brain.

He had to stop this before it was too late.

The drive into town felt interminable, even though he knew Taylor was pushing the limits of legality on speed the whole way.

A fat drop of rain splatted against the windshield, then another.

"Slow down," he told Taylor again, peering through the windshield at the dark gray sky. These late-spring storms came up fast, and they could turn the unpaved back roads into treacherous mud slicks in minutes.

Finally, they reached the white-painted brick building with the covered wraparound porch that housed the bank. And whatever hope Grady had held out died a swift, painful death.

Uncle Harrison's big black SUV was parked in its usual spot, and right beside it was Jo's battered blue pickup truck.

Taylor parked just as the sky opened up. Rain pelted down furiously and the wind picked up, whipping the HEART OF SANCTUARY banner that arced over Main Street.

"Stay in the truck," he told her.

Shooting him an incredulous look, Taylor opened her door and hopped out, holding the folder over her head to shield her face from the driving rain.

Grady didn't bother cursing again. It wasn't making him feel any better. Shoving out of the Jeep, he was soaked in seconds as he ran up the front steps of the bank to take shelter under the overhanging porch roof.

"Guess there's no point telling you not to come in with me," Grady said, bracing one hand against the bank door.

"You guessed right," Taylor told him.

Surrendering to the inevitable, Grady pushed inside the bank lobby. Violet Harvey, the lone bank teller working the counter, raised her pale brows and pushed her cat-eye glasses up her nose.

"Oh," she said in the vague, dreamy way that had given her a local reputation for ditziness. "Is it raining?"

Grady looked down at the puddle collecting under his boots.

Apparently deciding they didn't have the time or patience for stupid questions, Taylor ignored Violet and towed Grady toward the back of the lobby and down the hall toward her father's office.

Grady tipped his nonexistent hat to Violet, who shrugged and went back to the book she'd been reading before they busted in.

Taylor's grip on his sleeve tightened when they reached the dark wood-paneled door. Now that they were actually here, she seemed scared, the bow of her lips pulled into an unhappy curve.

"What if we're too late?" she whispered. "What if Dad thinks it's a great idea?"

"Then it'll be our job to explain how completely wrong he is." Grady didn't bother trying to work out a strategy—Taylor was about as likely to let him do all the talking as she'd been to stay in the truck—he simply put his hands against the mahogany and pushed.

The scene inside the office was almost identical to the nightmare scenarios that had been playing on an endless loop in his head ever since he saw the Windy Corner Bed & Breakfast picture.

Harrison was sitting on the green leather sofa in the corner of his office with Jo and Merry, while Ella stood before them, clearly in the middle of presenting her proposal.

All four of them looked up in startled surprise when Grady and Taylor barged in, but Grady only had eyes for Ella. The split second of guilt that tightened her pretty face nearly swiped his legs out from under him.

Even with the evidence mounted against her, he'd still wanted to believe that there was some big mistake, something going on that he didn't know about that would explain all this away.

But there wasn't.

"God," he rasped. "You're really doing it. You're trying to steal your mother's inheritance and turn this island into an amusement park for bored tourists."

Ella's eyes widened in an expression of such perfect shock, he almost laughed. Yeah, he'd been slow to catch on, but now that he knew the truth, he wasn't going to pussyfoot around.

"Grady, you don't understand," Jo started, half rising from the couch.

He silenced her with a sharp gesture, never taking his glare off Ella. "I understand plenty. This whole trip was nothing but an excuse to get in your good graces so Ella could steal Miss Dottie's house and turn it into a B and B. That's right. I know what you're up to." He dropped the folder Taylor had brought him on the low glass table in front of the sofa.

Ella flinched at the slap of the papers on the table, her face drained of color.

"Is that really what you think of me?"

In three steps, Grady was in front of her, close enough to reach out and grab her shoulders.

She gasped when he touched her, but he summoned his control and didn't squeeze bruises into her soft skin, didn't shake her. Didn't drag her close and crush that lying mouth under his.

He looked down at his scarred hands, bare to the world and nakedly sensitive against the cable weave of her yellow cotton sweater. "I thought you were the woman I'd work the rest of my life to be worthy of, the woman who made me want to be more than I thought was possible. Turns out, I couldn't have been more wrong."

Ella gasped in a breath, her face crumpling briefly before smoothing out into a blank mask. "Grady. You smell like a distillery."

He dropped his hands. "When the woman of your dreams turns out to be a nightmare? Yeah, you do a shot or two."

Ella went rigid in his grasp, "Are you drunk?"

"So what if he is?" Taylor piped up. "I drove."

"Honey, what's going on?" Harrison asked. "What are you even doing here? We're in the middle of a business meeting."

"We came to stop you," Taylor cried. "Don't listen to anything that bitch says—if you turn Windy Corner into a hotel, it'll wreck the whole island!"

Ella gazed into Grady's eyes as if waiting for him to leap to her defense. But he couldn't. Taylor was right, and the rage and fear thrumming through his blood locked his jaw shut.

"That's enough." Merry didn't raise her voice. She didn't need to—the furious intensity of her tone had every head in the office swiveling to her as she rose unsteadily to her feet, one hand pressed tight to the side of her pregnant stomach. "I don't care what you think is going on here. Nobody gets to talk about Ella like that."

"It's okay," Ella said, breaking the tense silence that followed. "She's entitled to her opinion."

That got his blood up all over again. "Gee, thanks. Except Taylor and I only get to have an opinion because she happened to find that folder in Jo's office. When were you planning on telling me about your little scheme? Oh right, you weren't, because you knew I'd never let it happen."

"Grady, calm down." Jo sounded appalled. "This isn't what you think."

Eyes glittering with blue fire, Ella went toe to toe with

him. "It's exactly what he thinks. I didn't tell him about my plans because I didn't want to deal with this exact tantrum. And I'm not having this out with you here— please leave."

Grady planted his feet and crossed his arms over his chest. "I'm not going anywhere."

Mouth a thin line, Ella pitched her voice so low that Grady almost had to lean in to hear her. "I realize you're angry with me. But I would have hoped, after everything I told you about my childhood, you'd have the class and courtesy to avoid a public drunken spectacle like this."

"For God's sake, three swallows of bourbon isn't enough to make me drunk," he protested, his insides squirming in an uncomfortable way at the honest betrayal on Ella's face.

"Good, then you can drive yourself home," she said, stepping back. "I'll walk you out."

Since what he wanted was a few minutes alone with her, that suited Grady just fine. "Let's go," he growled, turning on his heel.

Leaving the shocked silence of the office and striding across the mostly empty lobby, he threw open the front door and stepped out onto the covered porch with Ella right behind him.

Slamming the door after her, Ella turned him to face her with a surprisingly strong hand on his arm.

Grady stared at her in the storm-dark afternoon light as rain fell all around them, pounding on the veranda roof in a solid wall of sound. It was hypnotic, like the white noise of waves crashing on the shore, and without conscious planning, the question grated out of his raw throat.

"How could you do this?"

CHAPTER 28

How could you do this?

Ella almost wanted to laugh, because it was funny—those were the exact words echoing in her head.

But it wasn't funny ha-ha. Actually, she'd never felt less like laughing in her life.

His face was set in such stern, uncompromising lines, he looked like a stranger.

"I don't have to justify anything to you," Ella said. "This is business, between my mother and the bank. You don't actually have a say in what Jo Ellen does with her own property."

A curtain of windswept rain blew down Main Street, drowning out Grady's response. Good. From the snarl on his mouth, she didn't think she wanted to hear it, anyway.

He paced away from her to the veranda railing and back again, heedless of the rain lashing in the open sides of the porch and spattering him with droplets.

"Just tell me this—was any of it real? Or was it all research for your moneymaking plans?"

That dinged dangerously close to a sore, tender spot. "You did help me with research," she said cautiously. "But I've never lied to you. Not once."

Unless you counted lies of omission. Which she was still committing.

The cruel twist of his lips told Ella he was counting everything. "Noble of you. Except I never lied to you, at all. I opened up to you, I told you more than I've told anyone since I was in state-mandated therapy, trying to keep my job."

Pain clutched at her belly. "I know," she said. "And I listened to what you told me."

"No you didn't." He shook his head, shaggy rain-darkened hair spraying water droplets. "You couldn't have, or you'd know that this B and B idea is the last thing I'd ever want on my island. But you're going ahead with it anyway."

Torn between wanting to explain about Jo being in trouble and anger at Grady's blind refusal to consider that he might be wrong, Ella wrapped both arms around her middle. The wind had kicked up, chilly and damp, making her shiver.

"Not everything is about you," she said slowly. "But since that's all you want to talk about, let's be straight about what's really ticking you off. It's not the fact that I didn't tell you what I was working on; it's not even the B and B."

"No? From where I'm standing, that seems like plenty to be ticked about."

He swayed close to her and she smelled the sickening sweetness of whiskey again. Betrayal swelled up, fast, furious, and hardwired to the most primitive parts of her brain.

She narrowed her eyes. "You set yourself up as some Protector of the Island, like all you want is to keep it pure and safe for the horses—and maybe that's part of it. But what you really want is to keep the island a secret, your own hidey-hole where the rest of the world can never touch you. That might be understandable after everything you've been through, but it's no way for a grown man to live, Grady Wilkes. Especially not a man who expects so much courage and strength from everyone around him."

Grady went still, blinking in the dusky light, then turned on his heel and stalked down the veranda steps and out into the storm.

Disbelief propelled Ella after him. She gasped as the rain sliced into her, the wind cutting through her sweater and jeans like cold knives. "Don't you dare walk away from me," she shouted. "Can't stand to hear the truth?"

He stopped beside his Jeep. Over his shoulder, he said, "Maybe you're right about me. Maybe I'm trying to protect myself as much as I'm trying to protect Sanctuary. That doesn't change the fact that you're the one determined to destroy both of us."

Rocking back on her heels as if he'd slapped her, Ella thanked God for the rain. Grady would never know that at least half the wetness streaming down her cheeks was due to tears.

"If that's how you really feel, I don't think there's anything else to say."

His big hand clenched on the door handle, scars standing out white and livid. "This isn't over."

He was talking about the proposal, she knew—telling her he'd fight the B and B all the way. But when she said, "Yes it is," she meant something else entirely.

Ella was proud of how steady she'd kept the words,

when everything inside her was twisting in agony. "It never would've worked anyway. Relationships are hard. They take work, and guts, and hope for the future. I can't imagine going into one with a man who's so chained to the past that he's walled himself up on a four-mile-long spit of land completely cut off from the rest of the world. I was willing to change everything, try everything, risk everything for you—but you'd never do the same, would you?"

Those broad shoulders tightened, but Grady didn't turn around. Instead, he climbed into his Jeep and revved the engine before peeling out of the bank parking lot and down Main Street.

Ella stared through the driving rain until his taillights winked out of sight.

Numb, mind blank, she walked back toward the bank like a zombie. She nearly slipped on the wet wooden steps when she saw her mother and sister standing on the porch, waiting for her with identical expressions of outraged sorrow.

Ella squinted up at them, heart beating sluggish and off-kilter in her chest. "Should I . . . Sorry. Does Harrison have time to finish going over the plans now?"

Jo's eyes widened in amazement. "Honey, no. He's got your incredibly detailed, well-researched proposal. He can look it over and call me. You don't need to go back in there. Whether he decides to extend the loan or not, you've done enough for one day."

Sagging with relief—she really didn't want to see the triumph on Taylor McNamara's face—Ella leaned against the porch railing. "Okay. Then . . . I want to go home."

"Of course!" Merry hurried down the steps to wrap her

warm arms around Ella's rain-chilled shoulders. "Let's get you home, you need to get out of these wet clothes and get dry, before you catch a chill."

"Isn't that my line?" Jo herded them into the truck with a determined smile.

"Just practicing my mommying," Merry said breezily. Or as breezily as anyone could say while hauling herself up into the cab of a truck while very, very pregnant. It took the discreet application of one of Ella's hands to her sister's behind before all of them were settled in the dry, stuffy interior of the truck.

"You're going to be a great mom." Ella gave in to temptation and tipped over until her head was propped on Merry's shoulder. "I can't wait to come back to see it for myself."

Beneath her cheek, Merry froze. Ella felt it when her sister glanced over at Jo in the driver's seat.

"Well," Merry said, clearly feeling her way. "It would be super-efficient if you just stayed here. At least until the baby is born. It's only a few weeks away!"

Staring out the windshield at the water-blackened tree branches waving wildly in the wind, Ella swallowed until the pain in her chest was compressed into a hard lump just under her breastbone. "I can't. I've got a real life back in D.C.—one that I've neglected long enough. I thought maybe . . . I had a reason to stay. But that was a fantasy. And now that reality has set in, I need to get away."

"But—" Merry started, high-pitched and unhappy, but Jo cut her off.

"We understand. Don't we, Merry? And I'll always be grateful that you spent this time here."

Driving down a pitted country road with these two

women, one she'd loved her entire life and one she'd only begun to learn to love, Ella felt her chest constrict until her bones pressed on that hard knot of pain.

"I'm glad, too," she said thickly. "More than I can say. And I'll visit when I can. But right now, I need to leave."

Tears threatened in Merry's shaky voice. "Right now?"

Ella breathed out a shuddery sigh, eyes open and blank on the stormy sky, seeing nothing but Grady's hard, accusing eyes. "When I said I wanted to go home, I meant to D.C. When we get back to Windy Corner, I'm packing. I'll catch the afternoon ferry to the mainland."

Merry's arm stole around her, squashing Ella to her side. "Okay," she said, and Ella almost smiled, picturing the Brave Little Toaster expression on her sister's face. "But you have to promise to come back the minute—the second!—I go into labor. I'm not kidding. I know we've had our differences since we came to Sanctuary, but there's no one in the world I can count on the way I count on you. You're my rock. Baby and I are going to need you."

Ella sat up so she could return the hug. Merry immediately burrowed into her, the way she used to when they were little kids.

"I promise I'll come back for the birth," Ella said, pressing a kiss to the top of Merry's head. She caught Jo's soft smile across the cab and added, "But until then, you'll be in good hands."

Rain and wind kept Ella from hearing Jo's swift, indrawn breath, but she saw it. And even though her mother never took her eyes off the treacherously slippery roads for an instant, Ella knew Jo had heard and understood.

Satisfied, Ella went back to looking out the window.

She was watching for something in particular—something she desperately wanted to see one last time before she left Sanctuary Island.

And as the truck veered slowly around a curve and the road opened out onto the western wetlands, Ella got her wish.

On a sand bluff overlooking the ocean, the stark black figure of a horse stood limned in storm light against the rushing clouds. She kept her gaze on that figure until the flash of lightning out over the water highlighted him in a rush. It was the stallion she'd seen that first day, the leader of the wild horse band, with the long black mane.

He reared and pawed at the hard-packed sand before loping down the small hill to rejoin his mares, and Ella felt the pain in her chest ease by a fraction.

No, she'd never regret her time on Sanctuary Island. This place had taught her to face her past, to open her heart, and given her a new dream . . . when she'd believed herself long past the age of dreaming.

It had taught her to love.

Maybe that love hadn't worked out—and oh, the thought of Grady still cut at her like a knife. But even with the pain of that loss so fresh and raw, Ella couldn't bring herself to be sorry she'd met him.

Whether he believed it or not, he'd changed her life.

Grady drove with relentless precision, yanking the Jeep back in line every time it tried to fishtail along the sloppy back roads to Ben's house.

The bourbon had worn off completely right around the time Ella called him a coward.

That wasn't exactly what she said, a tiny voice tried to

tell him, but Grady downshifted and clenched his hands around the wheel to get it to pipe down. Maybe she didn't say the word "coward" but they were both thinking it.

Hell, maybe she was right. He probably needed to work on the whole never-leaving-the-island-again thing ... even if the very idea made his guts do a sick, roiling tango.

Bottom line: it didn't matter. She could try and turn it around on Grady all she wanted. Nothing justified what she'd tried to do.

All in all, Grady had never felt so sober in his life—a state he hoped to change, as soon as he got to Ben's place.

He didn't want to be alone right now, and God knew Ben wouldn't hassle him with a lot of questions and attempts at comfort. That's why they were friends. Ben never held back his true opinions to spare someone's feelings.

His brand of harsh, unvarnished truth was exactly what the doctor ordered. Grady wasn't sure he could take comfort right now—anything softer than a punch in the mouth was liable to shatter him.

Like Grady, Ben had elected not to live in the most heavily populated part of the island, along Main Street or on the western shore, where Harrison and Taylor lived. In fact, the winding road to Ben's cabin took Grady up past the turnoff to Wanderer's Point.

Luckily, navigating the road took every scrap of his concentration, so it was easy to avoid looking up to the ridge where he and Ella had spent that warm afternoon.

Where he'd told her how he got his scars ... and that he hadn't left the island in five years.

She'd seemed so understanding and compassionate that day, her gaze like a caress, her smile telling him everything would be okay. And when she'd leaped off the cliff and into the water, he'd felt alive in a way he hadn't experienced in years.

But Ella Preston was a liar, he reminded himself as he turned down Shoreline Drive, where Ben had chosen to build his farm at the edge of the maritime forest.

Ben was leaning on his porch railing and sipping from a chipped blue mug when Grady slammed out of his Jeep.

"Tell me that's something stronger than coffee." Grady loped across the yard and took the porch steps in one bound.

"It's Irish coffee," Ben replied, watching Grady shake himself dry like a golden retriever. "You look like you could use one."

"Or ten," Grady agreed, throwing himself down on the porch swing and riding out its creaky protests with a sigh. "What are you doing out here?"

"Watching the storm roll in. Looks like a big one."

So far it had mostly been rain and high winds, but as Ben disappeared inside—hopefully to pour a round—lightning flashed, followed by a clap of thunder cracking nearly overhead.

"More Irish than coffee in mine," Grady called, rubbing his hands through his wet hair. He was cold and wet, but he didn't mind it. The physical discomfort was something else to focus on, a decent distraction from the chaos of emotions throbbing in his chest.

"You'll take what I give you and like it, since I'm waiting on you hand and foot." Despite his annoyed tone, Ben was careful as he handed over the mug full of steaming coffee laced with sweet, smooth Irish whiskey.

"Hey, I didn't want to come inside and drip all over your pretty, pretty floors."

"Just because you're happy living in a man cave-slash-survivalist bunker doesn't mean we all have such low standards." Ben had put in reclaimed pine hardwood, the wood carefully culled from derelict barns and farmhouses all over Virginia, and he was fanatical about taking care of them.

"Pipe down, princess." It was an old, old argument between them, and he should've known Ben would recognize a halfhearted response.

Pausing with the mug at his lips, Ben sent him a glance over the rim as he settled into the hand-carved rocker he'd accepted in lieu of payment when Phil Hubbard's prize goat broke a horn. "Something on your mind?"

Grady took a healthy swig of his Irish coffee and hissed as it scorched down his throat. "I don't want to talk about it."

See, this was why Grady came here. Instead of prying, Ben shrugged and went back to watching the storm. The rhythmic creak of his rocker punctuated the steady drum of the rain, the occasional boom of thunder.

Precisely because Ben didn't push, Grady found himself bursting out with, "Ella and I had a fight."

"She finally figured out you're a loser, huh?"

The barb should've been blunted by the fact that Grady knew Ben was a rock-solid friend whose crusty exterior hid a depthless, unshakable loyalty and a sneaky, backhanded kindness—but it was aimed a little too well at the open wound Ella had left behind.

Grady must have flinched visibly, because Ben's abstract smirk sharpened into real concern.

Huffing out a breath, Grady palmed the hot back of his neck. "Yeah, pretty much. I guess we were both disappointed—because she turned out not to be the woman I thought she was, either."

"You've only known each other about five minutes," Ben pointed out, kicking back to prop his bare feet up on the porch railing. "It's not surprising you'd still be uncovering new quirks."

"Three weeks, not five minutes, and I'd say we got to know each other pretty well. I mean, we spent most of that time joined at the hip."

Ben snorted. "Woof."

"Not like that," Grady protested, surprising himself by laughing. The end of the laugh caught in his chest like a cough or a sob, but still, it was better than the dazed, incoherent anger and betrayal he'd been mired in since he left Ella standing in the rain.

"I didn't get to know Ella as well as you did," Ben said with a significant eyebrow arch, "but when we met up to go over stuff last week she seemed okay. I mean, I didn't like her, per se—"

"But you don't like anyone," Grady filled in as his mind snagged on the rest of Ben's statement. Dread and dismay filled him in a nauseating rush. "Tell me she didn't drag you into that damn Windy Corner proposal. What lies did she use to get you to help her?"

Ben's feet thunked on the porch floor as he sat up with a scowl. "You don't like her idea?"

Grady leaned so far forward, the swing almost dumped him out. Wrapping cold fingers around the chain that hung the swing from the porch ceiling, he said, "Do I like the idea of a bunch of strangers roaming all over Sanctuary, messing with the wild horses? No. I don't. I can't believe you do. Has everyone on this island gone completely nuts?"

Blinking at the snarl in Grady's voice, Ben said, "I would have thought out of everyone on Sanctuary, you'd be first in line to go in with Ella on this thing. It's right up your bleeding-heart savior complex. But man, even if you don't want anything to do with it, you're not saying you'd let a woman like Ella go because she wants to help people? That's cold, even for me."

The coolness in Ben's tone wouldn't seem out of place to most people, but Grady knew him well enough to tell—Ben was disappointed. In Grady.

Feeling like he'd been sucked into a *Twilight Zone* episode, Grady shook his head. "I'm sorry. On what planet is opening a B and B going to help people?"

"What are you—" Ben cocked his head. "I mean, I guess there might be clients who'd need long-term care, and a place to stay while they finish out their sessions. Ella didn't really talk to me about that part of it—she only asked me for advice about what it would take to get the center up and running, what changes the stable facilities would need, and the ongoing medical costs of caring for therapy horses."

The words cracked through Grady like a hot poker through a piece of charred kindling. "Therapy horses."

"Yes," Ben said slowly, the way he talked to people he considered too stupid to treat as adults . . . so, most people. "Therapy horses. For the Windy Corner Therapeutic Riding Facility. Which, to quote Ella's proposal, aims to provide equine-assisted therapy to wounded warriors and others suffering from anxiety, depression, and PTSD."

Boom.

Grady had no idea if the thunder was overhead or *in* his head. All he knew was that somehow, he'd made the worst mistake of his life.

CHAPTER 29

"Wow." Ben stared, his ice-gray eyes for once completely free of mockery. "You really *are* a loser."

Grady dropped his face into his palms, the full realization of what he'd done crashing over him now that he'd recounted the whole ugly thing to Ben. "Worse," he groaned. "I'm a complete asshole."

Ben kicked the rocker into furious motion, the way he did when he was thinking. "It sounds like you were both as dumb as a couple of boxes of hair about this whole thing. Yeah, you shouldn't have jumped to conclusions, but why the hell didn't she call you on it? All she had to do was show you her actual proposal and she could've rubbed your face in your complete wrongness."

Pressing the heels of his hands so hard into his eye sockets that colors and light burst behind his lids, Grady ground out, "That's what you would have done."

"Damn straight."

"Ella's not you," Grady said, breathing out and standing up to dig his cell phone out of his pocket. "She puts on a tough act, but she's soft underneath. God, the things I said. I've got to talk to her."

"There's no way she's going to pick up," Ben predicted sagely.

"Right. Because you're such an expert on women." Grady shot his friend a narrow look while the phone rang and rang and rang. "How many times were you out at Jo's barn this last week? Five, six? And usually you're there—what? Once a week, tops? And even with all that, you haven't said more than a dozen words to Merry Preston."

The rocking chair jerked to a stop. "Shut the hell up."

"I'm only saying . . ." Grady started, then swore when Ella's voice-mail message started playing in his ear. "She's not answering. I'm going out to Windy Corner."

"Good, get off my porch. Jackwagon," Ben grumbled, still a little red at the tips of his ears. He stood and snatched up Grady's mug, tossing the rest of the Irish coffee out into the rain-soaked yard.

"Seriously, man, thanks," Grady started to say, but broke off when Ben held up an imperious finger and tugged his vibrating cell phone from his jeans.

"Speak of the devil," he murmured, staring at the phone screen.

Grady stiffened. "Ella's calling you?"

"It's Jo's landline," Ben corrected briefly. "Hello?"

"Ask her how Ella is." Grady crowded close, ignoring Ben's irritated glare. "Is she upset?"

Ben didn't say anything, though—apparently Jo was talking too fast for him to get a word in edgewise. Grady could barely make out the panicked tone of her voice through the receiver.

But he could read the answering shock and fear that

flashed across Ben's face as clear as day, in the instant before it changed to fierce determination.

"How long between contractions?" Ben snapped out.

Grady frowned and racked his brain for which of Jo's mares might be going into labor.

"What's up?" he asked, but Ben was already striding into his house and reappearing a few moments later with the frayed canvas case that held the tools of his trade.

"Keep her calm. I'm on my way." Ben tucked the phone in the back pocket of his black jeans and started patting himself down, looking for his keys.

"Which mare is in trouble?" Grady vibrated with impatience. Every beat of his heart increased his need to get to Ella, to apologize, to grovel if he had to. "Come on, hop in the Jeep, I'll give you a ride. I'm heading over to Windy Corner anyway, and the trailer on your truck is going to handle like crap with the roads so bad."

Ben shook his head with a frustrated grunt before finally unearthing his keys from a zipper compartment on the side of his medical kit. He jumped down from his porch and headed out into the rain toward his truck. "Not a mare. Merry."

Shock paralyzed Grady on the top step for a good five seconds. "No way."

"Three weeks early and moving fast," Ben shouted over his shoulder. "She was having pains all day but didn't tell anyone, the little idiot. No time to drive her down to the ferry, much less all the way to Harbor General. I have to get over there."

Finally forcing his heavy legs into movement, Grady strode after him. "I'll come with you—"

"No." Ben tossed his kit in the truck and faced Grady.

"Jo needs you to go down to the ferry and try to hold it. Buddy's not answering his phone, but you know how the cell reception is down at the pier."

"I thought you said there wasn't enough time . . ."

"Not for Merry." Ben hauled himself up into the truck cab and started the engine with a roar. "Ella left Windy Corner fifteen minutes ago, planning to take the afternoon ferry over to Winter Harbor."

Grady's heart sank like a boulder dropped into a lake. "She's leaving Sanctuary."

She's leaving me.

"But Merry's asking for her," Ben said, as if that sealed the deal. "So you need to go get her. Now."

Grady was moving before Ben finished talking, cold rain stinging his bare skin and weighing down his clothes.

But that didn't matter. Nothing mattered but getting to Ella before the ferry left the island.

Ella held tight to the hard plastic arms of the copilot chair and muttered a fervent prayer that this old bucket wouldn't shudder to pieces around her.

Beside her, the grizzled ferry pilot was less silent, and a lot less prayerful. He was wearing a different bowling shirt from the one he'd had on when they took the ferry onto the island three weeks ago. This one was a solid, shiny sky-blue and had BUDDY emblazoned across the back under the unlikely team name THE SALTWATER COWBOYS.

The foul-smelling, unlit pipe clamped between his lips hadn't changed.

Wincing as he turned the chilly air blue with another streak of swear words, Ella gritted her teeth. "I thought you said the storm wouldn't hit until after we made it to Winter Harbor."

She'd been nervous when she got to the dock and saw the islanders' powerboats moored there tossing in the wind like toys in a splashing toddler's bathtub. But Buddy, the pilot, had spat on the ground at his feet and told her if she'd quit dithering and hurried up, they'd be fine.

Once Ella deciphered the thick Virginia drawl that made it come out sounding more like "If you harry up, we'll be fan," she bit her lip and boarded.

It might not mean much, considering she'd probably be back on the island in less than a month for her niece or nephew's birth, but right now, Ella needed the distance. She needed to feel in control of her destiny.

Making the choice to go back to real life and the real job waiting for her might not fill her with happiness. But at least when it came to the job, she got out of it what she put into it. Her personal life had never worked that way— she didn't know why she was surprised it hadn't gone well this time, either, but she was. Surprised, sad, and hurt.

Lightning zagged through the clouds over the water and she jumped in startled surprise. Buddy cast her a grouchy look that made her think he was reconsidering letting his sole passenger sit in the glassed-in cockpit with him, out of the wind and rain. "First time my knee's been wrong in twenty years."

Ella's fingers went white-knuckled. "We're out here on the open ocean in the middle of a thunderstorm on the advice of your *knee*?"

Looking taken aback at the shrillness of her tone, he said obstinately, "It acts up when a storm's coming in. Was fine at lunch, so I figured we had time. Figured wrong."

"Oh my God." Ella moaned, squeezing her eyes shut as the ferry rocked sickeningly through the choppy waves. "We're going to die."

"No we ain't." Buddy clamped the pipe stem between his gristly jaws. "I've got league tonight."

Great. If she made it through the next hour, she was going to owe it all to Buddy's dogged determination to get to his weekly bowling night.

Ella checked her phone again. The cell service on Sanctuary was never great, but with the interference from the storm, "not great" had been downgraded to "downright abysmal."

Who would she call, anyway? She certainly didn't want Merry traipsing around the island in this weather, or Jo driving that broken-down old truck on the roads that had almost defeated Ella's trusty rental sedan.

Grady.

She closed her eyes and pictured him the way he'd looked that first day, his muscular thighs gripping the horse's flanks, his shoulders broad enough to block out the sun when he rode up to interrogate her about her intentions toward Jo.

Funny. Ella had been so sure they'd moved past that initial distrust—but apparently it had been lurking underneath everything, every conversation, every kiss, every caress.

Gripped by nausea, she opened her eyes and stared sightlessly out the rain-smeared plate glass enclosing the cockpit.

The ferry pitched alarmingly, giving a shuddering clank that stopped Ella's breath for a moment before the lights in the cockpit flickered and went out. The eerie darkness was such a sudden shock that it took a moment to realize there was a reason she could hear her own heartbeat thudding in her ears.

The constant grinding throb of the ferry engine had stopped.

And in the instant before red emergency lights buzzed on, Ella knew that if she had even a single bar of signal and could make one last call, in spite of everything, it would be Grady Wilkes she reached out to.

CHAPTER 30

Grady made the hard right into the dock parking lot, cranking the wheel so sharply that the back end of the Jeep swung out in an uncontrollable arc.

But he was a man on a mission. His grip never wavered, all his focus on getting to the dock before the ferry cast off.

She'll still be there, he'd told himself over and over on the drive from Ben's cabin. *Buddy knows better than to make the run to Winter Harbor in weather like this. He'll wait it out.*

She's not gone.

Ella couldn't be gone—Grady had too much to say to her. And on top of everything else, he knew she'd never forgive herself if she missed the birth of her niece or nephew.

And God forbid anything should go wrong, but Grady didn't know if Ben had ever assisted with an unplanned home birth of a human being rather than a calf or a foal.

Ella needed to be there, that's all there was to it.

But when he reached the shore, the ferry was nothing but a black smudge bobbing against the darkness of the waves in the distance.

Unable to believe it, Grady parked and jumped out of the Jeep before he'd made a conscious plan.

All his plans had centered on getting here in time. As if his body hadn't gotten the message that it was too late, he found himself running, feet slapping through puddles and skidding on the slurry of gravel and mud coating the parking lot.

He ran down the pier through the forest of tall sailboat masts, their sails all packed away tightly, the colors painted on the sides of the powerboats a blur in his peripheral vision.

Lungs contracting like a bellows, Grady pushed himself to the limit, racing to the end of the wood and concrete pier, fifty feet out over the churning water.

He caught himself against a short pylon wrapped with thick rope, his eyes still on the ferry in the distance and urgency firing his blood.

This was as close as he could get to her.

Wiping rain out of his streaming eyes, Grady panted through the slashing pain and frustration.

Wait. Something's not right . . .

Shaking his head to clear it, Grady screwed his eyes shut and opened them again to check that he was seeing what he thought he was seeing.

He might not have set foot on that ferry personally in five years, but there wasn't a soul on Sanctuary who hadn't memorized its schedule. The comings and goings of the ferry were part of the rhythm of island life—and as Grady stared at it now, his overloaded brain flashed a warning that there was something missing.

Lights. The ferry was equipped with safety lights fore and aft, and in cloudy conditions, the cockpit at the aft end of the upper deck was always lit like a beacon.

Right now, it was dark.

Fear reached up from Grady's gut to choke him, but he hardened his jaw and forced himself to concentrate on the ferry's movements.

In the minute or so since he'd parked, the ferry hadn't moved any farther away.

That, plus the lights being out—the ferry had lost power.

Ella, and whoever was on that ferry with her, was marooned in stormy seas halfway between Sanctuary Island and Winter Harbor.

Years of training kicked in smoothly, as if Grady had never left the task force. No cell service on the dock, so he loped back up the dock to his Jeep and whipped out his CB radio to call it in to the Coast Guard. He reported that the ferry didn't appear to be in distress, apart from the loss of power. The dispatcher sounded harried—no doubt the Coasties were spread thin by the storm.

He wouldn't interfere with an official rescue op, but he wasn't going to sit on his hands and wait, either. In most cases, he'd be the first to strongly advise a civilian to keep out of it and let the pros handle the situation—because nine times out of ten, a civvie who rushed out to save a friend or family member in trouble ended up needing rescuing himself.

But Grady Wilkes was no civilian. And he had a perfectly seaworthy boat tied up at the dock, waiting to take him out to Ella.

Thank God he'd never dropped the habit of keeping the task force essentials in his kit. Grady grabbed his tool bag out of the back of the Jeep. Unzipping it, he did a quick double check—yep, flashlight, rope, signal mirror, knife, first-aid kit nestled in the corner of the bag next to the leather roll of screwdrivers and wrenches.

Grady slung the bag over his shoulder and moved quickly down the dock to the slip he'd rented for his sport boat. After years of tinkering and polishing, maintenance and hanging out, his feet carried him there without conscious thought. His hands remembered the motions, knew how to untie the lines, and cast off from the dock.

He'd tossed his tool bag into the open bow and vaulted into place behind the custom steering wheel before it hit him.

The minute he turned the key in the ignition and motored away from the dock would be the first time he'd left the safety and security of Sanctuary Island in five years.

Grady waited for the panic to slam into his chest, stealing his breath and flipping his stomach like a hamburger on the grill, the way it had every other time he'd tried to step foot off the island.

But it didn't come.

Maybe the panic couldn't get through the adrenaline careening through his bloodstream. Or maybe even his stupid, broken brain knew better than to allow an irrational fear to stop him from rescuing Ella.

The perfectly tuned engine roared to life at the flick of a switch, and Grady pushed back from the pier.

After all, he thought grimly as he put the full strength of his shoulders and back into fighting the surf, the slippery, wet steering wheel wrenching against his grip, his safety meant less than nothing if Ella was in danger.

Peering through the wet strands of hair clinging to his forehead at the helpless ferry in the distance, Grady muttered, "I'm coming for you, Ella."

Ella left Buddy in the cockpit trying to call for help on his radio. Both of their cell phones had lost signal before they even left the harbor, and she'd long ago passed nervous and was hurtling straight into freaked the heck out.

Keeping one hand on the rough wall to steady herself, Ella made her way down to the lower level. She'd stowed her suitcase in the backseat of the rental car, and she wanted to have it with her in case the Coast Guard or whoever sent a rescue boat. She wanted to be ready.

Mostly, she wanted to do something, anything, instead of sitting around tracking the rudderless drifting of the creaky old ferry.

It was dark in the narrow metal stairwell, lit only by the sullen red glow of strips of emergency LED lights. Ella gripped the handrail against a particularly heavy swell, the floor rocking under her feet and sending her stomach tumbling.

Please let me almost be there, she pleaded silently, fumbling down the last few steps toward the cavernous blackness of the lower deck where her car was parked.

The emergency lighting appeared to end at the bottom of the stairs, Ella noticed, squinting. Cautious but determined, she moved forward—and gasped when she stepped down onto the last stair and splashed up to her ankle in icy water.

Heart hammering, she scurried back up a few steps and groped for her phone. Still no signal, but when she turned it face out, the light from the backlit screen illuminated enough for her to see the water lapping fitfully at the hub-caps of her rental car.

Giving her suitcase up as a lost cause, Ella scrambled up the stairs as quickly as she could. She had to let Buddy know what was going on, so he could tell the Coast Guard to harry the hell up, because, oh God—

"Water!" she gasped out, hanging on to the metal door frame of the cockpit by her fingernails. "There's a leak . . . or something."

Shooting her a sharp look from underneath his bushy gray brows, Buddy said, "You sure?"

"There's a sloshy puddle in my right shoe," Ella told him, "and my rental car is floating better than the ferry. Yes, I'm sure."

"How much?"

Being forced to think and answer questions was actually helping her calm down. "About a foot, maybe? At least eight inches."

Buddy held the radio up to his mouth and relayed, "Yeah, we're taking on a little water, too."

"Copy that," came the tinny voice over the receiver. "This is the second call we've received about your situation. We'll send a boat out as soon as we can to tow you in. Sit tight for a spell. Over."

Before Ella could politely, calmly inquire exactly how long "a spell" might be, Buddy muttered something about checking out the damage and headed down below, leaving Ella alone in the cockpit.

Just as she was contemplating whether she'd be able to steer this thing if Buddy somehow knocked himself unconscious before the power came back on, her phone buzzed in her pocket for the first time in an hour.

Signal!

Not enough bars for a phone call, she saw as soon as she pulled the phone out. But a couple of text messages had gotten through. They were both from Jo.

Merry in labor. Had cramps all day, thought it was just braxton hicks but no, real deal! Ben is here, says everything will be fine, but she needs you.

And then, from a few seconds later, *We both do. Come home.*

Everything in her body went taut. Rushing to the radio, she picked it up and started mashing buttons, trying to get the stupid thing to power on so she could hail someone, anyone, to get her off this bucket right the hell now.

After a long minute of frantic switch-flicking, all she could hear was the raspy sound of her own panicked breaths, punctuated by the occasional roll of thunder.

This wasn't getting her anywhere. Even with the rational voice in her head cautioning her that the smart thing would be to wait for the Coast Guard to show up, Ella ducked out of the cockpit and into the driving rain to search the upper deck for something, anything, that might help her.

At the first sign of trouble, Buddy had hauled out the flotation devices, so she was already wearing a bulky orange life vest. She found the rest of them in a plastic box under one of the bench seats and briefly, hysterically, considered lashing twenty or so together to make a raft.

She slid the bin of orange vests back under the bench and kept looking. Heaven help her if she found a lifeboat, because Ella was afraid she'd have a really hard time talking herself out of that one.

Mind filled with images of her sister crying through contractions, asking where Ella was, she slid on the slippery deck as the ferry lurched precariously atop the waves. Adrenaline spurting, lungs squeezing, hands shaking, she clung to the railing for dear life and shook her head to dispel the odd ringing in her ears.

If this is what a panic attack feels like, she thought dazedly, *no wonder it stops Grady from leaving the island.*

Rain pelted her already chilled flesh, stinging like a shower of pebbles, but she couldn't give up. Merry needed her.

She could almost hear her sister calling out for her, *Ella,* over and over and over.

Wait. That wasn't just in her head. Someone was yelling her name.

Blinking water out of her eyes, Ella leaned over the railing and stared. That was it, she'd gone nuts. There was no way she was seeing that.

Grady Wilkes, soaked to the skin and battling a huge ocean swell in a tiny powerboat.

Joy, relief, and pure terror collided in a dizzying rush. "Grady!" she yelled down to him, her shout nothing but a thready whimper against the fury of the storm. "Oh dear God, be careful!"

At any moment, he could be dashed against the side of the ferry, his boat shattered into shards of fiberglass, and Grady tossed down into the depths. But he didn't seem afraid—his grim concentration never wavered while he carefully pulled alongside the ferry and did something complicated with a rope and his other hand.

The maneuver ended with his boat attached to the back of the ferry somehow, and with one burning look up at Ella, Grady disappeared behind the corner of the bigger boat.

Rushing to the back of the ferry as fast as she could—which wasn't all that fast, since she was working against the pitch and sway of the boat—Ella arrived just in time to reach out and grab Grady's wet, straining arm as he hooked it over the top rung of the safety ladder.

Heart in her mouth, Ella gasped in a strangled breath and wrapped both her arms around his broad chest in a desperate embrace.

"Ella." His voice was a guttural growl so low, it rumbled through her like the thunder overhead. Slinging one leg over the top railing and planting his booted foot on the deck, he crushed her closer, his mouth hot against her chilled cheek.

His lips moved up her cheekbone to her temple as his hands swept over her shoulders, mapping the curve of her waist and the flare of her hips as if checking for injuries. "Are you okay?"

"I'm fine," she all but sobbed, overwhelmed. "What are you doing out here? I thought you couldn't take your boat out, that you'd panic . . ."

Grady pulled back far enough for his eyes to devour every inch of her no-doubt pale face framed by stringy, bedraggled hair. He didn't seem to notice that she must look like a drowned cat.

One of those impossibly warm, broad-palmed hands came up to thread through her hair and push it back from her forehead. "Guess I never had the right motivation before."

Everything inside her thrilled toward him for one glorious moment, before reality came crashing back in.

Remembering the way they'd parted, Ella was abruptly aware of how tightly she was hanging on to this man who'd basically called her a money-grubbing opportunist.

She jerked out of his arms and stood on her own, ignoring the reflexive tightening of his grip. "Come on, get all the way onto the deck. Not that it's so much safer up here than you were down there. In fact, let me get you a life vest and then we should probably head straight back down the ladder."

"The situation here doesn't look too bad," he said, scanning the deck. "You're probably better off waiting for the Coast Guard—I sent up the distress call as soon as I saw the ferry had lost power."

"Thanks," Ella said. "But unless your boat has sprung a leak, it's definitely safer than this ferry."

CHAPTER 31

It turned out that the ferry was, in fact, sinking . . . but very slowly. Buddy, who'd come back up to the cockpit to report on their status to the Coast Guard, nearly threw a fit when the Coasties radioed saying they expected not to have a rescue boat free for another hour, but to keep them apprised of any changes in the situation.

Shivering even while wrapped in the silvery survival blanket from Grady's kit, Ella sat in the copilot seat with a dangerously pigheaded look on her pretty, chalk-white face.

"I'm not waiting another hour," she announced firmly. She didn't look at Grady.

After that first, ecstatic moment, Ella hadn't met his eyes once.

Trying his best to be the calm, sane voice of reason even though he'd never felt less sane in his life, Grady said, "Ella, I know you want to get to Merry, but you're not going to do her any good if you manage to get yourself injured making the trip back to Windy Corner. The

Coast Guard is the most capable, safest option right now. They'll be here in . . ." He checked his watch. "Less than an hour, now."

"And then what?" Ella said, staring out at the still-raging storm. "They'll mess around trying to get the ferry's power back on? Who knows how long that will take. And then they'll tow the ferry back to Sanctuary, which probably won't be a fast process, either."

Buddy took the pipe out of his mouth and pointed the stem at the windshield. "Nope. They won't be towing us to Sanctuary."

Ella's head swiveled to him so fast, it made Grady's neck hurt. "What? I have to go back to Sanctuary! My sister is in labor, about to have a baby with a freaking veterinarian as her attending physician!"

Buddy's brow wrinkles creased even deeper than usual. "That sounds like a made-for-TV movie."

Ella snorted. "Welcome to my life. But you see why we have to get the Coast Guard to tow us back to Sanctuary."

"Can't." Buddy shrugged.

Ella threw up her hands, the blanket sliding down to pool around her waist. "Seriously? Your bowling league is more important than woman in premature childbirth?"

Grady had no idea what bowling had to do with anything, but he figured it was time to step in before Ella popped the ferry captain a fast one on the jaw. "If the Coast Guard can't get the power on, the ferry will have to go to the big docks at Winter Harbor to get repaired. We don't have the resources on Sanctuary."

That brought Ella's gaze to him at last. Her blue eyes pierced through him as she stood up, kicking free of the survival blanket. "Then it's settled. You have to take me back in your boat."

Alarm chilled down Grady's spine. "Ella, it's not safe."

"It was safe enough for you to come out here just to check on us, even though you'd already called the Coast Guard," she pointed out through a clenched jaw. "I'm not going all the way to Winter Harbor—I'd never make it back to the island in time to be there for Merry. And I promised her I wouldn't miss this."

All his training told him he had to convince her to wait for the professional rescue. "Be reasonable—I only took the boat out because I had to make sure you were safe. When I first called it in, the Coast Guard couldn't raise y'all on the radio, and no one knew what to think. Anything could've happened, there could've been a medical emergency—Buddy might've had a heart attack!"

"Hey, leave me outta this," Buddy protested.

Ignoring him, Grady glared at Ella. "I'm trained to deal with situations like that," he reminded her. "The Coasties were a long ways out, and I was on the spot and able to assist. I had to come."

"Why?" she asked, squaring off with him. "Why would it matter to you, what happened to a sneaky, lying, conniving bitch like me?"

Grady felt every ugly word like a hammer strike to the gut. "I never said that. Don't put words in my mouth."

"Well now." Buddy coughed, sidling toward the door. "Think I'd better go check on the lower deck again."

Grady barely noticed when the ferry captain slipped out. All he could see was the naked pain drawing Ella's features tight.

"Fine," she conceded tightly. "You're too much of a Southern gentleman to call me a bitch. You only implied it. And you haven't answered my question. Why bother making your first trip off the island in five years, in dangerous conditions, for a woman you think so little of?"

"Because I was wrong." His voice was loud in the close confines of the cockpit, but he was having a hard time regulating it. "I was wrong about your proposal and I was wrong about you."

Instead of melting into his arms the way he'd half hoped she might, Ella stiffened as if someone had tied a plank to her back. "Someone showed you the revised proposal."

"Ben told me about the therapeutic riding center," Grady admitted, that feeling of amazement at her bold, innovative ideas washing over him again. "It's going to be incredible."

She lifted her chin and stared him down. "It will still bring strangers—outsiders!—to your precious island."

That was true, but Grady found that he couldn't begrudge these particular strangers the chance to find the same healing he'd found on Sanctuary. "But they'll be people who need help, who are looking for something to get them through the worst times of their lives," he said, emotion clogging his throat. "That's what *makes* Sanctuary so precious, at least to me. It's helped me so much. I love the idea of it helping other people. And I want to be a part of it, if you'll let me."

Desperate calculation entered Ella's narrowed eyes. "You admit you misjudged me."

It was a relief to shoulder the blame so completely. "Yes. I should've trusted you. After everything, the time we spent together, the things you made me feel—I'm an idiot. I'm sorry."

Her eyes flickered, but otherwise her set, determined expression never changed. "I don't need your apologies.

What I need is a ride to Sanctuary Island." Ella stalked closer and poked a stiff finger into his chest. "I've never broken a promise to my sister. I don't intend to start now. And you *owe me*. So pay up and get me to Merry."

Whatever hope he'd held that if he could only find Ella and tell her he was sorry, everything would be magically fixed—that hope was dashed against Ella's single-minded focus on her sister.

Disappointment cascaded through him along with a sense of loss so vast and deep, he nearly staggered. But Ella was right. He did owe her, and Merry was in trouble. That had to take precedence over whatever was happening between Grady and Ella.

And if nothing else, Grady acknowledged silently, he owed Ella for the understanding and compassion that had enabled him to find his long-lost confidence—because he knew, without a doubt, that he could get her back to Sanctuary safely. No matter what happened, he was equal to it.

She'd given him that. The least he could give her was the chance to fulfill her promise to Merry.

"Get your things," he said, watching as gratitude dawned over her like a sunrise. "I'm taking you home."

On some level, Ella was aware that she was engaging in what Adrienne would call "risk behavior," in her very best prim therapist voice. But Ella felt like a robot who'd been issued an overriding directive, a mission that took precedence over everything, including her own safety and happiness.

Merry was in trouble. Ella had to get to her. End of story.

It had to be the end of the story, because there was no

room in that narrative for daring rescues by handsome handymen who'd overcome years of fear and conditioning to save her. There was no room for wondering what really motivated said rescue—guilt? Remorse?

She couldn't even begin to contemplate the possibility of something deeper.

Ella was holding it together with a wish and a prayer as it was—the fear for her sister and the new life struggling into the world right this very second overpowered everything else.

Anxiety about purposefully lifting her leg over the side of the upper-deck railing and starting the slow, wind-buffeted climb down the ferry ladder to Grady's boat? No big deal.

Awareness that Grady was no more than a foot below her on the ladder, strong arms ready to catch her if she slipped? Nonexistent.

Really.

And once they were both finally in the Stingray, feeling the intense roll of the lightweight craft in the storm-tossed waves, was Ella afraid?

No. There was no time for fear, no time for doubts. When Grady shot her an assessing glance from behind the big steering wheel, she lifted her chin and tried to project poised, unshaken resolve.

Not the easiest image to conjure up when your teeth were chattering and you had to curl your ankles around the seat supports to hold yourself bodily in the boat as it bounced and jumped over the water, but Ella managed.

The bone-jarring journey back to Sanctuary was a dark dream full of saltwater spray, mind-numbing cold winds, and tense silence from the man driving the boat.

And once they were back on solid land, it didn't get a

whole lot better. The land wasn't all that solid, for one thing, and it certainly wasn't dry. Although it helped a lot to get into the Jeep and out of the rain.

Grady cranked the heat to high and took no chances with the sticky clay slurry that passed for the road through town and out to the eastern shore of the island where Windy Corner stood.

Ella bit her lip against the urge to tell Grady to drive faster. The look of grim resolve and intense concentration hardening his features told her he was pushing the Jeep as far as he safely could.

The one time she sighed and unconsciously drummed her fingers on her impatiently jiggling knee, Grady took his gaze off the road ahead for only a split second to sear her with a glance.

"Don't ask," he growled. "I won't risk you."

That was all he said, but it sent more warmth through Ella than the most powerful blast of heat from the Jeep's hardworking vents.

"Thank you for doing this." Ella pressed her fingers against the damp cotton of her khakis, needing to fill the silence. "I know I forced you into it against your better judgment. But Merry and I—"

"She's going to be okay." Grady's confidence seeped into Ella's heart, giving it a lift. "Ben actually went to medical school and did a surgical residency at some fancy-pants hospital before he quit to go to vet school. He's a good man. I'd trust him with my life."

Ella took in a shuddering breath. "That makes me feel better. Merry and I have been on our own for a long time, the two of us against the world, and even though I know she's not alone, she's with Jo, I just . . . I need to be there."

She ran out of steam, her mind crowding with images

of Merry screaming and working to bring her child into the world. After a heartbeat, Grady downshifted and said, "It's okay, I get it. There are a few people I'd do pretty much anything for, too."

He didn't look at her, but Ella swallowed hard. She had a feeling she might be one of those people for Grady.

But she didn't have time to think about what that might mean, or what she should do about it, because the Jeep finally made it out of the pine copse, and they were there.

The veterinarian's dilapidated truck with the shiny horse trailer attached sat out front. Ella's exhausted heart picked up speed, pumping what felt like pure, undiluted adrenaline through her body.

Grady threw the Jeep into park and Ella wrestled free of the seat belt and tumbled out the door, soaked shoes sloshing and sliding in the mud as she ran to the porch and vaulted over the hole she'd made in the steps that first day.

Stopping inside the front door, Ella shouted for her sister.

The house echoed with a resounding silence that sent a chill all through her—or maybe that was the draft blowing in from the door as Grady followed her into the house.

"Merry?" she called again.

The only response was a thin, high-pitched wail that sent a thrill of fearful anticipation through Ella's limbs.

"It came from Jo's room." Grady prodded Ella's frozen body in the direction of the hallway to the back of the house.

He kept one warm, reassuring hand at the small of her back all the way down the hall. It was only Grady's support that got her to the door of the room she'd slept in that first night. That seemed like a lifetime ago.

"I can't believe we made it," she whispered, staring at the chipped white paint of the door frame.

"Aren't you going to go in?" His voice was as gentle as his touch.

"I'm scared," she admitted with a watery laugh. "Stupid, huh? I wasn't scared before when I should've been. I think it was because I knew you'd get me here in one piece."

His fingers twitched against her back, curling as if he wanted to hold her more tightly. "And I did."

"Whatever's on the other side of that door," Ella realized, looking up at Grady's shadowed face. "You can't protect me from that. If it's bad—there won't be any way to rescue me. I'll have to face it."

"We'll face it," he told her, turning them both so that her back was to his strong chest and his voice was a puff of warmth against the sensitive shell of her ear. "Together. You're not alone."

It wasn't entirely true. Nothing between them was resolved—they weren't together, not really. But for this one moment, Ella took the sentiment as it was intended, as a gesture of support and solidarity, and she let it buoy her up enough to take a deep breath and push open the door.

The thin cry came again, and this time Ella could see—it wasn't her sister making the heart-wrenching sound.

She stood in the doorway with Grady at her back, all her heart and soul zeroing in on the tiny scrap of an infant shaking its miniature fists in red-faced rage at the world.

It took Ella a moment to realize there was anyone else in the room, but at her sister's happy, exhausted cry, Ella's focus zoomed to Merry, lying sweaty and pale against the pillows of the four-poster bed.

Jo, who'd been holding Merry's hand, jumped up and hurried over to grab Ella into a tight, rib-cracking hug.

"Merry's okay," Jo said as Ella drew in a breath that turned into an embarrassing sob. "It's a boy! They're both doing great."

"Thanks to Ben," Merry said tiredly, her eyes never leaving the dark-haired vet at the foot of the bed as he attended silently to the squalling baby's umbilical cord.

Ben snorted. "Nature took its course. I was just there to play catcher."

His voice was gruff and dismissive, but Ella noticed the care he took in swaddling the baby in a soft towel, and his light, almost reverent touch when he lifted the squirming bundle of infant onto Merry's heaving chest.

Merry's thin arms came up to surround her baby boy as Ben stepped back, and the look that passed over her damp, wan face . . . Ella couldn't hold back her tears.

Jo, who'd linked arms with her, squeezed Ella and pulled them both to the bedside as Merry lifted one trembling finger to trace the softness of her newborn son's cheek.

"Hi, Baby," she said, her voice so full of wonder and love that Ella felt her own heart swell. "I'm your mom."

"Come on, Grady," Ben said gruffly. "Our work here is done. Time for nature to take its course again—that kid needs to eat."

"We've got it from here." Jo was already sliding an arm behind Merry's shoulders, readying the pillows. Ella leaned over the bed and hugged her sister and tiny nephew close, gentling them into a more upright sitting position.

She lingered for a moment, anticipating the rightness, the completion, of having everyone she loved in the circle of her arms, Ella's entire heart contained in a single embrace.

But as much joy poured through her in this moment with Merry and her baby, and their mother close by and smiling down on them with tearful happiness, Ella was conscious of something missing.

Looking around, she saw that the men had slipped out of the bedroom.

Grady was gone.

Her heart gave a painful throb of longing, and Ella closed her eyes against the knowledge that without Grady, there was no such thing as complete, perfect happiness.

CHAPTER 32

The storm blew itself out, the black clouds rolling out over the white-tipped waves to reveal the spectacular purples and oranges of an island sunset.

Grady sat alone on the front porch of Windy Corner, staring out at the world washed clean. Ben had gone back into the house ages ago. His terse, grouchy friend had made a production about it being a chore to take care of two completely healthy people like Merry and her new baby, but Grady noticed Ben hadn't left her bedside for longer than twenty minutes since he first heard she was in labor.

As for Grady, he wasn't sure what he was waiting around for, other than a hope to be useful.

Right, his sardonic inner voice muttered. *It has nothing to do with wanting as much time as you can get with Ella before she leaves Sanctuary for good.*

Whether she wants to see you or not.

The bang of the screen door brought Grady's head up like a stallion sensing danger to the band.

Or maybe danger to my heart, he thought as Ella stepped out onto the porch.

His blood throbbed through him in a completely involuntary response to the slim shape of her, dressed in one of Jo's old flannel shirts and a pair of faded jeans. Her face was a just scrubbed pink, her dark, wavy hair sleeked back in a wet ponytail.

She'd showered, Grady realized, which of course meant that his internal vision was nothing but images of Ella sliding her soapy hands all over her naked body when she sat down on the top porch step beside him.

Hunching slightly, Grady waited for her to tell him again that it was over, to leave and not come back—or worse, for her to thank him.

He didn't want her to feel grateful. He wanted her to understand that he would do anything he could to make her happy for the pure joy of seeing her smile.

As always, however, Ella Preston defied all of Grady's expectations.

With a sigh, she wrapped her arms around his elbow where it rested on the knee closer to her, and leaned her forehead against his bicep.

"You left the island," she said, her voice muffled in the still-damp cotton of his T-shirt. "You got in your boat and came after me."

Grady shifted uncomfortably—but not enough to dislodge her from where she clung to him. "I didn't have far to go," he pointed out. "What, a few hundred yards offshore? Didn't even make it to the mainland."

"You would have, though."

The certainty in her voice stopped his breath. "I would've," he agreed hoarsely.

She lifted her head to stare him in the eye. "If I'd gone

all the way back to D.C., you still would have come after me."

Grady shook his head. "How can you know that?"

The left side of her mouth quirked up into a humorless smile. "It was never about how far you were willing to go—it was about taking that first step."

The realization that she knew him this well, understood him better than he'd understood himself for a long time, and he'd known her and trusted her so little that he'd accused her of trying to steal her mother's inheritance . . . Grady swallowed against the surge of regret in the back of his throat.

"I'm sorry." He had to say it again, even though she hadn't wanted to hear it before. "The things I said to you at the bank . . . I can't believe I was such a jerk."

She sighed, her eyelashes fluttering down and concealing her expression. "I can. With the information you had? It was pretty damning. After all . . ." She took a deep breath and turned her head to stare out at the rain-sparkled tree line. "I did put that B and B proposal together. It was my work, and I tried hard to sell Jo on the idea."

"But you thought better of it," Grady argued. "If I couldn't have faith in you, I should've at least gotten all the facts before I accused you of anything."

Pulling her arm back, Ella angled her body to relax against the porch railing. Without her pressed to his side, Grady felt the cold of the evening breeze through his wet clothes more keenly.

"What reason did I give you for that kind of faith?" Ella asked frankly, her gaze open. "I slept with you, but I refused to talk about what was going on with us. I didn't tell you how I was feeling, about you or Jo or anything—I didn't say a word about how close I was to chucking it all and staying on Sanctuary."

Pain shafted through Grady's chest. "You wanted to stay here."

He'd been so close to having everything he wanted, and he'd ruined it.

"I wanted to stay with you," she corrected softly. "But I was hideously afraid of admitting it. Of taking that first step away from the security I worked really hard for, into a scary new life I never planned on."

"And now?" Grady could hardly breathe.

She laughed and tipped her head back against the railing, exposing the slim, pale column of her throat, the tender hollow where her heartbeat sped. "I'm still afraid," she confessed. "But if Merry can decide to raise her son on her own . . . if you can overcome years of fear . . . how can I be less brave?"

Grady didn't dare to hope. "What are you saying?" he demanded, needing to hear the words.

Tipping her chin over her shoulder at the hole in the porch, Ella said, "The last time I took a first step this big, the world fell out from under me. But you dived in after me and pulled me up. And I guess what I'm saying is that I don't know what life has in store for us, or exactly how we're going to work out the details, but I want to take all my first steps from now on with you at my side. And I want to be the person who picks you up, when you fall."

Grady stood, heart thundering, and bent to grab Ella under her knees and arms. He hauled her up to his chest, holding her like a bride. She made one startled squeak, then twined herself around him like a climbing rose.

"Where are we going?" she asked, as he marched down the drive toward his Jeep.

"I need to do bad, bad things to you, and I'm not going to be able to do them in your mother's house."

"And . . ." She frowned down at where they were pressed so tightly together. "Oh my gosh, you haven't showered yet? Grady! You need to get warm and dry, I can't believe you. You have to take care of yourself."

"The shower is an acceptable setting for the bad, bad things," Grady allowed.

Her smile was radiant, glowing brighter than the fading sun. Then she bit her lip and he almost dropped her as every drop of blood in his body rushed south.

"After the shower and the . . . bad things," she said hesitantly.

"I'll bring you back here." He got them to the car and deposited her on her feet. "We'll be gone an hour, tops. You'll be back in time to take your turn with the crying baby and the midnight feeding, I promise."

"I love that you know what I was going to ask. But actually." She backed against the side of the Jeep, keeping Grady from getting the door open. "Ben says after the work they did today, Merry and the baby will both probably sleep hard. And she's got Mom there. She's fine."

Thoroughly distracted, Grady wedged a leg between her thighs and made a cradle of his body, leaning into her. "Mom, huh?"

"Just something I'm trying out—telling the people in my life what they mean to me," Ella said breezily, her eyes bright in the blue light of dusk. "So far, it's working out fairly well."

He stared down at her from inches away, close enough to share every breath—and still he felt himself straining toward her, wanting to merge as close together as possible. Wanting to become one.

"Maybe a couple of hours," he amended as his gaze dropped to her lips. "It's going to take at least an hour for me to kiss every single inch of you."

"That doesn't sound like such a bad, bad thing," she said. He loved it when she went a little breathless like that.

"Oh, it gets worse," he promised, his heart stuttering into overtime. "Because after I kiss you all over, I'm going to tell you exactly how much I love you. That's going to take . . . considerably longer than an hour."

Face shining with happiness, Ella beamed up at him. "I can probably find room in my schedule for such an interesting topic. How long do you think you'll need?"

Grady traced the delicate line of her jaw, pushing his fingers into her hair and cupping the shape of her skull in his palms. "I don't know," he said, mouth dry. "Pencil me in for the rest of your life."

Laughing softly, Ella looped her hands behind his neck and pulled his mouth down to hers.

The taste of her was explosive, sweetness bursting across his tongue like the first bite of a late-summer peach. Before he lost himself to it completely, Grady dragged his head up to gasp against her cheek. "I don't mean you have to stay here forever. I know you've got that job you love in D.C.—I can move there, or we can keep the cabin here and split our time, because with Merry and the baby and your mom and everything . . ."

"Shhh," Ella crooned, going up on tiptoe to kiss his lips closed. "That means—so much to me, Grady. Just knowing you're willing to uproot your whole life like that . . . But for once in *my* life, I don't want to plan exactly how this is all going to work. We'll figure it out as we go. But whatever happens, we're spending most of our time on Sanctuary Island."

His throat closing with emotion, Grady nuzzled into the soft, scented warmth of her neck. "Look at you, Miss City Mouse, talking about living out here on this nearly inaccessible backwater of an island."

"How could I not want to live on Sanctuary Island? This place changed more than my life, it changed me." Ella surged against him like the tide. "I love it here. Almost as much as I love you."

Jo dropped the cordless phone in its cradle and twitched the parlor curtain back into place. Briefly, she wondered what her aunt would think of all this.

Knowing Aunt Dottie and the somewhat tumultuous history of the Hollister women, she'd be cackling in delight at having an unwed mother in the master bedroom and a canoodling couple in the driveway.

Jo was too tired at the moment to work up a cackle, but the glow of satisfaction she felt at the way everything was working out went bone deep.

She'd made a lot of mistakes in her life—too many to name—but somehow, through luck or grace, she'd been given a chance to make things right. And now that Ella was all but settled, her thoughts turned to Merry.

Sweet, bright Merry.

Wandering back to her bedroom, Jo leaned silently in the doorway and watched the way Ben's face went soft and helpless when he looked at Merry and her baby cuddled on the bed.

Merry seemed to have eyes for no one but her son. She'd counted every perfect finger and tiny, rosy toe.

She'd inspected the whorls of his little ears, the dimples at his knees and elbows, and laughed over his shock of black hair.

But she hadn't named him yet.

"I've been calling him Baby for so long," she'd told them earlier, "I can't think of any boy names! Xavier? Lancelot? Spike?"

"Whatever you choose will be wonderful," Ella had said loyally before exchanging a worried glance with Jo.

Please, anything but Spike, Jo remembered thinking.

Busying himself packing up his medical kit, Ben missed the way Merry's gaze darted to follow him as he moved around the room. But Jo saw it.

And she saw the way he stiffened when Merry spoke into the peaceful silence.

"What's your middle name, Doc?"

Wariness dropped over Ben's face. So wary, that one, always ready to fight. "Why?"

Merry rolled her eyes. "I'm not going to steal your identity or something. Come on, answer the question."

"Alexander."

A thoughtful look crossed Merry's face. "Alex. Ooh, or Zander. I like it."

"Like it for what?" Ben grumbled, bent over his canvas satchel.

"For Baby," Merry said placidly, smoothing her son's hair so that it lay flat against the tiny skull for a moment before springing up into its natural Mohawk again.

Ben froze, wrist deep in his satchel, his gray eyes wide and shocked. Jo had to smother a grin at the naked amazement on his face.

"Alexander Hollister Preston," Merry mused, and now Jo was the one dropping her jaw in amazement.

Clearing her throat, she stepped farther into the room, barely aware of Ben standing stock-still at Merry's bedside, as if he'd been turned into a statue. "I like it," Jo told her daughter.

"I want him to know where he comes from," Merry said, a slight frown creasing the space between her brows. "Even without his dad, he's got lots of family. Plenty."

"More than enough, some people might say." Ben went back to packing his med kit, bending his head down so that they couldn't see his face. But Jo could hear the smile in his voice. "People who've met the Hollisters, for example."

Ignoring the sass, Jo sat on the bed beside Merry and leaned over to get a better look at baby Alexander's buttoned-up eyes and stubby black lashes. "He does have plenty of family here on Sanctuary Island. I think he'll even have an Aunt Ella around most of the time."

"Really?" Merry's grin was tired but brilliant. "Yay!"

"And while we're dishing out good news," Jo went on, excitement simmering under her skin, "I just got off the phone with Harrison. The bank will extend me a loan—we'll get to keep the house."

Merry caught her breath, eyes shining. "Oh, Mom. That's wonderful. And the therapeutic riding center will be such a great thing for the island!"

"It'll be a lot of work." Jo tucked a lock of hair behind Merry's ear. "But it's work that's worth doing. Especially if it means we can stay in the house that's been in our family for almost a hundred years."

Outside, the storm had lifted and the call of birdsong could be heard in the trees. The conversation with Harrison had been good, and Jo felt a sense of new possibility unspooling before her like a ball of yarn.

Alexander opened his little mouth in a big yawn that screwed up his whole chubby face. Eyes almost dropping closed with exhaustion, Merry sighed.

Before her grandson could settle into a real squall, Jo picked up the precious, kicking bundle and said, "Here, let me. I'll walk with him."

Grady and Ella would be home soon, and if Jo was any judge of attraction, there was more than bickering going on between Merry and Dr. Ben Fairfax.

Walking over to the window, she stared out at the roofline of the stables in the distance, behind the pines. A new business, a new family, a new chance with the man she'd loved for a decade.

And another generation of Hollisters would grow up at Windy Corner, on Sanctuary Island.

Read on for an excerpt from

SHORELINE DRIVE

the next captivating romance from Lily Everett,
available soon from St. Martin's Paperbacks:

Rain lashed across the cracked windshield of Dr. Ben
Fairfax's ancient pickup truck as it roared over the pitted
inland roads, churning up mud and gravel as he raced
across Sanctuary Island.

Ben raked wet hair out of his eyes and tightened his
grip on the steering wheel. A single thought repeated itself over and over in his head.

Get to her. Get to her. Get to her.

He bared his teeth at the clash of thunder that rocked
his truck, rattling the state-of-the-art large-animal trailer
hooked to his back bumper.

*Go ahead and do your worst. Nothing's going to stop
me from getting to Windy Corner in time.*

The same cold wash of fear he felt when he got the call
from Jo Hollister froze his belly again, but there was no
time to fool around with doubts and worries.

Meredith Preston was in labor. At least three weeks
early, in the middle of the worst spring storm he'd ever
seen roll in off the Atlantic Ocean. And according to Jo,

her daughter's contractions were approximately three minutes apart and lasted a full minute each.

No time to get Merry to the ferry that would shuttle her the hour from Sanctuary Island to the big hospital in Winter Harbor, Virginia. No telling if the ferry was even running in this weather.

No choice but to step up and do what he could to make sure both mother and new baby made it out of this alive.

Which wasn't all that different from Ben's normal practice—he'd helped countless mothers deliver healthy newborns over the course of his seven years on Sanctuary.

Of course, most of those newborn babies had been foals or calves. There was the occasional lamb or goat kid.

Animals were easy. Even when things went wrong, they knew what to do—lie there and let Ben handle the situation. People were more annoying, which was why he tended to avoid them.

Not an option tonight. He had to push everything aside and focus on helping Merry.

Even though the last time Ben had been involved with a human birth was before he'd chucked it all to study veterinary medicine and he hadn't been the attending physician. He'd been the father.

Grimly beating back the dark surge of memories, Ben refocused his gaze on the road.

I was better off when all I was thinking about was getting to Merry's bedside.

With that in mind, he pushed the grumbling engine as hard as he dared, making the half hour trip from his farm on Shoreline Drive to Jo Ellen's big, dilapidated plantation house on the northeastern end of the island.

Hauling his canvas duffel off the truck's bench seat, Ben tore up the wooden porch steps, heedless of the rain. He swerved to avoid the ragged, gaping hole in the sagging boards and crashed through the front door just as thunder boomed overhead.

Silence.

Ben stood in the dim hallway for an instant and held his breath, listening. A soft murmur of voices from down the hall had his adrenaline pumping and instincts clamoring.

Merry.

Shoving down the terror and worry, Ben gritted his teeth. He had to get these . . . feelings under control. Merry's life, and the life of her soon-to-be-born baby, depended on Ben keeping a clear, level, unemotional head.

So what if Merry was pretty, and his body reacted inconveniently to being around her. He'd been attracted to women before. Sure, maybe never one as sweet, vivacious, and universally adored as Meredith Preston, but all that meant was that she was even less likely to ever think about a man like him that way.

Rationally, he knew he needed to get over this ridiculous infatuation. And since Ben was a man who prized rationality, he would. End of story.

Braced and ready, he opened the door. Meredith Preston paused in her pacing of the hardwood floorboards, one hand at the small of her no doubt aching back, the other arm hooked around her mother's strong shoulders.

"Up and walking? Good," Ben said, moving to lay out his medical instruments on the dresser top.

"I didn't know what else to do." Jo sounded more afraid and uncertain than he'd ever heard her, the tremor in her voice noticeable even for a man who did his level best never to notice other people's emotions.

"I'm fine. Oh," Merry gasped out. Her pretty, even features tightened as a spasm of pain gripped her abdomen. With a clinical eye, Ben took in the hectic flush over her high cheekbones, the rapid throb of the pulse at the hollow of her throat. The bow of her back and the whiteness of her knuckles as her bloodless lips moved silently to count out the seconds of the contraction.

Without conscious thought, Ben moved to her and nudged Jo gently out of the way just as the contraction released Merry. Exhausted, she swayed on her feet. Ben caught her as gently as he could, supporting her weight against his chest, and froze.

He had his arms around Merry Preston.

Shaking his head to rid it of the frustratingly persistent thoughts, Ben slanted a glance at Jo, wringing her hands a few feet away. "Can you boil some water for me? And we'll need clean towels or sheets, a big stack."

Looking grateful to have a task, Jo straightened and leaped for the door. "Yes! Sure, only . . . Merry, honey, I hate to leave you."

Merry lifted a shaking hand to wipe her damp, dark hair off her sweaty forehead and attempted a smile. "It's okay, Mom. Dr. Fairfax will take care of me."

But as soon as the bedroom door shut behind Jo, Merry pulled away from Ben. He tried not to notice how empty and cold his arms felt.

Irrelevant.

"Ready to get back in bed?" he asked mildly, hands out and ready to steady her if she wobbled. "You can walk some more, if you want."

"What I want is to get this kid out of me." She panted

for a moment, then looked up at him from under her dark, sooty lashes. Ben read the fear and nerves in her gaze as clearly as if she were shouting it in his ear. "You can do this, right?"

Foregoing the usual sneer at anyone who questioned his incredibly overqualified competence, Ben still couldn't quite force the gentle, soothing bedside manner they'd talked about in his residency program.

There was more than one reason he'd dropped out of the surgical program and redirected toward veterinary medicine.

"Yes," he told her, giving it to her straight, no waffling. "I've delivered healthy babies in far worse conditions than a clean, dry, warm, well-lit room."

Not human babies, but he had enough sensitivity not to remind her of that. The brief flash of humor in her blue eyes said she hadn't forgotten, but her only response was to climb up onto the high mattress and settle in the nest of downy white pillows.

"Birth is birth." Ben rolled up his shirtsleeves and went back to setting out his tools. "It's the first clue we get that life is going to be messy and painful, but it's not complicated."

"Unless there are complications." She sounded calm, but Ben saw the way her fingers clutched, white-knuckled, at the quilted bedspread. "I'm three weeks early."

He wanted to tell her to stop worrying, the baby was done cooking and everything was going to be fine—but he wouldn't say that until after he'd examined her.

It was weird, almost like an out-of-body experience, to stare down at Merry's pale, strained face and the taut, swollen line of her stomach. Sometime between entering the room and this moment, he'd made the switch in his head.

Merry wasn't a person right now. She wasn't the woman who reminded him he was human and made him want to snarl and snap and avoid her for it. She wasn't beautiful or sexy or funny or vivacious or stubborn or kind.

She was his patient, and she was in pain. Nothing else mattered.

The next hour passed in a blur. Merry showed a surprising amount of backbone and determination for someone who generally faced the world with a smile and a twinkle in her eye. She battled her own body and the forces of nature to bring her son squawling into the world.

Hands moving on automatic, the dance of his fingers and muscles a response choreographed by hours of practice and an unswerving instinct, Ben was there for all of it. For Merry's heaving breaths and near-silent cries of pain to her exhausted, incandescent smile when he laid the naked, squirming infant on her quivering stomach.

No matter how many times he witnessed it, Ben knew he'd never get tired of the rush he felt at the awe-inspiring spectacle of birth. What he'd told Merry was true—it was painful and messy, for sure.

But it was also the closest a man like Ben was ever going to get to touching pure joy.

There was a lot of confusion and chaotic happiness, Jo Ellen crying and her older daughter, Ella, rushing in dripping rainwater all over the floor with Ben's best friend, Grady Wilkes. Lots of hugging and explanations and chatter, and Ben didn't bother to follow any of it. He'd get the details from Grady later.

In the meantime, Ben would do his damnedest to allow the peace of the moment to wash through him like a wave over the beach. And like the ocean, he couldn't help coming back again and again, just to make sure Merry and the baby were still there, still breathing, still okay.

When the conversation turned to names, Ben busied himself with packing away his medical kit. He didn't want to hear Merry talk about the baby's mysterious, absent father.

Not because it bothered him. It was more that it was boring. Predictable. Merry had fallen for an asshole—any guy who let his beautiful, sexy, very pregnant girlfriend traipse off without him was, by definition, an asshole—but if he ever showed the least bit of interest in her and the baby, she'd probably go running back to him. Statistics didn't lie.

Except it turned out that she didn't intend to name her son after his father.

"What's your middle name, Doc?"

Her voice was awfully chipper for a woman who'd been holding back screams for the last two hours.

"Why?" Ben countered.

Merry rolled her eyes. "I'm not planning to steal your identity or something. Come on, answer the question."

Ben paused, debated. Couldn't come up with a reason not to tell her. "Alexander."

She got that thoughtful look on her bright, open face.

And that was it. Merry's son was named Alexander Hollister Preston.

Preston, which meant she wasn't giving him the biological father's last name. Hollister, which meant she wanted him to have a connection to her mother's family.

And Alexander—nicknamed Alex within an hour of being born—for Ben.

He really didn't know how he felt about that.

At some point after Grady and Ella cleared out to let

Merry get some much needed sleep, Jo excused herself to take a phone call in the front parlor, leaving Ben to watch over her daughter and new grandson.

"Thank you." Merry sighed, eyelids fluttering as she struggled to stay awake with her son lying on her chest under the sheet.

"You said that already," Ben reminded her, but his usual sharpness was blunted around the edges. He felt . . . softened. By exhaustion—now that the adrenaline was draining out of his system, he was aware of every ache and pain—but even more, by the simple happiness glowing in the depths of Merry's bright blue eyes.

Propping his hip on the edge of the bed, he tried to let the unfamiliarity of wanting to be nice settle in his chest. "Besides, the hard part was all you. You did very well."

Merry gave him a slight smile. "You're not as much of a dick as you want everyone to think you are."

"No, I really am," he told her honestly. "Doesn't mean I can't give credit where it's due."

Beneath the sheet, baby Alex snuffled against Merry's breast and made a sound that was like nothing so much as a piglet rooting for its mother's milk. Merry winced as he latched on, an odd expression on her face.

"Hurts?" Ben stood up, ready to dig through his canvas bag for . . . what? He didn't exactly keep plastic nipple guards in human sizes on hand.

"A little. It's weird." She let her head fall back against the headboard with a muted *thunk*, stars in her eyes. "But kind of satisfying."

You're going to be a good mother, he wanted to say. Ben clamped his lips shut stubbornly. Sentimental idiocy. There was no guarantee Merry would be any better at parenting than anyone else.

The only guarantee was that she'd mess up that kid the way all parents messed up their kids, even the loving parents. Maybe especially the loving parents.

But at least she'd have the chance to try and get it right.

A familiar ache swelled and bloomed under his breastbone like a spreader inserted between his ribs, cracking him open wide.

Dr. Ben Fairfax stared down at Merry Preston nursing her baby for the first time and, all of a sudden, he knew exactly how he felt about having that kid named after him.

He liked it.

But it wasn't enough. He wanted more.

Merry yawned, a real jaw cracker, without a trace of self-consciousness, her deep blue eyes hidden under the sweep of long lashes a shade or two darker than the roots of dyed-pink hair over the pillow. Alex was an impossibly small, perfect bump under the sheets.

Ben stood there and let the wave crash over him.

I want Merry and Alex to be my family.